That Feeling

Slade Brothers Second Generation - Book 1

Alexis Winter

Edited by Michele Davine
Illustrated by Sarah Kil
Photography by Wander Aguiar

Copyright © 2022 by Alexis Winter - All rights reserved.

In no way is it legal to reproduce, duplicate, or transmit any part of this document in either electronic means or in printed format. Recording of this publication is strictly prohibited and any storage of this document is not allowed unless with written permission from the publisher. All rights reserved.
Respective authors own all copyrights not held by the publisher.

A wonderful thank you to my amazing readers for continuing to support my dream of bringing sexy, naughty, delicious little morsels of fun in the form of romance novels.

A special thank you to my amazing editor Michele Davine who I would be COMPLETELY lost without!

Thank you to my fantastic cover designer Sarah Kil who always brings my visions to life in the most outstanding ways.

And lastly, to my ARC team and beta readers, you are wonderful and I couldn't do this without you.

XoXo,
Alexis

Chapter 1

Tyler

"Tyler, you'll be manning the mechanical bull this year."

I tip my hat at Miss Bellows as she reads off the volunteer duties for the annual Fall Fest in Grand Lake.

My father's brewery, Slade Brewing, donates the beer tent every year for the fest, and most of us Slades spend at least a few hours volunteering. I usually drive the tractor for the hayrides, but my cousin Axle took that over this year.

"You ready to spend the day surrounded by screaming children, big brother?" Trent nudges my arm with his elbow. "Maybe it'll finally light a fire in those Levi's of yours and you'll give mom and dad their first grandkid."

He doesn't look up from the phone he's furiously typing on.

I chuckle and shake my head. "And why is that left to me? You're the one with the fancy job and six-bedroom house."

"Could've been your job, remember? Still can." He smirks, his hand clapping around my shoulder before he spots our dad, Drake, and makes his way over to him to most likely *talk shop.*

Trent's not wrong. His title as the CEO of Slade Brewing International could have been mine, and according to my parents, *should* have been mine. But the idea of being glued to my phone all day while jet-setting from one meeting to another makes my skin crawl.

As the oldest son and heir to the Slade Brewing empire, I get that I probably let a lot of people down when I took over the family ranch instead, but I don't regret it. Over the last 20 years, the ranch has expanded to 30,000+ acres, nine cowboys, three ranch hands and hundreds of heads of cattle. Someone had to take it over, and it was the one place I always felt I could make a difference.

Financial reports and projected earnings always instantly bored me. I'm still on the board of the company and always will be, so it's not that I don't care about it or don't want it to continue to be one of the most successful breweries in the world—I just don't want the title or responsibility of CEO. Besides, Trent came out of the womb ready to take that bull by the horns.

I grab a cup of coffee from the refreshments table supplied by Violet from the Bean & Bun bakery in town and walk over to where my dad and Trent are deep in conversation. My dad has a telltale deep V between his brows as Trent gestures animatedly with both arms.

"I'm telling you, she's an expert. She's young, but that's what this company needs right now, especially with the recent success of our new seltzer line." My dad nods at Trent's comment.

"You guys really can't not talk business, can you?" I say, walking up beside them.

"I'm just telling dad about the new employee who's starting on Monday. I'll introduce her to everyone at the board meeting and she'll introduce our new social media initiative. I'm telling you, it's going to be a game changer. She's fro—" The phone in his hand rings, pulling his attention away from finishing his sentence as he steps aside to answer it.

"That boy is going to have a stroke if he doesn't relax," my dad grumbles.

That Feeling

"That's why you'll find me out in the pasture. I'd rather herd cattle than people."

We stand shoulder to shoulder, silence settling over us as we watch families mill about the fairgrounds. My dad smiles and waves at a few people, which is a little funny considering that before I was born, he hated this town and everyone hated him.

We're not from Grand Lake. Virginia Dale is about three hours north, but my family's reputation was set in stone back in the early 1900s when their land ownership was brought into question, something that's long since been squashed thanks in part to my mom, Celeste—a bulldog of a lawyer who came to Virginia Dale as my dad's new lawyer and never left.

"Your mother ran into Selma the other day. She was asking about you."

I take a long sip of coffee. My dad has a knack for saying way more than he actually says. His words always carry a much deeper message, even if it's only a sentence or two. But I'm really not in the mood to discuss Selma again.

"Well, if Selma has questions about me, she can come to me."

"No second chances there, huh?"

"Nope."

"Okay, son," he says, patting my shoulder, letting me know he understands and that the conversation is over . . . or so I thought. "Just go easy on your mother if she brings it up to you. She just wants grandkids and it can make her a little shortsighted at times."

He gives my shoulder a quick squeeze before walking over to man the beer tent.

"What do I get if I win?" The teenage boy I just explained the ride to narrows his gaze at me as I hand him the glove to ride the mechanical bull.

"Bragging rights, kid." I step over to the controls as he hoists himself up onto the bull. I know for a fact he won't make it eight seconds; they never do.

Sure enough, about three seconds in, he's on his back on the cushions surrounding the bull.

"That's not fair!" He slams his fist down before standing up and walking back to me to return the glove. "That's so unrealistic."

"Unrealistic? You ever ridden a real bull, son? A real one would break your back and gore you faster than you can blink. Bessie here is a cakewalk."

The kid looks at me with horror before bolting over to his group of friends.

"Gee, you really have a way with kids. You're a natural."

I turn to my right to see where the breathy voice is coming from when my eyes land on a pair of brand-new shiny cowboy boots on bare, shapely legs.

"Best they know the truth. You can get seriously hurt or killed out here if you don't respect the land and the animals." I shake out the glove and stare across the field. "Had to deal with it firsthand with these damn transplants and tourists," I mutter slightly under my breath but loud enough that she hears.

"Even the fake mechanical ones?" She's being sarcastic and I won't lie, it's fucking sexy. I like a little attitude in a woman. Makes it challenging.

I turn my attention back to the bull, trying my damndest not to notice the way her plump ass fills out her tight denim shorts. Her lips are a shiny red, matching the print of her flannel shirt and her fingernails.

"So what do I get if I win?"

I turn back to face her, an eyebrow instinctively rising as I give her an obvious once-over. "You're going to ride the bull?"

"Yeah," she shrugs, "why the hell not?"

She takes off her fake cowboy hat and situates it between her thighs as she pulls her long blonde hair up into a high ponytail, her curls bouncing at the end.

That Feeling

"Just don't seem the type."

She crosses her arms over her chest, pushing her full tits together right in my line of vision. She juts out one hip, cocking her head to the side.

"Oh yeah? And what type do I seem like?"

I can't help but chuckle as my eyes drop back down to her boots. I make no effort to hide my gaze as it slowly travels up her curvy body, pausing briefly on her full hips.

I wonder what it would be like to grip those hips as she rides me.

"Like a little tourist who's wearing a costume of what she *thinks* Colorado people dress like."

"You seem to like it." A coy smile spreads across her lips as she reaches for the glove in my hand.

"You're just missing a cow-print vest and a six-shooter, little miss tourist." I smile and she looks at me questioningly. "Then you'd complete your look of Woody from *Toy Story*." She rolls her eyes as I let out a hearty laugh.

"Give me that!" She snatches the glove from my hand and tugs it onto her manicured fingers. "I've gotten several compliments on my outfit today, so you can suck it."

"Oh, I don't doubt that, sweetheart. I bet everyone was really impressed with your Amazon cowboy hat and belt buckle."

"Stop flirting with me and go over the rules so I can ride this damn bull."

*Flirting? She thinks I'm flirting with her? Wait . . . **am** I flirting with her?*

"Make sure that glove is on your dominant hand; you'll grip the strap with that. Your other hand has to be in the air and can't be touching the saddle or any part of the bull. You can squeeze the bull with your thighs, and here's a tip: Try to move your body with it, otherwise you'll just get thrown off and it'll hurt like hell. I'll flip the switch and you try to stay on, simple as that."

"So, you never answered me. What do I get if I can last the entire time?"

"Same as everyone else," I say, "bragging rights."

She tilts her head. "That's not going to work. We need something that will motivate me."

I hesitate because I know I shouldn't be flirting with the guests, let alone someone who looks at least a decade younger than me. But I ask anyway . . .

"What do you want?"

She taps her chin and squints one eye like she's deep in thought. "A date."

"Done," I say, and she instantly lights up. "I've got half a dozen cousins who would kill to go on a date with you."

She gives me a look that tells me I can jump up my own ass, and I laugh.

"With *you*."

"Now, why would a pretty young woman like yourself want to go on a date with an old man like me? I could be a serial killer."

"I guess it would make for an interesting date then."

She's quick.

Feisty.

The type that if I had to bet, always gets what she wants.

"Fine. If you can last the entire time, I'll go on a date with you."

"And it's eight seconds?" she asks.

I nod. "That's the goal. Most people can't last more than three."

"Good thing I'm not most people," she says in that breathy tone again as she steps forward, pausing an inch away from me. "I've ridden things *much* longer than eight seconds." She drags her teeth across her bottom lip and—*fuck me*—it sends a lightning bolt to my cock.

"We'll see about that." I turn, hoping my hardening dick isn't visible in my jeans. I watch out of the corner of my eye as she tosses a long leg over the saddle and pulls herself up onto the bull.

Goddamn, I'd love to see her do that stark-ass naked.

"You ready?" I ask, trying to get my mind out from between her thighs.

That Feeling

"Wait! Toss me my hat," she says. I reach down where she left it and walk it over to her. "I feel like I need to wave it in the air as I ride this bad boy. Get that full Colorado experience, ya know?"

I roll my eyes and walk back over to the controls, ready to flick the switch and put her in her place . . . on her back.

The bull starts slowly, but with a few quick bucks and twists, it's running wild. A huge smile spreads across her face as she squeals. I glance at the stopwatch.

Four seconds already.

She rolls her body with the bull like a pro, even keeping a firm grip on her cowboy hat that she holds high over her head.

I look at the watch again. Six seconds.

Shit.

I check the controls and she's on the hardest setting. She whips forward then backward, falling to the side of the bull before landing on her back in a heap on the ground. Laughter erupts from her as she stumbles before standing up to run over to me.

"What's the time?" she asks breathlessly, her ponytail falling haphazardly to one side.

We both look down at the watch where I've stopped it.

"Nine seconds!" she shouts before dancing in place. "Looks like you owe me a date." She shoves her hands into the back pockets of her shorts as she looks up at me, her chest rising and falling rapidly with excitement. It's just now that I'm noticing how much my 6'3" frame towers over her.

"Looks like I do," I say, still in disbelief.

"I'll come find you later to set it up." She pulls the ponytail out, her hair falling in shiny waves down her shoulders, before putting her hat back on. She takes a step away before turning back to look at me over her shoulder. "Not too bad for a *little tourist*, huh?" She winks before walking off.

I'm clenching my jaw tightly. I don't know what just happened, but it's been a long while since I've had that kind of visceral reaction to someone. I didn't even get her name and I'm supposed to take her on a date.

I shrug it off. I live three hours from here and there's no way in hell she's even heard of my town or knows where it is. I'll be long gone tonight and I'll just be that mysterious cowboy who promised her a date then disappeared. A fun story for her girlfriends back home—wherever that is.

I try to focus the rest of the day, but it's hard knowing she's somewhere around here. Every once in a while, I catch myself glancing over my shoulder trying to find her.

By the time I'm done for the day, the sun is setting and I'm exhausted. Ranch life never sleeps, so I know I have to be up bright and early tomorrow morning . . . and I still have a long drive back home tonight.

I turn off the bull and leave the key with Miss Bellows. Normally, I'd walk around and tell my dad and brother I'm leaving, then say a quick "good night" to my cousins, aunts, and uncles scattered around here, but I don't want to risk being spotted by what's-her-name from earlier trying to nail down the details of our *date*.

I tip my hat down a little lower and pull my jacket tighter as I walk across the field toward my truck. I reach for the handle just as I hear the crunch of gravel. The steps quicken as I swing the driver's side door open.

"You're not trying to bail on me, are you?"

Fuck. She found me.

"Wouldn't dream of it," I smile as I turn around to face her.

"You sure? Kinda seems like you are." She steps closer to me and I close the door, casually leaning against it with my shoulder.

"You having second thoughts?" I ask, hoping she says *yes*, but she slowly shakes her head *no*.

"Tomorrow night? I'll meet you at the Lariat here in Grand Lake at 7. Deal?"

She's doing that thing again—shoving her hands into her back pockets as she bites her bottom lip. She looks up at me through her

That Feeling

eyelashes as she steps a little closer, her breasts so close to touching me, I can feel heat radiating off her body.

She knows what she's doing to me. It's evident by the little smirk on her face. "How do I know you won't just stand me up?" she asks.

"You don't."

I can smell her sweet perfume. I'm clenching my jaw again, but I can't will myself to relax when she's standing this close to me.

"Maybe I should entice you not to flake on me." Her words are barely above a whisper as she rises up onto her tiptoes and places her lips ever so softly against mine. She leans against me—her breasts smashing against my chest—and I swear I can feel her nipples harden. She breaks the kiss, stepping back just as quickly. "See you tomorrow."

She spins on her heels to leave, and I know I shouldn't, but I dart my hand out and grab her arm. I pull her back toward me, with the sound of her breath leaving her body in an audible huff as she slams against me. I spin her until her back hits the door of my truck and I plant my hands on either side of her face. I lean in, taking her lips with my own. My tongue snakes inside her mouth, lapping at her. She whimpers and nips at my tongue, causing me to pull back.

"Maybe I should entice you to not fucking tease me," I say through gritted teeth as I press my hardening cock against her lower belly.

She giggles and I drop one hand to her shoulder, running my fingers over it and up around her neck. I watch as her smile fades, her mouth falling open as her eyes grow heavy-lidded in an instant. It only spurs me on as I tighten my fingers a little, the pads pressing firmly against her warm skin.

"And how would you do that?" Her eyes are still locked on mine, and it makes me want to exert dominance, control her.

"Maybe I should bend you over the bed of my truck and really test your earlier statement about being able to ride something a lot longer than eight seconds."

She swallows, and I can feel her throat constricting against my hand that's still wrapped around her.

"Or maybe," I say as I lean in and nip at her earlobe before sucking on it, "I should have you drop to your knees and see if you suck as good as you run your mouth."

She brings out a side of me I haven't expressed with anyone before. I don't even know her, but something about her makes me want to strip myself bare and lose myself in her.

I can feel her trembling against me. I'm not sure if it's from fear or excitement or both, but instead of finding out, I release her, stepping back to put some space between us and regain control of myself and the situation.

"Tomorrow night," I say as I reach around her to open my door again and climb into my truck. I don't look back—I just leave her standing in the parking lot as I head home.

I feel like a complete asshole knowing full well I have no intention of following through on our date plans. It's not that I don't want to, it's just that I have no interest in getting involved with a tourist who will just be gone in a week or two. I did that a lot in my twenties and it seemed fun at the time—the no-strings-attached sex and all—but it just left me feeling empty. The sex was mediocre at best and often unsatisfying . . . although with her, I can just about guarantee it would be fucking amazing.

I turn up the radio and let my mind drift to the million and one things I have to get done before I head into the office tomorrow for our quarterly board meeting. Trent has some new endeavor to present to us, and a new staff member to onboard. Once I make it home, I shower, eat some leftover pasta, and pass out.

I'm up before the sun, like clockwork. I have a cup of coffee, some oatmeal, and fruit, then head out to check the cattle and get the cowboys going for the day. Ranching ain't for the weak of heart or mind. It's tough and lonely, but I find serenity and peace in riding my horse through the pasture as the sun comes up over the mountains.

By the time I've made the drive into the brewery office, I've been

That Feeling

up for more than three hours. Ranger, my right-hand rancher and cousin, doesn't need much direction when it comes to managing the cowboys and the day-to-day tasks. He knows that when I go into the office, he can reach me if need be, but more than likely he'll be just fine.

"Mornin'," I say to my brother as I walk into the boardroom and head straight to the coffee and donut station—the one good thing about coming into the office.

"Good morning, sunshine!" Trent slaps me on the back, his annoyingly chipper voice right in my ear. "Nice to see you in the office; glad you dressed the part."

"What's wrong with what I'm wearing?" I take a bite of my donut and look down my body at my black jeans, boots, and flannel.

Trent just laughs and steps over to where several other board members have gathered, including my dad and my Uncle Colton.

I grab my coffee and take another bite of my donut, taking a seat at the table. I don't socialize much at these things, not because I'm too good for them, but because I hate talking business. I stay up-to-date on all of the brewery-related decisions and finances, so I'm not just a useless vote on the board who collects a dividend check every month. I care about this company; it's my dad's legacy, after all. I just don't like all the small talk and office bullshit.

"Good morning. Got a little glaze on your lip."

A familiar breathy voice pulls me from my thoughts as a warmth spreads through my body. Instinctively, I put my hand up to my lips to wipe away the sugary crumbs from my donut as I whip my head to the right ... and there she is.

Little miss tourist sitting at my boardroom table.

Chapter 2

Brooklyn

The look on his face right now is priceless.

"The fuck are you doing here?"

"Well, that's one helluva way to greet your new boss," I say with a smile.

"Excuse me?" The donut in his hand is paused halfway to his mouth and I can see his brain trying to figure out what's going on. It's cute, and I'll savor it a few more seconds before he finds out who I am and what I'm doing here.

"Do you have an issue with having a female boss, Mr. Slade?" I bite the end of my pen, goading him. "That's not very progressive of you."

"What the fu—Trent, what's going on?" He drops the donut and stands up, shooting his chair across the floor.

"Hey, I see you've met our new social media strategist." Trent gestures toward me as he walks over to where Tyler is standing. "Brooklyn, this is my older brother, Tyler. Tyler, meet Brooklyn."

I can see the wheels turning in Tyler's brain as he's still trying to figure out what the hell is going on.

That Feeling

"Why'd she say she's my new boss?" Tyler looks frantically to Trent for clarity, and it causes both of us to laugh.

"She's kidding, Tyler." Trent arches an eyebrow at his older brother. "Your last name is the one on the building, remember?" He playfully taps Tyler's elbow before walking to the front of the room to start the meeting.

"Good morning, everyone. This is our Q3 board meeting for Slade International Enterprises. I want to start out by introducing our newest team member, Brooklyn Dyer." Trent gestures toward me and I offer up a pleasant smile and wave.

"I met Brooklyn this last spring at the annual wine and spirit trade show back in Chicago. She was basically running the entire thing and went above and beyond to make sure every booth had what they needed and then some. When we ran into a small emergency, Brooklyn herself ensured it was resolved."

I blush a little at Trent's words. He's not wrong, though. We were severely short-staffed for that event, and while I was only supposed to be managing the social media aspect of the event, I took over a lot of the organization and day-to-day duties.

"She not only graduated top of her class from Northwestern in both undergrad and grad school, but she was also hired by the Chicago Cubs before she even graduated. Brooklyn is the younger generation that will breathe new life into this company."

The men in the room actually applaud, leaving me to fiddle nervously with the pen in my hand.

I can feel Tyler looking at me. I glance up just in time to catch his eyeline. He leans over so he's close enough to whisper. "Should I mention that you're also an accomplished mechanical bull rider?"

I glance back to Trent, pretending to ignore Tyler before raising my hand. "I'd also like to mention that I was able to ride the mechanical bull for a full nine seconds at the annual Fall Fest in Grand Lake yesterday, one of my proudest accomplishments."

The room erupts with laughter and clapping. "She's already

fitting in out west," an older white-haired gentlemen says with a smile.

I lean back in my chair and slowly swivel it so I'm clearly looking at Tyler. I give him my best smile and flick my hair over one shoulder.

"She can give you all a much better introduction and insight into her first project here. Brooklyn?" Trent stretches his hand out to his side for me to come join him.

"Thanks, everyone, for the warm welcome. It truly means so much to me coming into such an established and successful company like Slade Brewing International." I turn to Trent, who is about to take a seat. I grab his arm to stop him.

"I want to say a massive thank you to you, Trent, for taking the time to talk to me at the trade show in Chicago and for having faith in me so quickly by offering me this job. I can't thank you enough."

The members clap again and I can feel Tyler's eyes on me. I look over to where he's sitting and his gaze has fallen to where my hand still rests on Trent's arm. I instantly let go of it, his eyes finding mine.

When I saw Tyler at the Fall Fest, it was the first time I'd seen him in person. Through my research of the Slade family and business, I'd found a few photos of Tyler that instantly made me curious about him. He's obviously attractive, tall, and built like he works the land. He's rugged with dark brown eyes and even darker hair. Today he's clean-shaven, but yesterday he'd had a few days' worth of growth that had me wanting to reach up and feel the scruff.

I couldn't find an exact age, but I know he's at least mid-to-late thirties. I've always had a thing for older men. Today is the first time I'm noticing the gray coming in a little at his temples and the smile lines around his eyes. It gives him character. He looks exactly like a younger version of his father, Drake, who is by far the most handsome 69-year-old I've ever met.

I have to will myself to look away from Tyler—the moment feels so intimate and everyone's witnessing it. I can feel a small bead of sweat at my hairline. It's funny how I felt so in control of the situation last night when I was shamelessly flirting with him, but in the light of

That Feeling

day, in his boardroom, I feel like I'm two seconds away from becoming a puddle on the floor.

"Like Trent mentioned, I'm from Chicago, born and raised. Go Cubbies! I studied marketing and social media in college. Growing up with the internet and right on the bubble of social media, I feel like it really allowed me to fully immerse myself in this world and know what people are looking for when it comes to advertising, engagement, etc."

I keep my eyes moving from person to person around the table, avoiding settling on anyone for too long.

"During my research, I was incredibly impressed with how quickly Slade Brewing International grew from a microbrewery with two beers into an international beer and liquor company that now offers very high-end small-batch whiskeys, plus more than seven beers and even more seasonal beers, and now seltzers. Not to mention the presence you have not only inside Colorado, but across America. Since Slade is the official beer of the professional sports teams here in Colorado as well as on tap in several chains throughout North America, I think the new contract we just signed with Top Tier Foods Limited will take us to heights we've never imagined."

I grab the remote control from the table and click it, changing the screen behind me from the Slade Brewery emblem to my first slide.

"Here you can see the list of restaurants and bars owned by Top Tier, along with the number of locations they have in each state. While we're rolling into these restaurants and bars with on-tap options, tastings, and branding, I'll be heading up a massive nationwide campaign that will introduce us and our partnership with these restaurants."

I work through my PowerPoint, my nerves decreasing as I see the genuine interest and surprise by the members around the table. I'm a confident woman and I know I have the work ethic and knowledge to be successful at this job, but it's always intimidating when you're trying to convince a room full of men—some old enough to be your grandfather—that you know what you're doing and can be trusted.

"I'll be heading up an intense campaign over the coming weeks and months that will focus on getting the Slade name out to a wider audience—one that isn't just beer or whiskey drinkers. With the extremely successful launch of the Mountain Waters Seltzer line in June of this year, we can strategically focus on marketing to millennials, a practically untapped market with Slade beverages."

I finish up my presentation then exit the room so that they can carry on with their quarterly meeting. I walk down the hall to where my new office is located. Thankfully, Trent gave me a tour earlier this morning.

I take a seat in my chair and let out a long sigh. I've been incredibly tense and nervous about that presentation for the better part of a month.

My view is breathtaking. Coming from Chicago, a lot of people think a view of the lake or a view of the skyline is breathtaking, but this view blows all of that away. It's what I've been dreaming of. I may only be 26, but I've spent my entire life in the city and I'm ready for a slower-paced life I can actually appreciate. I make good money, but I've always been too busy to actually enjoy that privilege.

"You killed it!"

I spin around in my chair, my thoughts interrupted by Trent standing in my doorway.

"Did I?"

"Absolutely. They couldn't stop talking about how impressed they were with you and your 'gumption,' as my dad likes to say. I told you they'd be on board with it."

I feel my shoulders finally fall from my ears as a genuine smile spreads across my face.

"Now we just have to convince Tyler about the plan," Trent says tentatively.

I grimace at that thought. I know I can be convincing, but this is work. I'll keep it professional and not flirt my way into getting him to be on board with what Trent and I talked about.

"Oh, speak of the devil. Hey, Tyler, come here for a second!"

That Feeling

Trent is looking over his shoulder back down the hallway. A few seconds later, Tyler is the doorway and Trent is ushering him into my office.

"We have something we want to run by you."

Tyler's hat is pulled down a little lower today, but I can still see his eyes under the brim. He does that thing again that's so weirdly sexy, leaning his shoulder against the door jamb. He casually crosses his arms over his chest and it emphasizes his bare forearms. His sleeves are rolled up and I can see the dark hair peppering his tan skin. He has forearms like a baseball player, something I didn't notice last night when he had his long, calloused fingers resting against my neck. Instinctively, I reach my own hand up and rest it delicately at the base of my throat, and it instantly garners his attention. His eyes settle on my hand before slowly raking up to my eyes.

Goddammit. Why does it feel like this man is always undressing me with his eyes?

"Make it quick. I've got to be at a cattle auction in Fort Collins in less than an hour." His tone is clipped, his deep, gravelly voice doing all sorts of things to my insides.

I glance quickly at Trent then back to Tyler. "Okay, here goes." I place my hands on my desk, folding then unfolding them. "We want you to be the face of Slade Brewing International."

"The what now?"

"The face. Like, the spokesperson. You remember the Marlboro Man?"

Tyler's head slowly falls back and he lets out a full belly laugh. "Funny. He put you up to this?" He points to Trent then shakes his head before pushing off the doorway. "I gotta get goin'."

He turns to leave but I stand up. "It's not a joke, Tyler. We're serious."

His eyes dart from me to Trent, who gives him a huge grin and grabs his shoulders.

"Time to get a haircut and some new clothes, brother. You're a model now."

Chapter 3

Tyler

"Abso-fucking-lutely not," I say matter-of-factly at their ridiculous suggestion.

"Why not, man? It's not like you'll be signing autographs and dodging the paps. It's just some photos for social media."

"Because I fucking said *no*. I don't want my face all over social media and I don't have the time for any of that shit. We have, like, 30 cousins. Why can't you go pick one of them?"

"We at Slade feel li—" Brooklyn starts, but I cut her off.

"*We?*" I interrupt.

"Yes, *we,* Tyler. She works here now. She's part of the Slade Brewing family."

"You gotta be fucking kidding me." I know I sound petulant, but what the actual fuck? "This broad shows up like two days ago and she's already calling the shots around here?"

"That's her job, Tyler. Don't be an asshole. She is extremely successful in her field and I promised her she'd have our full support in whatever decisions she decides are best."

"Well, that's on you. I never promised shit!" I can feel my blood

That Feeling

pressure rising. I pull off my hat and run my hands through my hair. Trent's not wrong about me needing a haircut.

"Look, Tyler," Brooklyn starts, "I'm not trying to step on your toes or come in here and piss you off, but I am damn good at my job and I need you to trust me on this. I know I'm just a *broad*, but I've got balls."

I stare at her. She crosses her arms, letting me know she's serious and she's standing her ground. I respect that.

"I didn't mean it in an offensive way. The broad comment, that is," I elaborate. She raises both hands as if to say she understands. "Why me?"

"You're the center of the Venn diagram."

I run my hands over my face. "The what now?"

Brooklyn reaches for her iPad, flipping open the cover and turning it around to face me. She tilts her head around the screen to zoom in on a particular chart. "Based on the demographics of people who drink Slade beer, whiskey, and seltzer—"

"God, not another PowerPoint, please."

She snaps the cover closed. "Okay, so we took several polls and we know that we have a very solid base with baby boomers and Gen X-ers with our whiskey and beer offerings, and we've had a massive increase in sales with millennials lately with our new seltzers and some of our IPAs and craft-style beers."

"I still don't see how I fit in here. Obviously, I like the stuff too." I feel like an idiot but I'm not seeing her point.

"The older generations are pretty solid whiskey and beer drinkers. They like the idea of a rugged, self-made man who still works with his hands and has a simple life. Then we have the younger generations—the hipsters, the ones who love a family-owned business and are opting out of having children to adopt animals and homestead. That's trending like crazy right now."

"I'm *trending*?" I shake my head. This is a hard lifestyle; the kids nowadays have no idea. I stand up and put my hat back on.

"Ranching ain't a trend. This is my life and I'm not going to pimp myself out to cater to some naive idea of what mountain life is like."

"Just think about it, Tyler. You don't have to make a decision right now," Trent says as he steps aside so I can leave Brooklyn's office.

I'm frustrated. I'd like for it to just be accepted if I say I don't want to do something. I'm all for being a team player, but I like my privacy and my quiet life on the ranch. The last thing I want is a camera crew in my face telling me to smile and showing me how to pose.

I check my phone. I'll just make it to the cattle auction in time. I send a quick text to Ranger letting him know I'm on my way.

"Tyler, wait!" I turn around to see Brooklyn power walking in her high heels across the parking lot.

Damn, how'd I miss how fucking sexy her legs look in that skirt and those heels? I shake my head as if that will clear the thoughts from my head. Now that she works for my father's company, that fantasy is over.

I don't stop walking until I get to my truck. She's right on my heels, panting from the slight jog.

"Altitude," she says, trying to catch her breath.

"I need to get to work, ma'am." I reach for the handle of my door and pull it open.

"Ma'am? I wasn't ma'am last night when your tongue was down my throat."

I slam the door closed.

"That how we're gonna play it?"

She shrugs. "I'm not playing anything."

"Good, let's keep it that way, because I'm not the type you want to fuck with, sweetheart. Last night? Didn't happen. You work for my company, you're far too young for me, and most likely, you'll be long gone from here inside of a year."

"You good now? Got that off your chest?" She's back to having her impenetrable facade up. "I have no interest in fucking with you, and you're what? Maybe 10 years older than me? I don't have daddy

That Feeling

issues, Tyler, so my guess is, I'm not your type. Now can we get back to business for a minute before you leave, or is there some other vague threat you want to toss at me?"

I run my tongue over my teeth so I don't grab her and finish what we started last night. I've known this woman less than 24 hours, and already I feel myself losing my grip on reality around her.

"You've got two minutes."

"I'm sure you're used to saying that to women."

I can't hold back my chuckle. "There's that tongue again," I mutter, but she just carries on.

"A few months ago, when Trent and I first started coming up with this campaign, he sent me a photo of you."

I furrow my brows. "Why?"

"Because he saw what my vision was and knew you'd be perfect for it. I took that photo and did a poll of more than 1 million followers on social media, and you beat out 11 other guys by 94%." She says each word slowly and emphatically.

"You might not think that's anything big, but trust me, it's huge. The people have spoken, Tyler, and they want you as the face of the Slade empire. And you're *actually* a Slade, so honestly, it would be crazy to hire a random model for it."

She's not wrong there, but still, this is all too much. She must see it on my face, because she reaches out and places her delicate fingers on my hand that's still resting on the door handle.

"If you promise to think about it, you don't have to take me on that date tonight."

I roll my eyes. "That wasn't going to happen anyway."

"Yeah, I figured. Wouldn't be the first time someone stood me up."

I give her a sideways look. "You've been stood up before? Hard to believe."

"Why? What's that supposed to mean?"

"You know, you don't have to be so defensive all the time. It just means that a woman who looks like you . . ." I stop myself as my eyes do that thing again where they slowly climb her body.

"A woman who looks like me what?"

The warm smile and the way her eyes go soft remind me to rein it in.

"Nothing. I'm late for the auction." I pull my door open and climb inside. "I promise I'll think about it." I reach for the handle to pull the door shut when I see a small, satisfied smile spread across her lips, and it makes me pause. "Was this your plan?"

Her smile fades slightly. "My plan?"

"Throwing yourself at me at the fest last night. Make me think you're into me so I'll be more agreeable to your request?"

"You think you're being agreeable?" she scoffs but doesn't answer the question. I hook an eyebrow at her. "No, that wasn't my plan, and for the record, I didn't *throw myself* at you."

"You begged me for a date. I'd say that's some pretty hard throwing."

"Don't you have an auction to get to?" She rolls her eyes and crosses her arms across her chest, narrowing her gaze at me. "I can promise you one thing, Mr. Slade. I've never begged a man for anything and I never will."

Fuck me.

If she only knew all the ways I've already imagined her begging. I bite down on my tongue to keep from saying something that will embarrass both of us. I chuckle under my breath.

"You've never met a man like me before, Miss Dyer."

I shut the door and start the truck. Almost made it out of here without this damn woman getting under my skin.

Almost.

Chapter 4

Brooklyn

The sun isn't up yet. I can just see the orange glow beginning to illuminate the peaks around me. I'm not usually one for being up this early, but a sunrise over the Rocky Mountains is worth it.

I yawn for the third time in a row as I pull down the long road adorned with a massive wooden archway.

"Slade Ranch," I read the sign aloud as I squint to try to make out if that's a house or a barn I see straight ahead.

I roll down the window of my Toyota 4Runner. Other than the crunch of gravel beneath the tires, it's eerily silent out here. I close my eyes and take in a few deep breaths of the crisp morning air. It's early September here, so the mornings and evenings have started to bring frost and a chill to the air—though by midday, it'll be in the high 70s with sunny skies. While I've only lived here for two weeks, I feel like I've already gotten a taste of Colorado's unpredictable and ever-changing weather.

My phone dings. It's a text from my younger sister, Mallory. It's just after 6 a.m. here, which means it's 7 a.m. back in Chicago, where I'm sure she's already at her vet office for her residency.

Mallory: *Hey sis, miss you! Hope you're having a great time in Colorado. Give me a call so we can catch up. Love you.*

I smile as I type out a response.

Me: *Miss you too lil sis. I'll give you a call soon so we can catch up. Lots to share! XoXo*

Mallory and I have always been close. Leaving her back in Chicago was the hardest part of my decision to move out here. I almost didn't take the job at Slade Brewing, but Mallory refused to let me give up my dream to stay close to her.

"Brook, who knows where life will lead me when my residency is done here? You know I've always dreamt of working with horses, and Chicago isn't exactly overrun with stables."

She grabs my shoulders and gives me a little shake.

"I'm serious. You go meet some sexy cowboy and pave the way for me to come out to Colorado in a few years."

I laugh when I recall our conversation. The reality is, she was serious. I don't doubt that whether I'm out here or not, Mallory will find her way out west someday.

I finally reach the end of the long driveway and put my SUV in park as I look out the windshield at the large custom-built home. It's stunning. The wraparound porch has a railing made of logs and a few rocking chairs. There's a wool blanket thrown over the arm of one of the chairs and a table next to it that looks like a tree stump. Whoever designed this house perfectly nailed that upscale rustic lodge look.

I climb the stairs and approach the door with a hand raised to knock when it suddenly swings open, and I'm greeted by a shirtless Tyler.

"The hell are you doing here?"

His dark hair has flopped down over his forehead. He runs his fingers through it, brushing it back off his face. He lifts his other hand and quickly pulls on a flannel shirt, but not before I get to admire the way his chiseled body ripples with the movement.

"Good morning to you too." I give him a sincere grin but he doesn't reciprocate.

That Feeling

"How'd you know where I live?"

"Not hard to Google *Slade Ranch* or ask anyone who lives within a hundred miles of here." He just stares at me. "Trent told me. Can I come in?"

He steps aside and allows me to walk through the doorway. His flannel shirt is still hanging open. I quickly glance down to see a trail of dark hair that runs down his chest, dipping beneath his jeans that sit so deliciously on his hips.

His eyes catch my gaze and his fingertips quickly work to button the shirt. "Didn't expect anyone this early," he mutters, shutting the door behind us.

"I know it's early, but I also know that you guys tend to be up before dawn and all that. I also know you're busy, so I figured we could run through some things before the campaign launches in 10 days."

"Campaign?" He scratches at the back of his head like this is the first time he's heard about it.

"Yes, the campaign, Tyler. The one where we agreed you'd be the face of Slade Brewing International?" A coy grin slowly spreads across his face. "Oh, you're a funny guy, huh?"

He walks toward the kitchen. "I'll put some coffee on."

"I'm actually surprised it's after 6 a.m. and you're not out in the pasture already," I say, glancing around the great room. The ceilings have to be at least 12'. The large exposed wooden beams draw your eyes upward to a massive floor-to-ceiling window that overlooks the property. It's absolutely breathtaking.

The house is decorated very tastefully and way more professionally than I had expected from Tyler Slade—a man whose closet seems to consist solely of jeans, flannels, and cowboy hats.

I grab the bag I brought in with me and pull out my iPad and portfolio and lay the boards across the coffee table.

"Well, it is Sunday. I tend to get a later start on Sundays," he says from the kitchen. "Cream and sugar?"

"Yes, please." I open my iPad and pull up my strategy plan. A framed photo on the coffee table distracts me and I pick it up. It's a group of probably 25 people. I spot Tyler pretty quickly in the background next to Trent. It must be the entire Slade family.

"But I did get up at 5 a.m. and tended to the horses before coming back to bed . . . what the hell?"

I glance up as he walks back into the room with a mug in each hand.

"What's all this?"

I take the coffee from his hand and inhale it briefly before taking a long sip. "This is our roadmap." I take a seat on the couch and pat the cushion. "I promise not to bite."

He takes a seat next to me and I try not to notice the heat I feel radiating off his thick thigh that's almost touching mine.

"Okay, so I already have everything scheduled for our social posts. We know what the captions and hashtags will be, which days and times the posts will go live, etc. Right now, we're kind of working a little backward. I've already hired a photographer from Denver who will take all the photos for Instagram, the website, and Facebook, and film any videos for Instagram and TikTok."

"TikTok? You're just making shit up now."

I look at him a little sideways. "TikTok? You've seriously never head of TikTok?"

"No, and saying it multiple times doesn't make it any clearer." He stands up and walks over to the window. I can tell he's already feeling overwhelmed.

"It's a video social media app, and the videos last anywhere from a few seconds to a few minutes long. It's extremely popular right now and an amazing marketing tool."

He nods his head, keeping his gaze out the window as he drinks his coffee.

"I don't have any social media—never have, never will." He looks over his shoulder at me as he says it.

"That's fine; we don't need you to have your own. The whole point of this campaign is that it's all hosted on the Slade Brewing

That Feeling

International social media pages and you're just the face." I smile at him genuinely, hoping I can relieve some of his anxiety and apprehension about this whole thing.

"I don't know," he mutters, "it all just feels too much. I'm a really busy man, Miss Dyer, and none of this—" he motions toward the media boards on the coffee table, "is real. This is all just a bunch of curated, made-up shit to sell something. It doesn't mean anything."

I try to remain calm and not take his words too personally, but the fact of the matter is this is my entire job and he knows it. The least he could do is try to be a little understanding even if he doesn't understand it all. To belittle my profession feels extra shitty.

"Well, how about this . . . you don't have to worry about any of it. I'll tell you well in advance whenever I'll need you for a photo shoot and where you need to show up. I'll handle everything else."

He chews his bottom lip as if he's contemplating my offer.

"Ranger and Decker have already agreed to step it up and pick up any slack around the ranch when you have to step away for the shoots."

He whips his head around, his eyes narrowing on me. "My cousins? They don't know how to run the place without me. Sure, they're my right-hand guys, but I need to be here."

"I'm not saying they can run it without you, but they did assure me they can handle the day-to-day stuff for at least a few hours at a time if you need to step away."

Jesus, with Tyler it's like trying to walk on eggshells and stroke an ego at the same time.

"You should've let me talk to them about it."

I smile and nod. "You're right; I'm sorry."

"I'll have a conversation with them—make sure they can handle it." He places his coffee mug on the end table and crosses his arms over his broad chest. "If I do this, I don't want any pressure from you or anyone to do anything else. I won't have my own accounts and I won't be talked into it. What matters to me is this ranch and my family. I don't give a shit about any of this pointless TikTack or Instagram whatever, understood?"

My patience is running more than a little thin with Tyler's attitude and constant waffling on this whole thing—not to mention this new need to invalidate my job and make it clear to me that he feels like it's pointless.

I slam the cover of my iPad closed and reach for the media boards on the table. "You know what, Tyler? I think I've changed my mind. Sorry to have bothered you about all this." I stuff the boards back into my bag, followed by my iPad.

"Huh? I said I'd do it."

I hoist the bag up under my arm as I pull the strap up my shoulder, "Oh, I heard you. You not only went out of your way to let me know how pointless my job and entire career is, but clearly, you don't think you need me or this for your family business, so I'll be on my way."

I walk toward the front door.

"Brooklyn, wait." Tyler follows quickly behind me.

"It's fine, Tyler, honestly. I have no doubt Trent will be more than willing to step in. I know he's insanely busy as well, but this campaign and the direction it could send your company in means a lot to him."

"I didn't mean to make you feel like your career is pointless . . . that's not what I intended."

I reach for the front door handle. "It's fine. Besides," I turn my gaze over my shoulder and drag my eyes up his body like I've seen him do to me several times, "you two look so much alike I doubt anyone will even notice he's not you."

I pull the front door open but Tyler's hand is on it in a flash, slamming it shut as he steps forward.

"I'll do it."

I glance up at him, and his lips are inches away. I can feel his chest hit my arm as his breathing grows rapid.

That Feeling

"I've got two inches on him and 20 pounds of muscle. People would have to be fucking blind not to see that."

I shrug nonchalantly. "Maybe, but it's a risk I'm willing to take if it means working with someone who doesn't have his head so far up his ass he can't see the bigger picture for his family business."

I pull on the door again, but he straightens his arm so I can't open it. He extends the other one too, so now both hands are flat against the door behind me. I twist my body around until my back hits the door.

He bends his elbows an inch, bringing his nose almost to mine before gritting out the words, "I said I'd fucking do it."

And just like that, I got Tyler Slade to do exactly what I wanted without him even realizing he was being played.

He might think I'm just a young woman from the city who's way outside her element, but he's got it all wrong . . . he's just met his match.

Chapter 5

Tyler

I want to lean down two more inches—close the distance between our lips—but I know it's a bad idea. I see her throat tighten as she swallows, and the tip of her pink tongue darts out to wet her lips.

"It's not a good idea." My voice sounds thick with desire . . . no use trying to hide it.

"What's not a good idea?" She's teasing me again.

"You and me."

I do nothing to put more distance between us. Instead, I dip my head just a little lower, my hair falling down. Her eyes shift upward at the movement. I take a second to admire those eyes—the vibrant green with little flecks of gold.

"I wholeheartedly agree," she whispers. "I'd never recommend getting involved with your boss."

I chuckle—somehow Brooklyn referencing me as her boss has the opposite effect. Now it sounds sexier and even more exciting, like it's forbidden.

"Especially since I'm a woman in a male-dominated industry. If people knew I already kissed my employee once bef—"

I jerk back. "Your employee?"

That Feeling

"Yes, I'm *your* boss." She says it like I'm an idiot for getting it wrong.

"Ha! Last time I checked, little lady, it's *my name* on your employee contract and *my name* on the family business."

She steps around me and straightens her back. "Yes, but this is my campaign, my department. You're the talent and I'm the boss."

She is not backing down from this.

"What do you mean you've already kissed me? I kissed *you* that night."

Her mouth falls open with a laugh that comes out in the form of a huff. "No, you didn't. You were trying to run away and I found you at your truck." She points her finger at my chest as she takes a step toward me. "I kissed you!" She shoves the tip of her finger against my chest and I don't know why, but I reach out and grab it, pulling her until she crashes against me.

"That wasn't a kiss. It was a peck, so it doesn't count."

"Man, you really cannot ever be wrong, can you?"

We're chest-to-chest, neither of us conceding.

"What's your size?"

"Hmm?"

"I need to go shopping for your looks before the photo shoot on Tuesday. Shirt, pants, shoes ... I need it all."

The moment is ruined, and I'm reminded that I've signed up for this ridiculous circus. I step back and run my hands over my face a few times.

"Look, the only way I'm doing this is if I get to wear my own clothes."

She tosses her hands in the air and lets out a frustrating grunt. "Can't you ever just be agreeable? Forget it! I'm going with Trent."

"Hey, don't you want this to be authentic?" She tilts her head as if she's going to hear me out. "If you want me—a rancher or 'homesteader' or whatever the trendy term is right now—to be out there, showing everyone how it looks to work the land, it should be authentic. And that includes my clothes, my cowboy hat, and my boots that have a fucking history of walking this land, of breaking horses, of building this home you're standing in."

She lifts her eyebrows as she motions with her finger. "*You* built this?"

"Yeah. My dad and brothers helped, plus a couple cousins, but yeah, we Slade men have built all of our homes. This ain't some Hollywood cowboy show where we spend a million bucks to hire some fancy crew. We take a lot of pride in everything we do. We chose every damn tree we took down on this property for this home." I run my hand along one of the exposed beams that runs down to the floor. "Nothing went to waste."

"Okay, let's see what you're working with then. Show me your closet." She smiles at me as she puts down her bag by the front door and points toward the staircase, taking a few steps. "Bedroom's upstairs?"

I jump in front of her, holding up my hands to stop her. The thought of Brooklyn Dyer in my bedroom has my brain thinking all sorts of things it has no business thinking.

"Just hold on a beat." I try to come up with an excuse as to why that's not a good idea, but I'm drawing a blank. Bottom line is, I'm the one who insisted on using my own clothes and she seems to be obliging. "I, uh—I haven't made my bed yet."

"Seriously?" she laughs.

Yeah, I sound insane. "Fine, this way."

We walk up the stairs and I glance over my shoulder to make sure she's following me.

"I'm actually shocked there isn't an antler chandelier or, like, a giant moose or bear head on the wall above the fireplace."

We both glance over at the massive stone fireplace she's referring to. The stone not only encompasses the fireplace and hearth, but it runs all the way up the wall to the ceiling.

"When I pulled up this morning, I thought for sure it would look like Gaston decorated the place."

"Gaston?"

That Feeling

We take a right down the hallway until we hit the end, where the master bedroom is. I pause briefly. "Yeah, like in *Beauty and the Beast?* When he's singing, he says, 'I use antlers in all of my decorating'?" She sings it, gesturing with one arm as I stare at her blankly. "Come on . . . Gaston?"

I bite back a smile at how cute she looks. "Nope, no clue." I open the door to my bedroom and we both step inside.

"Holy shit," she whistles, "this room is bigger than my entire apartment back in Chicago." I watch her as she does a lap around the room, poking her head into the bathroom before I hear her gasp echo off the tile floor.

"You have a clawfoot tub?" Her head shoots back around the corner.

"Yup, my mom picked that out, actually." I follow her into the bathroom and watch as she softly runs her fingertips over the edge of the massive tub. "Had it custom made since I'm too tall for the typical old-fashioned ones."

"Your mom has excellent taste."

She's silent again, taking in the unobstructed mountain view from the large bay window on the far side of the bathroom.

"No neighbors," she gestures with her chin. "Was this place originally going to be yours or your parents'?"

"Mine." I push off the wall and point over my shoulder. "Closet is this way."

I don't mind her questions, but I'm also not interested in getting into a discussion about my plans for this place or why I live alone in a 5,000-square-foot house. Naturally, those are the types of questions that follow.

"Hmm, okay," she says, flipping through my shirts. She dives right in, pulling different hangers and opening drawers. She groups several shirts on an unused portion of the closet rod. "Only jeans?" she asks, pointing to some drawers.

I shake my head *no*. "There are a few non-denim options in there. Not sure if they still fit."

She pulls the drawers open and grabs a few pairs of jeans and a pair of Dockers. She steps back and stares at the selection of clothes she's assembled.

"I don't think we need shoe or hat options . . . we'll just use the same boots and hat you always wear."

"Told you I had options," I smirk.

"I'll be out there." She points back toward my bedroom and makes a beeline out of the closet.

"Wait, what's going on?" I ask, following behind her.

She takes a seat on my unmade bed. "You're trying on the clothes so we can style some outfits."

She's clearly confused as to why I'm confused, but all I can focus on is the fact that she's sitting on my fucking bed. She leans back a little, resting her hands by her hips.

"Why do you need me to try stuff on? I'm in jeans and a button-down right now, and those are just different variations of this." I motion to my body.

"I'm the professional, remember? We agreed. I say 'jump' and you do it." She bats her eyelashes at me.

"I don't remember agreeing to that."

She's standing her ground. She casually crosses one of her legs over the other, her tanned knee poking out from a large rip in her jeans. Her lips aren't cherry red today. I'm not sure if she has anything on them—they're just a shiny, rosy pink. Still tempting as fuck and has me wanting to taste them again.

"Fine."

I step back, reaching up to unbutton my shirt. I maintain my eye contact with her as I undo one button after the next. I grab the open lapels, roll my shoulders, pull off the shirt, and toss it toward her.

"Clothes are in there." She points toward the closet as I drop my hand down to the waistband of my jeans.

She's trying hard to keep her eyes on mine, but I watch them flick downward momentarily. I undo the button and zipper and hook my

That Feeling

thumbs like I'm about to pull them down when her throat constricts again. This time her eyes drop and don't come back up.

"Sorry, boss, forgot I have to keep things professional." I walk back into the closet and I can feel her eyes burning into my back. It's cute how she thinks she has the upper hand in this.

I pull my jeans down and kick them to the side, pulling on a pair of the Dockers and grabbing one of the shirts.

"Pants are a little tight," I say as I walk out of the closet and back into the room. "Might have to buy new ones."

She stands and walks over to me. "What are you—?" She circles me slowly and I swivel my head around in a circle to follow her. "Pants aren't too tight, trust me. Can you tuck the shirt in?"

I nod and tuck it in. She disappears into the closet, returning a few seconds later with my hat and boots.

"Need to see the whole thing."

"Well?" I ask after putting on the entire outfit and feeling pretty fucking silly doing this in my own home.

Brooklyn tilts her head as she looks me over before stepping closer. She reaches around my neck, adjusting my collar. I can smell her perfume and it's sexy and almost has a spicy note to it. Suddenly I feel like sweat is beading on my brow. She must notice, because she starts asking me questions—trying to intimidate me.

"Younger women make you nervous?"

"No."

"Powerful women intimidate you?"

"Only my mother." That makes her smile.

"This one is a keeper, hold on." She turns around and grabs her phone that she's placed on my bed. "Just stand there." She holds the phone up and I hear the camera shutter sound.

"Did you just take my picture?"

She doesn't look up from her phone. "Yeah, need it for the photo shoot. That way we'll know the looks and can easily grab them so you can change between shots."

I nod. This actually makes sense. "So am I trying on the rest of these? Because I've got some cattle I should attend to."

"Yes, and Ranger and Decker are covering things on the ranch until 8, so we have plenty of time."

We repeat the process of me trying on the clothes while she snaps photos of them once she has them nailed down.

"So, what made you want to focus more on the ranch than the brewery?"

Her question takes me by surprise as she organizes the clothes into the outfits after I finish trying them on.

"Just wanted something different," I shrug. "Trent was always better at the CEO stuff than I was, and he seems to thrive on it. Seemed like the best option was for him to take over the brewery."

"You ever wonder what your life would've been like if you'd chosen that path?"

I can feel my brow furrow as I think through that question.

"Nah, I'd just be in everyone's way." I shake my head.

"Well, for what it's worth, I don't think Trent or your dad would ever feel like you're in the way at the office."

I can feel myself getting irritated. I'm over trying on all these clothes and having someone suddenly show up and start telling me what to do. I also don't appreciate her trying to play therapist or whatever the fuck she's doing.

"I can manage my life and relationships just fine, Miss Dyer."

"Sorry, I didn't mean to get involved. You're right." The silence is short-lived. "Was your dad disappointed when you didn't choose the brewery?"

I toss the last shirt on the bed. "Did they hire you to psychoanalyze me or something? You show up here and somehow force me into doing this stupid model shit, and now you want to corner me before 8 a.m. in my own damn home and ask me if I regret my life choices? For fuck's sake!"

I don't know why I'm yelling. This whole exchange escalated in a

That Feeling

matter of 30 seconds and it's totally on me. But now I'm mad that I'm mad.

"I didn't *force* you—"

"You did, actually! You told me I didn't have to take you on a date and then threatened to go after Trent instead."

I hear it.

I sound crazy and her expression tells me she hears it too.

"I threatened you? And now I'm going after Trent? Just because you're weirdly jealous of your own brother and insecure about your decisions doesn't mean it's my fault. You made a commitment to me about this, so we're going to see it through, but I've heard you loud and clear. This," she motions between us, "will stay strictly professional and I won't dare try to get to know you a little even though we'll be working closely together. Excuse me for being friendly."

This is what I needed: for her to realize that I'm not just a fun time while she's here in Colorado. I'm not just some guy she can flirt with to not feel lonely or goad into doing what she wants.

I won't be toyed with and tossed aside.

I don't chase after her when she grabs her phone, walks out of my room, heads down the stairs, and slams the front door.

Chapter 6

Brooklyn

I don't look back as I slam Tyler's front door and march to my SUV, throwing it in reverse and spitting gravel as I take off back down the long driveway.

I didn't force him into this. In fact, I gave him an out this morning. Sure, I was trying to tease him into agreeing when I made the Trent comment, but the truth is, if he had said, "Yes, please go with my brother," I would have. I would have dropped it and called Trent in a heartbeat, because this campaign has to get off the ground ASAP and I don't have time to babysit or seduce some grown-ass man into it.

I reach the massive archway again and bring the truck to a stop. I roll down the window again and listen to the soft sounds of a few birds singing and the wind winding its way over the mountains.

"Ugh!" I let out a grunt and grip the steering wheel before turning around and driving back up to the house.

I knock on the door and a minute later, a surprised Tyler is answering it again.

"Look, I refuse to work in a hostile environment. I don't want to force you to do anything you don't want to do, so this is it. This is the last time I'll offer you an out. If you don't want to do this, it's fine,

That Feeling

honestly. But if you do want to commit, then no more whining about how *pointless* or *stupid* you think this is. This is my job. I was hired to do this and I love it. I take it very seriously and I will always do my job to the best of my ability. I expect you to be professional and not act like a child who didn't get his way."

Tyler is standing there as I speak, his face unmoving. He's gripping the door in one hand while his other is on the door frame—looking effortlessly casual while my stomach is in my throat.

"I'm a friendly, outgoing person," I continue. "I know I'm young, but I'm not naive, and I can do this job and do it well. I'm not saying we need to be best friends, but I'd like to know that I can be myself around you and not worry that you're going to bite my head off or belittle my work or complain about how much you hate everything we're doing."

He nods his head slowly.

"So, deal?"

"Deal. You're right. I did agree to this and need to act like an adult."

I nod. "Thank you. Now I'll be out of your hair." I thumb over my shoulder and turn to walk back to my still-running vehicle.

"And Brooklyn?" I turn back around. "I didn't mean to hurt your feelings. I'm sorry."

I let out a small sigh of relief and offer a slight smile. "All good. I'll be here at 5 p.m. on Tuesday evening with the photographer. Leave those clothes organized in the outfits we decided on, okay?"

I wave and step back down the porch stairs. When I shut the door of my truck and slide it into gear, he's still standing in the doorway staring at me.

There's something so fascinating behind Tyler Slade's cold exterior and those dark brown eyes—something that makes me want to strip him bare, layer by layer, and lose myself in him. A warmth forms between my thighs and winds its way up my body till it settles in my chest. It's a feeling I never even experienced with my ex, Neal.

The warmth dissipates the moment Neal's name pops into my

head. Sweet boy-next-door Neal, who can charm anyone's mother, connect with their father, and end up best friends with their siblings.

Neal, who could always talk me into staying when my heart was telling me to leave.

"How could you want to walk away from us? We're meant to be together, Brook. We love the same movies and music, have the same friends—hell, we even met at our favorite restaurant. You can't break up this dynamic duo. What would everyone say?"

He would hold my hands and pout his lips, his eyes growing big and round like a puppy's. I can remember thinking that none of those things really matter if you're not in love with the person, but I wasn't ready to admit that to myself, and everyone always says love is a choice.

"You just have to choose to love him," my mother told me.

Everyone thought we were perfect together, and from the outside looking in, we were. We never fought, we didn't have insanely differing beliefs or backgrounds, but for all the things we *were*, on my end at least, we weren't in love.

He was a comfort.

I loved him at first. Truly, I did. But something I've come to realize is that I loved him in the capacity I could at the time.

We connected so well and laughed so much. It felt like the universe was giving me the "perfect" guy and I would be an ungrateful, selfish bitch if I didn't recognize that this was a man who would make a loyal husband and loving father someday. So I ignored my gut and said *yes* to a first date and several more after that until we were officially a couple.

Maybe I was childish for walking away and leaving it all behind, but I couldn't accept a ring and a marriage proposal when I didn't feel a spark or connection when he kissed me. I'd close my eyes and try so hard, but it was never there.

I was starting to believe that the whole chemistry and "sparks" feeling was all a bunch of manufactured bullshit from Disney . . . until Tyler Slade's lips touched mine.

That Feeling

I feel my shoulders fall as I pull onto the main road and head toward my office. Because even if Tyler Slade is who I'm meant to love, it doesn't seem like he feels the same way.

"Okay, now look at me but right past me."

Kevin, the photographer I brought in from Denver, snaps several more photos as Tyler stands with one thumb hooked in the belt buckle of his jeans while the other holds a bottle of Slade whiskey.

"Perfect, yes, just like that."

Kevin is moving around him, trying to capture as many angles as possible with the slowly setting sun. I try not to stare at Tyler, but it's hard. I keep glancing down at my phone, pretending to reply to emails even though I've tried to read the same one probably half a dozen times already.

I finally give up and turn my gaze to Tyler. He's wearing some dark, worn jeans with a red and green flannel shirt with hints of yellow. His hat is pulled down just low enough that if he tips his head, it hides his eyes.

"Okay, now let's try a few with you on the horse, and then some leading the horse."

He nods and walks over to where Misty is tied to a post. He strokes her nose a few times, pushing her mane out of her eyes as he leans in and whispers something to her. She nods and makes a grunting noise like she understands him as he unties her reins and walks her back to where Kevin and I are standing. It's mesmerizing to watch how he can so easily communicate with her.

"She seemed to understand you."

"She does. Takes a lot of trust-building."

He hooks his foot into the stirrup and reaches up to grab the top before effortlessly swinging his leg overtop of her before situating himself in the seat.

I take a step back as he walks her in a few circles.

"Keep doing that," Kevin says, crouching down to snap more photos. "Look off into the distance." He snaps a few then looks through them.

"Tyler, try to relax a little. Even with your hat on, it looks like you're furrowing your brow like you're angry or confused. We want to convey ease and comfort. Find a point and focus on it. Kevin looks over his shoulder at me. "Better yet, look at Brook. Try to maintain eye contact with her."

His eyes settle on mine and I feel my stomach clench. I suddenly feel the urge to look anywhere but Tyler's eyes. Meanwhile, his eyes feel like they're burning holes in my retinas—like he can read my soul.

"Perfect. Now a few with you and the horse standing still. Maybe have the reins in your hands."

Kevin snaps a few more then instructs Tyler to slowly start walking toward me while maintaining eye contact again.

"You doing okay?" I ask softly as he comes to a stop right in front of me. "May I?" I say, reaching out my hand toward Misty.

"Yeah. I'm okay . . . just angry-looking, I guess." He has a slight smile when he says it and relief washes over me. I guess I didn't realize how tense I've been through this whole shoot worrying if he's pissed or about to walk away.

"You're doing great. You seemed to drop your shoulders and relax once he said to find a focal point."

Misty's nose feels soft like velvet as I stroke it.

"She likes you," he says, and I look up to find him still watching me.

"At least someone here does," I mutter half under my breath.

"You think I don't like you?" Tyler pulls his hat off and runs his hands through his messy hair.

"Seriously? I wouldn't say you hate me, but I wouldn't say you were anywhere near the ballpark of *like*." I shrug and stuff my hands into the back pockets of my jeans. It inadvertently thrusts my chest out and I see his eyes drop for just a second.

That Feeling

"Okay, people, we're going to lose the light if we don't finish up." Kevin's voice interrupts our quiet moment.

"Interesting," Tyler murmurs as he takes the reins and starts to pull Misty away. He juts his chin out a little, pulling his bottom lip between his teeth like he's thinking. "Guess I'll have to work on that then."

Is he flirting with me?

We finish the shoot and Tyler says he'll meet us back at the house after he puts Misty away.

"You heading back to the motel with me?" Kevin asks as I help him load his equipment into the back of his truck.

"Maybe. I'm going to ask Tyler really quick if he wants to grab dinner, so he can probably drop me off after."

Kevin gets a devious look on his face. "You little minx . . . I knew there had to be something between you two, because the sexual tension felt like a ten ton elephant out there!"

I roll my eyes and put a finger to my mouth to tell him to hush. I glance over my shoulder as Tyler approaches.

"Tyler Slade, a pleasure, sir. You are a natural star, I'm telling you. If you ever want to do, like, a Slade Brothers calendar, call me."

Tyler laughs as they shake hands and Kevin excuses himself to give us a moment.

"He is right, ya know. Once you let your guard down out there, it looked really effortless. So, hey, can I buy you dinner at the Forks?"

"I'm not sure that's a great idea." He does that sexy thing men do where they run a hand over their scruffy beard.

God, this man gets sexier with every interaction. I'm kind of kicking myself for not taking him up on his offer the first night we met.

"Why not?"

"You know why."

I wrinkle my brow. "I don't, actually."

I'm playing coy, but I'm also a little curious, because while we flirted that night at the Fall Fest, I was the one chasing him and doing the flirting. I was the one who recommended a date as the prize for riding the bull. And I meant what I said earlier about him not liking me. At this point, I feel like an annoying little gnat always buzzing around him.

He gives me a look. A look that says, *you know exactly why*.

"Oh, come on, we work together; it's merely a professional courtesy. It's the least I can do. I promise I won't jump you."

He shakes his head and lets out one of those sexy, grunty laughs while he kicks at a rock on the driveway. When he looks back up at me, his eyes seem darker, hooded . . . lustful.

"Fine. But I wasn't worried about you doin the jumpin', darlin'." He gives me a wink. "I'll grab my keys."

I thank Kevin and let him know he can take off as Tyler reemerges from the house and nods toward the garage around the back.

The door is already open and I walk around to the passenger side of the Super Duty F-350 truck. I'm reaching for the handle when Tyler's shoots around me from behind. I whip my head to the side and almost hit my nose on his chest as he leans forward to open the door.

"This isn't a date, you know," I say as I step one foot onto the running board and grab for the handle on the inside of the cab.

"Not about being a date; it's about being a gentleman. Common courtesy."

He places his hand on my lower back as I hoist myself into the truck, his fingertips gliding softly against my shirt as I turn and take a seat.

"Men don't open doors for women where you're from?" He fires up the truck and puts it in reverse.

"I mean, yeah, some do, I guess, but that's usually on dates. Most of the time it's just a first or second date thing and then it goes away." I shrug.

"Sounds like you're dating the wrong kind of people then."

"I just think it's a generational thing. Guys my age don't really care about stuff like that."

That Feeling

He glances over at me briefly. "I realize I'm a decade older, but I can tell you that a real man will open doors for you and pull out your chair no matter what generation he's from. It's about being a man and not a boy. Chivalry doesn't go away with time—at least not if it's genuine."

"It seems I've hit a nerve. This is the most I've heard you talk." I smile at him so he knows I'm just teasing. "Trust me, I want those things. I just haven't experienced them, so I guess I just thought it was an old-timey thing. Maybe I'll meet some chivalrous cowboy out here who will show me how a real man treats a woman."

I say it half as a joke. He doesn't respond, but I swear I hear the leather of the steering wheel twist beneath his hand as he grips it tighter. We ride the rest of the way to the restaurant in silence.

―――

"So why did you take the job here and leave Chicago?"

I dunk a French fry into ketchup and pop it into my mouth, chewing it thoroughly as I think about how to answer that question.

"Why not? It was an amazing opportunity. I was born and raised in Chicago and I know I can always have a job there. It's a major city and I'm well-connected, but I wanted something new. I wanted a new environment and a new challenge."

He nods as he swallows the bite of his steak sandwich. "You running from something?"

"What? No, why would you ask that?"

He tosses his napkin on the table. "Because I don't get why a cosmopolitan woman like yourself would move to the middle of butt-fuck nowhere."

"Well, if you haven't been in my shoes, then you might not ever get it. Living in a major city can be exhausting and—weirdly—incredibly lonely." I see him raise an eyebrow as soon as I say it, and I wish I could take it back. Not a can of worms I want to open up just yet.

"It won't last."

"What won't?"

"You. Here. You'll miss the convenience of the city and want to go back. Nothing wrong with that. We all come from somewhere." He leans back in his seat and finishes off his Pepsi.

"Maybe, maybe not. For now, I'm happy here and loving it. I'm not focused on the next step. Plus, you might not know this, but Trent offered me a very competitive benefits package." I wriggle my eyebrows and giggle.

I can tell the joke didn't land by the expression marring his face. He sits back up and places his elbows on the table.

"You dating my brother?"

My smile instantly falters at the suggestion. "Trent? Your bro—*no*. No, I'm not dating him and that's not why I got the job."

He raises his hands. "Okay, I'm sorry. I've struck a nerve with you now. I didn't mean to insinuate that that's why you got the job. You two just seem—close."

"We get along really well and he trusts me, which means a lot. But also, I wouldn't have kissed you that night if I were dating him—or anyone, for that matter. I just want to make that clear."

"We've had this conversation and we agreed that what you did technically wasn't a kiss. It was a peck and it didn't count."

I laugh—a full, throaty, head-falling-back laugh, which in turn makes him laugh.

"You ready to head back?"

I nod and he tosses a few bills on the table.

"Hey, I said I was taking you to dinner." I pick up the money and attempt to hand it back to him, but he refuses to take it—instead he stands up and walks over to pull out my chair.

"A gentleman always pays too."

"Not if the woman offers. You know, this macho cowboy thing can come off as a bit toxic." I side-eye him as I reach for my wallet.

"Shanelle?" I say to the waitress, with the bill and my credit card in hand so Tyler can't pay. I turn to him. "If you really insist, you can always get the tip." I smile sweetly as Shanelle approaches our table.

That Feeling

"Oh, no worries, sweetie. It's been taken care of already." She gives Tyler a wink and he nods back at her as she waves and heads back into the kitchen.

"That *is* the tip," Tyler says, motioning toward the wadded bills I still have in my hand.

"What the hell? When did you pay?"

"Before we got here." He holds my elbow and ushers me out of the restaurant and back into the truck.

"I'm confused. What was that in there?" Then it hits me. "Oh, you own the place, don't you? Is there anything in this town you don't own?"

He grips the steering wheel with one hand and stretches his arm out over the back seat to check behind him as he backs up.

"Not much."

"You know you have a camera for that . . ." I point to the dash, but he doesn't seem to care.

"You own the motel?" I ask, ready to give him an earful about it.

He shakes his head *no*.

"I need an actual apartment, but strangely, there's hardly anything available around here. What's that about?"

"We've had a huge influx of social media strategists taking jobs out here to escape the big city."

"Oh, Mr. Funny Guy again." I slow clap at his sarcasm and we both chuckle.

This feels good. Easy. The worst part is, we have that chemistry. I know because I can't get the feeling of his lips off mine, but I can't act on it.

It's pitch black out now and I look out the window at the sky.

"I bet you can see so many stars and constellations out here." I'm talking half to myself, trying not to notice how the inside of this truck smells just like Tyler Slade. It doesn't smell like cologne; I can't imagine he's the type to wear it.

We pull into the motel and he puts the truck in park and removes his seatbelt. I turn to thank him when he opens his door and slides out, walking around to mine.

"Ah, forgot again, sorry," I say as he takes my hand and helps me down.

"What room?" he asks, and my mouth turns to dust.

"Sev—" my voice catches, "seven."

I thank him again for dinner and the ride as we approach my door. I see now that he was merely being a gentleman again and walking me to my door.

Thank God I didn't say something about coming inside or make a sex joke. I feel my cheeks redden for even thinking that was his intention.

"Have a good night, Miss Dyer," he says, tipping his hat and standing there until I close and lock the door behind me.

I lean against the door once I'm inside and take in a few deep breaths. I pull the curtain back just a centimeter so I can see through the crack as he walks away. Only, he doesn't get very far. He turns back around and returns determinedly to my door, lifting his hand to knock . . . but I don't hear anything.

I worry he's seen me, but he's not looking in my direction. He places a hand on either side of the door frame, gripping it tightly like he's trying to talk himself either into or out of his next move.

Either way, the knock never comes.

He pushes back from the door and walks away, leaving me standing there holding my breath.

Chapter 7

Tyler

"Walk the fuck away, man," I mutter to myself as I return to my truck.

Nothing good can come from one night of what I know would probably be absolute fucking heaven. It's not only that I'm too old for her—yeah, that's part of it—but I won't be the reason she runs away from Colorado.

I've done this song and dance before. I fell hard for a woman who came to town on the fringes of a divorce. Wanted a fresh start in someplace new and exciting and all that. She was looking for validation and an escape from reality, and I was looking for forever. Clearly, it didn't work out.

I won't be someone else's cowboy fantasy again. The romantic novelty of it all wears off pretty quickly when one harsh winter settles in and you realize there's no Amazon Prime.

"What do you mean you're not interested? It was written all over your face when you saw her again at the board meeting—the way you flew out of that room like a fox with his tail on fire." Trent laughs as he helps me unload the two new horses I bought at auction.

"'Saw her again'?" I pause and look at him.

"Yeah, she told me she met you at the Fall Fest the night before."

I shake my head. "You guys have a sleepover and paint each other's nails too?" I don't love the idea that Brooklyn is telling my brother stuff about us.

"Us"? What us?

"Oh, come on, man, don't be childish. She just doesn't know anyone here yet. She and I are friends is all. She didn't spill your secrets . . . don't worry." He slaps my arm before waving to Decker and Ranger as they approach. "Mornin', boys!"

"Mornin', Trent. Tyler, heard you got yourself a mare you're eyeballin'." All three of them burst into laughter at Decker's comment.

"Seriously? You too?" I roll my eyes and place the horses in the barn in their new stalls. "You guys are like a bunch of high schoolers, you know that?"

"Hey, man, we're just looking out for you. We think you should ask her out. What's the harm?"

I glare at Ranger. "I don't need you guys trying to set me up or whatever. Pretty sure I could handle gettin' myself a date if I wanted one."

"That's the problem, brother. You haven't been on a real date in what? A year?"

"A woman like that doesn't want to settle down in a small mountain town, trust me."

I motion for Ranger and Decker to help me toss a few bales of hay into the horse stalls, and Trent trails behind us.

"Doesn't have to be forever. Nobody is saying propose to her."

"You know I'm 10 years older than her, right?" I take off my gloves and shove them into my back pocket. "Besides, she works for

That Feeling

our company, Trent. Don't you think that's a conflict of interest or whatever?"

He laughs. "Oh, come on. You think us Slades adhere to any of that shit? Dad married his lawyer, Uncle Colton married his nanny, and Uncle Clay was Aunt Autumn's contractor. Besides, you're both smart enough that if after a couple dates you realize you don't want anything serious, you won't let it get in the way of the business."

"Funny how you forgot to mention that Uncle Colton's future father-in-law showed up to his house with a shotgun and Aunt Autumn's ex-husband showed up ready to kill Clay. I ain't looking to have a hole in my chest over something casual."

The guys finish up helping me get the new horses situated before Ranger and Decker head out to go check the first pasture.

"Back in an hour or so, boss."

I turn back to Trent, who's leaning against the door of his fancy SUV.

"Why don't you go focus on your own personal life? Y'all always act like I'm the only single one in this family when none of you are even close to getting married."

"I'm busy with the company," he replies, "and besides, as the oldest in the family, it's our right to razz you about still being single." He opens the door and rolls down the window. "Besides, I'm not technically single."

"Banging Claire Wells every time she breaks up with that tool, Brent, isn't exactly a committed relationship, bro."

"At least I'm gettin' some!" he shouts at me through the open window as he drives away.

I spend the next hour or so going over inventory, checking maintenance on a few machines, and sorting a few of the cowboys.

I can feel sweat running down the center of my back as I pull myself out from under one of the tractors as Decker and Ranger approach.

"Pastures look good, boss," Ranger says. "I let Carl and Teller know they can start moving the cattle with the others."

I wipe the dirt off my jeans when I see a truck approaching. "Thanks, guys. We expecting company?" We all three turn and squint to see who's approaching when I realize it's Brooklyn's gray SUV.

"The fuck is she doing here?" I mutter as I walk toward the approaching vehicle.

"Mornin', Miss Dyer. Help you with somethin'?"

She smiles as she exits her 4Runner and walks toward me.

"I'm here for the tour."

"Pardon?"

"Trent told me you wanted to show me the ranch?"

Of course he did.

"He's mistaken. Besides, it's a workday. Shouldn't you be at the office or something?"

She follows on my heels, ignoring my comment as I walk back toward a smiling Decker and Ranger.

"Morning, guys." She smiles sweetly at the two of them, who practically fall over themselves vying for her attention.

"Hey there, little lady, you're looking extra gorgeous today."

"You're too sweet, Decker, thank you. You men aren't looking too bad yourself. Except for Mr. Grumpy Pants over here." She tosses her thumb toward me and they laugh at the joke.

"Miss Dyer, as I said previously, Trent was mistaken. I'm too busy to give you a tour today. Sorry you drove out here." I tip my hat toward her and make my way to the stables to saddle up Misty.

"We can give you a tour."

That makes me pause. I glance over my shoulder and both of the cowboys are looking at me.

"Come on," Ranger loops an arm over her shoulder, "we'll leave Mr. Grumpy Pants to himself." He can barely get the words out, he's laughing so hard.

I saddle up Misty and work on breaking one of our most recent colts we bought at auction down in Texas.

I run through a few drills with the fiery little animal. We only

That Feeling

ever practice gentling around here—no breaking a horse's will with force. I let him see how I ride Misty, spend time brushing and petting his head, and let him wear a halter for a bit to get used to it.

I grab an apple from my bag and cut it into pieces, feeding a few slices to Misty and the yet-unnamed colt.

Brooklyn's loud laugh interrupts my focus and I glance over to see her touching Decker's arm as she tosses her head back. Her blonde curls tumble over her shoulders. I turn back to the horses. "Not your circus, not your monkeys," I say aloud, trying to remind myself that it's none of my business who Brooklyn wants to flirt with.

"Yee-haw!"

Ranger shouts and pretends to ride a horse in place with a lasso overhead. I can't hear what they're talking about, but he looks like a damn fool. I roll my eyes and try to focus on the task at hand, but I can't pull my gaze from Brooklyn's tempting silhouette.

She's wearing skintight jeans today—they're dark and stuck to her curves like glue. She's tucked in a long-sleeved black shirt that accentuates her tiny waist and ample tits. She's built like a screen siren from the '50s, and I know every single man in town has noticed.

I watch as Decker laughs and attempts to pull her in for a half-hug.

"That's enough," I mutter as I mount Misty and trot over to where they're standing. "Okay, wrap it up. They have work to do and you're distracting them. Guys, get up to pasture one and check on Carl and Teller."

"Sure thing, boss man." Ranger nods to me and then they both tell Brooklyn goodbye.

"I need to go check a few fences. Maybe you should get back to the office?"

She ignores my comment again. "You riding up there on Misty?"

"Yeah."

"Can I come?"

I sigh and pull my hat off in exasperation. "Woman, I've got more work than I have days on this earth. Can't a man just work in peace?"

53

Her countenance drops and I can see she's disappointed. Maybe she's not simply trying to annoy the hell out of me.

"Okay, fine." I dismount Misty and tie her reins to the hitching post outside the stables. "Let's go in here and get your horse saddled up."

"Oh, I'm riding alone?"

"No, I'll be with you." My brows knit together.

"It's just that . . . I've never ridden a horse before."

"Then why'd the hell you ask to come with me?" I'm now confused and a little frustrated. "And how the hell did you ride that bull so well?"

She laughs. "That. Well, I've been to Nashville more than a few times, and it was always something my friends and I did for fun after we'd had a few. Turns out, if you're good at it drunk, you're fantastic at it sober."

I nod. "So what are you wanting to do then? I need to get up there, and if you're too scared to ride alone, we can take one of the ATVs. I'll just need to put Misty up."

"No, no! I want to ride on Misty with you."

An instant sweat breaks out on my body at the thought of having her pressed up against me. I glance down at her thighs and then back up to her tits. How the fuck am I supposed to handle *that* body pressed up against me?

"Well?"

I shake the thoughts from my head as she looks up at me, wide-eyed.

"All right, fine."

She claps in excitement as we walk back outside over to Misty. I release her reins from the post and pull myself up onto her.

"Here." I hold my hand down to Brooklyn. "Put one foot in the stirrup—yup, like that—and grab my hand." She obeys and I pull her swiftly. She yelps and lands squarely on the saddle behind me as she tosses her leg over.

"You're going to want to scoot as close to me as you can. You can

That Feeling

squeeze your thighs against mine so you're not bouncing all over the place, and place your arms *tightly* around my waist. I mean it—I don't want you flying off the back and suing me."

"Damn, such a gentleman. Thanks for caring for my well-being," she giggles as she situates herself against my body.

I'm already regretting this. The smell of her shampoo permeates the air and the warmth of her soft tits is burning into my back.

The fuck was I thinking?

I'm half-tempted to fake an emergency.

"Move with the horse," I say as Misty walks slowly. "If you're too stiff, you'll just bounce up and down hard and it'll hurt. You'll be sore tomorrow."

"Wouldn't be the first time, Tyler," she says huskily in my ear.

I tap Misty with my foot to signal her to pick it up as we take off across the field, Brooklyn's high-pitched squeal echoing across the plains.

She's a good sport, and she even helps me check the fences for gaps and assists when I have to patch a few areas.

"This is breathtaking." She stares out over the pastures to the snowcapped peaks behind us.

"You think this is something? I'll show you a better view."

We take off across the pasture, not in a full gallop, because I know she's not ready for that yet. She's loving it, giggling and smiling the entire way. She's fearless and it's something I've always wanted in a partner.

"Oh wow," she gasps as I help her down from Misty, trying my damndest not to pull her against me. I release my hands from her waist as we walk up to the edge of the overlook.

"How'd you find this place?"

"Well, this land has been in our family for generations, so I spent a lot of time up here as a boy. My dad used to take Trent and me camping all through these mountains."

We both stand in silence as we take in the view of the valley below. There are a few clouds in the sky, but it's a crystal-clear day. I prop one foot up on a rock and lean my elbow down on it. I turn when I hear the camera shutter sound.

"You just take a picture of me?"

"Yeah, you look so at ease up here." She smiles at me softly and I return the gesture. "It'll be perfect for the campaign. You in your most natural element, completely candid. Those are always the best shots for catching emotion."

My smile falters when I realize the photo is just part of the job. I'm about to ask her if she's ready to head back when she asks me a question.

"So I know we talked about it briefly, but if you had to give one reason for why you chose ranch life over the brewery, what would it be?"

I think about it briefly. "No one answer, really. I'm not good with the politics and ass-kissing it takes to be CEO, and I sure as hell won't be tied to a desk. Not with views like this." I nod toward the valley. I don't know why, but I keep talking. "I like being in nature—it's my church, I guess. I like working with my hands and being around the animals. It's hard work but it's fulfilling and peaceful. Feeds my soul."

Something about Brooklyn puts me at ease. She asks questions like she's genuinely interested in me—not just trying to get a story. Silence falls between us and I feel like I've revealed too much of myself.

"Besides, this is my office. No corporation can offer me this."

"I feel you there, although the location of your headquarters provides amazing views out of my office window. Just . . . breathtaking. I know I keep using that word, but I can't think of how else to describe this place."

I watch her as the wind whips a few stray hairs around her face. Her green eyes sparkle in the sunlight. I want to grab her and pull her to me—to feel her petite body under my control as I make her fall apart.

"I always wanted to live in downtown Chicago growing up. Well,

That Feeling

first New York City, because I grew up watching *Friends*. I'm from the suburbs and I just thought having a penthouse apartment in the city with views of Lake Michigan and all the buildings would make me happy. Once I had that and my killer dream job, I'd be set."

"Did it?"

She looks over at me quizzically.

"Make you happy?"

She shakes her head *no*. "Maybe for a little while. But it was really just a Band-Aid for what my soul actually craved."

"Which was?"

"Freedom. Just following my heart and what I wanted to do rather than what I *should* do or what everyone expected me to do. My parents are from Illinois—my entire family is. My older brother Silas is a tax lawyer. He stayed in Illinois and got married and had two kids. He's a lot older. My parents got pregnant with him at 19 and then waited almost 10 years to have me and then my younger sister, Mallory."

I lean against a tree as I listen to her. She's still staring out over the mountains while she talks. I like that I'm getting this private view into her life. Makes me wonder if she opens up to everyone this way.

"She's a vet—or rather, she's doing her residency right now and then she hopes to come out here, actually. Her focus is on horses."

"You miss it?"

"Hmm?" She looks over at me.

"Home."

"Nah—not yet, at least." She shrugs as she takes a step toward me, reaching for my hat.

"What are you doing?" I grab her arm, pulling it away.

"I want to feel like a real cowgirl." My eyes drop to her pink lips that have curled into a seductive smile.

I pull off my hat and hand it to her. "Gonna take a lot more than wearing a hat and riding a horse for that."

She flips her hair and puts on the hat, taking another step closer. She leans in, pressing her delicate fingers against my chest.

"And what would it take, Tyler?"

Her chest rises and falls in cadence with her breath. I don't hide my eyes as they fall down to her cleavage.

"Don't tempt me, Brooklyn. I'm not a patient man."

"What kind of man are you?" She bites her bottom lip and slowly drags her fingers down my chest.

I grab her hand in mine right before she hits my belt buckle. I spin her around and press her against the tree I was leaning against. A small huff escapes from her lips at the force of her back hitting the tree.

"The kind of man you don't want to tease." I press my hardening cock against her, causing her lips to fall open. "You like to play games, don't you?" I thrust my hand into her hair, gripping the back of her neck as my hat tumbles to the ground.

"No," she whispers. Her eyes blink slowly, heavy-lidded with desire.

"I warned you last time, didn't I? I told you what would happen if you didn't learn your lesson about teasing me."

I tighten my grip on the base of her neck, causing her head to stay still. I tip my head down, dragging my nose up her neck till my lips are at her ear.

"What did I say I'd do?"

She whimpers as I flick her earlobe with the tip of my tongue, her hands reaching out to grip my shirt.

"Come on, little girl, I want to hear it. Where's that confidence now that I'm calling you on your bluff, huh?"

"I—I don't remember." Her voice is wispy as I drag my free hand up her body to cup her breast. I squeeze it softly before settling on her hardening nipple. I pinch it hard.

"Mmm, that's a shame. Guess I get to choose between the two options I told you."

She pulls at my shirt, trying to kiss me, but I yank her head back with my hand that's tangled in her hair.

"Tsk, tsk," I look down into her eyes, "I'm in control."

That Feeling

I step back and reach for my belt, undoing the buckle and zipper. Her mouth is hanging open as she watches me. She looks wild and wanton—the desire coursing through her veins has brought a glowing pinkness to her cheeks.

I reach beneath the waistband of my jeans and pull my fully erect cock out. Her eyes bulge and I laugh as I grip the base and stroke myself slowly—once, then twice.

"On your knees, sweetheart."

Chapter 8

Brooklyn

Something about the way he's commanding me makes me want to defy him, but I'm not sure he's the kind of man who would put up with that.

So, of course, I have to try.

"Make me." I say the words slowly and deliberately.

His eye twitches as he pulls his belt free from the loops of his jeans. In one swift move, he's lunging toward me, grabbing my arms and spinning me around so my back is against him.

"You're a defiant little thing, aren't you?" he grunts as he loops the belt around my wrists before pulling it tightly. He walks us forward until I'm in front of the tree, then spins me around. He forces me down to my knees and I almost stumble without the use of my hands.

"Let's see if we can break of you that."

It's exciting and intoxicating. I've never had a man take from me what he wants so unapologetically. There's no sweet talk or gentleness to his movements.

It's rough and awkward, and it causes a fire to ignite in my lower belly.

That Feeling

"Now," he tips my chin upward as he fists his cock, "you ready to obey and suck my cock with that smart little mouth?"

I nod but he demands more.

"Say it."

"I'm ready to behave," I say softly.

"Then get to work," he grunts as he parts my lips with the tip.

I'm already desperate to taste him. I can feel my need building as I take him in my mouth. A low moan falls from his mouth as I begin to slowly slide my lips up and down his shaft, swirling my tongue around the tip.

He leans forward, resting one hand against the tree as the other grips the back of my head. He begins to pull my face forward as he thrusts his hips, fucking my face. I can feel my eyes begin to water a little at how deep he's going.

"Ohhh God, yes, yes, yes." He grunts each time he hits the back of my throat.

I don't care that my knees are probably bloody from the rocks and sticks digging into them through my jeans. I don't care that I'm trying not to gag as he gets closer to finishing. I look up and watch the image of him with his head falling forward, his hair sticking to his sweaty forehead as his eyes squeeze shut.

"I'm gonna co—" He doesn't finish the sentence before I feel him running down my throat. He thrusts two more times before slowly pulling himself from my mouth.

I'm panting, trying to catch my breath as I look up at him. I'm sure my mascara is smeared and my hair is a disaster, but I couldn't care less.

I want more. I need more.

"I was wrong," he says as he reaches out with his thumb and wipes away the remnants of his release. "You suck cock way better than you run your mouth."

He smirks and helps me back up to my feet after righting himself. Neither of us speaks as he removes the belt from my wrists and pulls it back through the loops on his waist.

"Come here."

I reach down, pick up his hat, and hand it back to him. He takes it but grabs my hand in the process, looking at my wrist. He grabs the other and does the same.

"I'm okay," I say, reassuring him. Concern on his face tells me that while he acts like I'm nothing more than a blow job, he cares at a least a little.

"You sure?"

His eyes narrow on me. He reaches out a hand to smooth down my hair, his eyes burning into mine as he leans in. I think he's about to kiss me—the moment feels so intimate—but it's like he can hear my thoughts the moment I think that word. He pulls away and the moment is gone.

"Yeah. We should get back?"

He nods and helps me back up on the horse as we set out back to the stables.

"Where have you guys been?" Trent asks as we dismount Misty.

"Don't act like you didn't send Brooklyn here for a tour."

"I'm just surprised you actually obliged her," Trent laughs, slapping Tyler on the back as he leads Misty to her stall. "Dad's up at the pasture with Ranger and Decker. He said he'll be back down here in a while to help you with some delivery that's coming today."

Tyler just waves and walks Misty into the stables.

"Hey, I drove out here with my dad," Trent says. "Mind giving me a lift back to the office since we have that meeting with the Grand Lake Chamber of Commerce at 3?"

"Yeah, of course," I look past him into the stables to see if I can catch Tyler before we leave, "just give me a minute?"

I walk inside and find Tyler brushing Misty in her stall. I don't

That Feeling

say anything at first—I just watch the gentle moment between the two of them. The way she trusts him is magic.

"Hey," I say as he looks over his shoulder at me, "I'm going to take off, but I wanted to say thanks for the ride earlier and . . . uh, yeah." I feel like a silly schoolgirl. I can feel my cheeks growing red as I absentmindedly kick at nothing on the ground in front of me.

"You're welcome," he smirks.

"Would you want to grab dinner or drinks later? Or maybe tomorrow or something?"

He pulls up Misty's hooves and looks them over briefly before meeting my eyes. He smiles for a second before looking past me.

"For the campaign?"

"Uh, no, like, just socially." Surprised he's not catching on.

"I don't think that's a good idea, Brooklyn."

His curt response stings.

"Why not?"

He sighs in exasperation. "We've been over this."

I open my mouth to give him a piece of my mind and ask him if he's serious—especially after what just transpired between us—when Trent appears next to me.

"You ready?"

"Yes." I brush past him and out into the sunshine. I take in a deep breath and exhale audibly, allowing my shoulders to fall.

"Hey, you okay?" Trent jogs to catch up to me as we walk to my SUV. "I interrupt something back there?"

"Yeah, I'm good." I smile, trying to convey sincerity even though I don't feel it.

Trent furiously types out an email on his phone as we drive back to the office. I debate on if I should ask him about Tyler, but I don't want him asking me about earlier. In the end, my curiosity gets the best of me.

"So what's up with Tyler?"

"What do you mean?" he asks without looking up from his phone, his thumbs still furiously moving across the screen.

"Did someone rip his heart out or something?" I can feel Trent looking over at me when I ask the question. I narrow my gaze on the road and try my hardest to look and act casual about the subject matter.

"Dunno, really. He's a vault when it comes to his personal life. Otherwise, he's a softie. He tries to front that he's this hard-nosed asshole, but he's a teddy bear."

"Seems like a tough nut to crack." I try to sound nonchalant.

"Tyler has always done his own thing ever since we were kids. He's always known himself and what he wanted to do, and that was the ranch. Nobody could talk him out of it even though it's a hard life that's very demanding and leaves little to no time for a personal life. The land is his calling and he loves it, plus he's good at it too." I feel him looking at me again, but I keep my eyes trained on the road. "Just not sure there's room for someone else."

I know he's saying that last part for my benefit. Clearly my attempt to mask my ever-growing feelings for his brother didn't go unnoticed.

"As we've been discussing these last few weeks, the Grand Lake Library is hosting a fundraiser and the Slade brewery is providing all the drinks, but we also had another idea . . ." Milly, Trent and Tyler's cousin, pauses briefly for emphasis before arching her arms in a rainbow, "a bachelor auction!" she says with a big grin.

A few people chuckle in confusion, but most agree it's a great idea, especially since the theme of the fundraiser is "Nights in New Orleans."

"I think it's a fantastic idea and I can tell you with absolute assurance that it would be a huge hit on social media," I chime in.

"That's perfect, because I think we could really get some big donors from Denver and Boulder if we get the word out that some of

That Feeling

the Slade men will be on the auction block." She bounces her eyebrows at Trent.

"Don't look at me, 'cause there's not a chance in hell, but I can guarantee some of the others will gladly do it."

"Brook, would you be willing to put some feelers out to the guys?" Milly asks, and I agree.

We conclude our meeting and I get a chance to chat with Milly for a few. This is the first time I've met her in person, and she's just as lovely as she is on the phone. Her short brown bob is styled with blunt bangs that highlight her bright blue eyes. She explains how she fits into the Slade family—her dad Colton being the eldest of the Slade brothers. We promise to catch up over coffee so she can show me around Grand Lake the next time I'm in town.

I walk down the hallway to Trent's office and poke my head inside. "So what are your thoughts on this auction? Think it'll be a success?"

"Yeah, I do. I just won't be on the chopping block," he laughs. "I'm sure Ranger and Decker will gladly do it, along with my cousins Axle and Aiden."

I lean against the doorway and chew my lip, questioning my next suggestion. "Think Tyler will do it?"

That makes him laugh even harder. "Not a chance in hell, but it can't hurt to ask him. Honestly, you *should* ask him, because I want to hear his response."

I walk back to my office and pull my phone out of my pocket. I think about sending him a text but figure it would be easier to convince him on the phone, so I give him a call. It rings several times before going to voicemail.

"Hey Tyler, it's Brook. I had a quick question—er, favor—to ask. The Grand Lake Chamber of Commerce is doing a fundraiser for the library and they suggested a bachelor auction. So I volunteered you as one of the bachelors. Give me call back to discuss."

I hang up the phone and let out a shaky breath. You know what they say: It's better to ask for forgiveness than permission.

Let's just hope Tyler Slade is forgiving and willing to sell his sexy ass on an auction block. Then a tinge of jealousy creeps in and sours my stomach at the thought of a dozen other women bidding to take him out on a date.

Shit. What did I just do?

Chapter 9

Tyler

I twist off the cap on my beer and kick my feet up on the coffee table. All day I've been trying to force the images of Brooklyn on her knees in front of me out of my head. I even second-guess if it actually happened. For being the bossy woman who told me off just a few days ago on my porch, she was quick to let me take control.

I feel my cock twitch at the thought. I should have pushed her further—bent her over and taken her.

"Fuck," I mutter as I down half the beer in one gulp. Why the hell did I let myself know how good she was at sucking cock? Even with those full hips and an ass you want to sink your teeth into, I was doing a damn good job of convincing myself that she was nothing more than a pretty face.

Three quick knocks on the front door bring me out of my head. I glance at the clock, and it's nearly 9 p.m. The knocks sound again and I walk to the front door.

"You didn't call me back," Brooklyn snaps before I even have the door fully open.

"'Cause I ain't doin' it." I take another drink of beer. I know what she's referring to—that ridiculous bachelor auction. "Nice try telling me you already signed me up to do it, though, as if that would change my mind."

She nods but—surprisingly—doesn't press the issue.

"What's that smaller house on your property?"

"My old house." I lean against the door frame, letting her know I have no intention of inviting her inside. I'm a pretty disciplined man, but I know if I let her come in this house after what happened today, she'll be on her back, her knees, her side, and any other position I can bend her in.

"Lived there while we constructed this one. It's the original house my dad lived in before he built the house he's in now. Why?"

"You ever think of renting it out on Airbnb or Vrbo? Bet you could book it out a year at a time."

"And why would I want to do that?"

She shrugs. "Could be a good source of passive income. Maybe help cover your mortgage on this house."

"Don't have a mortgage on this house, darlin'. It's paid for. Trust me, the last thing I want is a bunch of tourists stomping around my land, disrupting my cattle, and filming their TikToks or whatever."

A smile spreads slowly across her lips. "You remembered TikTok." We both chuckle. "You're right, it would be annoying to have strangers all over your private space."

I should tell her it's late and I need to head to bed soon, but I don't want her to leave. I like this—whatever this is right now. Just talking to her about nothing.

"Can I see it?"

"Right now?"

She nods her head.

"Why? Needs some work," I lie, hoping it will deter her from wanting to see it.

"Well, if you didn't notice, I'm still living out of suitcases in the motel. I don't want to lease an apartment in town. I want my own space, ya know? Plus, out here I feel like it's that true Colorado experience. Remote and off-grid."

That Feeling

That makes me laugh. "You know it has Wi-Fi and cable hookups, right? Not exactly roughing it. If you want that experience, I'm sure I can let you borrow a horse and tent to go up in the mountains."

"Come on, humor me." She stares at me for a moment, and against my better judgment, I give in.

"Let me grab the keys and my boots." I walk back to the door a minute later and we head down the stairs of the front porch to the driveway. "We'll just cut across the field," I motion toward where I'm heading.

We're about 10 steps in when I look back to check which shoes she's wearing. "You need some boots if you're gonna be stomping around out here. Need to protect your ankles from the snakes."

"Snakes?" she yelps and grabs my arm, looking around frantically.

"Yeah, rattlesnakes like to hide out in the fields sometimes." She looks at me, petrified—her big round eyes unblinking. "Get on my back."

I don't have to tell her twice. I squat down and help her scoot herself into a piggyback position. I focus my attention on each step I take so I don't trip in the darkness. I'm also trying my hardest not to notice the heat radiating from her thighs, which are wrapped tightly around my body.

When we approach the house, I slide her down my back and pull the keys from my pocket.

"Oh, wow, it's so cute in here." She looks around after I flip on the light. I stay near the door as she walks through the kitchen-adjacent living room. She runs her fingertips over the back of the couch and then the mantle. "Even has a fireplace?"

She looks giddy, her smile never faltering as she walks into the kitchen then down the hallway into the two bedrooms.

"What work does it need?"

"Hmm?"

She pokes her head around the corner to look at me. "You said it needed work."

"Oh," I stumble, glancing around hoping to see something, but I don't. "Think my dad said something about it needing a new water heater and having some plumbing issues."

She ducks back into the bathroom and I hear her flush the toilet then turn on the water. A minute later, she's walking back out to the living room.

"Plumbing seems fine to me. Water even got hot pretty quickly."

I shrug as she closes the distance between us.

"Did you just tell me that to scare me off so I wouldn't ask about renting it from you?" Her hands are in her back pockets, her breasts almost touching me.

"Maybe." I don't know why I don't just lie again—tell her that, no, it does need work and I need to go to bed.

"Why?"

"I can't give you what you want, Brooklyn." I finally say the words.

"And what is it that you think I want, Tyler?"

I take a step back and look up toward the ceiling in exasperation. "Look, I don't have time for games. I've got a ranch to run and I can't get wrapped up in some young woman who ran away from her previous life because she was bored. One harsh winter here and you'll realize you really can't live without Amazon Prime and Sephora. I won't be standing here with a broken heart when you hightail it back to Chicago."

She giggles and I feel it in my chest. I hate that I'm starting to notice the little things about her—the way her skin crinkles around her green eyes when she laughs.

"And how do you know what Sephora is?" She reaches out her hand and places it against my chest. "I think it's cute that you're worried I'll break your heart." She steps closer and I can feel the door against my back. Her eyes are heavy and they drop from mine to my lips. She closes the distance between us, and just before her lips meet mine, I grab her hand that's on my chest and spin her around so she's pinned against the door.

I grab her other hand and pin both above her head.

"Why won't you kiss me?" she asks.

I drop her hands and place my palms flat against the door behind her. I want to kiss her. I've relentlessly thought of kissing her since the first night I met her, but I know that the connection I felt with her will come back the moment our lips touch again.

"It's just fucking. I'm not your boyfriend. I'm not even your friend."

She slowly reaches out her hand. My eyes don't leave hers as she drags her fingertips down my chest then straight beneath my waistband. I inhale sharply as her fingers wrap around my cock. She teases me, sliding her hand up and down my length agonizingly slowly at first before gaining speed.

"It can be whatever you want it to be if you agree to the bachelor auction."

I squeeze my eyes shut. I can feel my release building as her other hand undoes a few buttons on my shirt.

"Fuuu—," the unfinished word is garbled as she drags her tongue over my now-exposed skin.

She grips me tighter in her hand, releasing me fully from my jeans. She runs the tip of her thumb on the underside of my head and my knees almost buckle.

Am I really about to explode with a hand job?

I reach for her shirt and pull at it. "Wanna come on your tits," I say as I fail to remove the material from her.

"Are you going to agree to the auction?"

"I don't fucking care . . . I'll do anything . . . just don't stop." I'm practically begging. I can feel the pressure building and I close my eyes again as I prepare to come, but then she stops.

My eyes dart open. She's pulling her shirt over her head, exposing her full tits in a sheer pink bra. I immediately reach out to run my thumb over one of her nipples that's clearly visible through the fabric.

She reaches around and unclasps her bra, then the straps fall down her shoulders to the floor. The hunger I have for her takes over. I reach out both hands and grab her tits, bringing them to my mouth, where I voraciously suck and lick and nip at her.

Her hands work the button and zipper of her jeans. I take a few steps back and sit on the back of the couch, stroking myself as I watch her shimmy her hips back and forth to drag her jeans and panties down her thighs.

"Your pussy's wet." I nod toward the small dark spot I see on her panties.

She drops her hand down to where her thighs meet, running her finger over her folds before sliding it between them. Her eyes grow darker as she strokes herself a few times.

"Put your fingers inside you," I command.

She slides a finger up and down a few more times before obeying, sliding her finger inside once, twice, and then a third time. Her eyes close as her lips part.

"Now come here."

She removes her finger and takes a step forward. I reach out and grab the hand that was just pleasuring herself and bring it to my lips—wrapping them around her finger and sucking off her wetness.

She tastes better than I imagined: tart and sweet. I feel my chest tighten like I'm seconds away from tearing her in half. I narrow my eyes on her.

"You're about 15 seconds away from getting fucked hard, so if that's not what you want, you better walk out that door right now. You understand me?"

She doesn't flinch or run. I stand up and kick off my jeans, grabbing her around the waist and hoisting her up onto the small kitchen island.

"On the counter?" She yelps a little when the cold granite hits her bare backside, her tits bouncing with the movement.

"I'm about to eat a juicy pussy, baby. Where else but the

That Feeling

kitchen?" I sit on the barstool and forcibly spread her thighs apart, holding them in place as I run my tongue up her wet slit.

"Ahhh . . ." Her hand thrusts into my hair as she looks down her body at me. I keep eye contact as I swirl my tongue around her already-swollen bud. Her nipples grow even harder as her eyes flutter closed and her head falls back.

I don't relent. I devour her—her cries and groans only spurring me on as her back falls flat against the counter while her hands play with her tits.

"I'm close, don't stop," she pants as her thighs begin to quiver against my shoulders. Seconds later, her back is arching and her nails dig into my scalp as her orgasm tears through her body.

I don't waste time. I pull her still-trembling body off the counter and position her directly over my erect cock.

"Time to get fucked, baby." I grip her waist and slowly lower her down onto me. "Goddamn, you're tight." I can barely get the words out. I let out a shaky breath.

"You're too bi—"

I can't help but laugh. "It'll fit, sweetheart. Just relax and let me work it into you."

I lift her up and down slowly—each time a little bit more—sliding into her hot, wet sheath.

"You want me in this auction, you better work for it. Ride my cock." I feel her feet find the bar on the stool. She plants them then grabs the lip of the counter. She lifts herself up then lowers her body back down on me. "Just like that," I groan as she picks up speed.

I watch as her tits bounce each time she slides back down my shaft. I reach around and grip the back of her neck with my hand, helping her force herself all the way down as she takes all of me.

"Ow!" she yelps. "Too deep."

"You're fine, baby. You can take it. You're gonna take it," I say as I repeat the process.

Soon we're both panting and moaning. It's all I can do to watch her as she rides me in ecstasy. A bead of sweat falls from her temple, winding its way down her neck, where I lean forward and lick it off.

"Behind."

The word is barely audible, but I know what she wants.

"You want it deeper, don't you, you greedy little toy? You're my plaything, Brooklyn, my dirty little fuck toy." I feel like a man possessed. I hope I'm not scaring her with my words, but maybe I should. Maybe it'll show her that I'm not the man she needs.

I flip her around, keeping myself inside her as I lay her flat on the counter. I kick the stool away from me, and it clatters to the floor as I grab a handful of her hair and anchor her against the counter, pounding into her.

Not even 10 seconds later, she's exploding around my cock as I reach around and flick her clit. She grasps unsuccessfully at the countertop as her release pushes me to the edge. I can feel her pussy squeezing me.

I flip her back over just as I pull out and stroke myself, spilling all over her tits.

I walk to the bathroom and wet a hand towel. Neither of us speaks as I clean her off then softly place the cloth against her. She winces briefly.

"Too rough?" I don't make eye contact as I lean down to pull on my jeans.

"No, just been a while," she giggles, reaching for the bra I'm handing her.

I want to ask her how long, but then that makes me wonder about the last guy who was fucking her, and my stomach does an uncomfortable flip. I know she mentioned getting out of a long-term relationship with someone back in Chicago, but that's about it. I don't know who he was or how long the relationship was . . . and I don't want to know. The more I know about her, the harder it'll be to walk away.

We don't speak as we finish getting dressed. I grab the keys and usher her out of the cabin, walking slowly back up to her car. Clearly, she's not concerned about the snakes anymore—that or I fucked her senseless.

"I didn't come here to—"

I open her SUV door and she climbs inside.

"I don't need an explanation, Brooklyn. We're both adults and I said what it was between us. That's all the talking we need to do on the matter."

She nods her head and reaches for the car door. "Have a good night, Tyler."

"I'll have the cabin cleaned up and ready for you to move in by the weekend."

I close her car door and make my way back up to my front porch as she drives away.

I don't know what just happened, but I somehow agreed to not only let this woman live in a house on my property, but I also signed up for a bachelor auction and just had the most mind-blowing sex of my life.

"Gotta stop thinking with your dick," I mutter to myself as I head back inside to take a shower and pretend that tonight never happened.

Chapter 10

Brooklyn

"Mornin', Brooklyn. Got a minute?" I look up from my desk to see Drake Slade leaning against my door.

"Good morning, sir. Absolutely. Please," I say, gesturing toward the chair in front of my desk.

He tips his cowboy hat at me and takes a seat, casually crossing one of his long legs over the other. His black cowboy boots have seen better days, but if I had to guess, I'd say they're the same boots he wears every single day—just like Tyler.

"Things going okay with the social media stuff?"

I've learned pretty quickly that Drake Slade is a man of few words—similar to Tyler. They look exactly alike. Drake may be pushing 70, but he's still an imposing man who likes to keep his finger on the pulse of everything that's going on in his company.

"Yeah, things are going great. We have a second shoot with Tyler this Saturday at the ranch." I reach for my iPad and pull up the dashboard so he can see the metrics on the recent campaign. "You can see here," I say, pointing to specific numbers, "just how many new profile views and how much traffic we've had in the last seven days. You can also see here that the engagement is up by

That Feeling

almost 600%, meaning people are really resonating with what we're doing."

He pulls a pair of glasses out of his denim shirt pocket and perches them on his nose. "Mm-hmm," he says, squinting at what I'm pointing to.

"And it's not just traffic and engagement; we're seeing a massive spike in sales." I pinch the iPad screen and switch to our revenue report for the last week. "As you can see here from the report I got from Chuck this morning, our sales are up 38% in the last week alone. I will be presenting all of this information at our next all-hands meeting."

I can see the genuine shock on his face as his eyebrows shoot upward. "That's impressive, Brooklyn." He leans back in his seat and folds his glasses, putting them back in his pocket. "You liking it here at Slade?"

I nod. "Yes, very much. Everyone is extremely welcoming and helpful, and if I'm honest, they're super on board with having a young millennial woman run a massive social media campaign. Thought I might have to prove myself a little more out here. Honestly, sir, I can't thank you and Trent enough for bringing me on board."

"Well, I'm glad to hear it. Colton has been really impressed with you and so has Wyatt. Not that the others aren't—they've just been the most vocal about it."

He's about to continue when we hear some noise in the hallway.

". . . I also want you to meet one of our newest employees—oh, there you are, sweetheart," Celeste interrupts us as she waltzes into my office with another young woman next to her.

Drake's eyes light up the moment he sees her, and it's adorable. "Here I am," he says, standing up and walking over to his wife, who stands on her tiptoes to kiss him.

Celeste is impeccably dressed in a black dress with matching pumps and a simple pearl necklace. Her hair is swept up in a low bun at the nape of her neck.

"Adrienne and I need to run some contracts by you, so I'll meet you in your office shortly," Celeste says to Drake.

"Miss Dyer." He tips his hat at me before ducking out of my office.

"Brooklyn, I was hoping you'd be in. I wanted to introduce you to my niece, Adrienne. Her father is Hudson, Drake's younger brother. Anyway, she's currently interning with me at my firm and plans to take over being the Slades' in-house counsel someday."

"Hi!" I reach my hand out as I walk toward Adrienne, who has at least four inches on me. If she decided not to pursue law, she could certainly be a model. "Nice to meet you. I'm Brooklyn."

"Just thought it might be nice for you two to meet as two of the youngest ladies here at Slade."

"Nice to meet you too." Adrienne smiles at me. "I talked to my cousin Milly the other day and she's already singing your praises, so I'm glad I can finally put a face to a name. She also mentioned the three of us hanging out sometime soon?"

"Yeah, absolutely. She's wonderful and offered to show me around Grand Lake and take me out. Here, let me get your number." I reach for my phone and see I have a missed call from my sister. I slide open the screen and there's a text from her as well.

Mallory: *Hey, stop ignoring me and call me! Got a slow day and want to know what's going on in Colorado. Miss you!*

I type Adrienne's number into my phone then shoot her a quick text so she has mine. The ladies say goodbye and head over to their meeting with Drake. I have a few minutes before my next meeting, so I pull up Mallory's name and hit call.

"Hey, big sis, thought you fell off the face of the earth."

"Hey, I know, I'm so sorry." I rub my forehead, embarrassed at how long it's been since I've spoken to my little sister. It's very unlike us not to text daily and speak at least every other day. "Things have been crazy busy here, but in a good way. How's the residency going?"

"Oh, same . . . good, busy. I got to assist in some pretty serious surgical procedures and even took the lead on one."

That Feeling

I can hear the excitement in her voice. "That's amazing, sis! Seriously, I can't tell you how proud of you I am. Just the thought of all that science and blood makes me squeamish."

She laughs. "You're the brave one, just picking up and moving across the country at the drop of a hat."

"Yeah, or maybe I'm a coward."

"Coward? What makes you say that?"

I contemplate telling Mallory about things with Tyler then decide against it. If this is just a one-time thing—or hell, even a fling—I'll tell her about it when it's done. Talking about my feelings for Tyler right now would only solidify the fact that I have feelings for him, and I don't want to cultivate that any more than I already have. Not when he's made it clear that he thinks I'll be gone by next year.

"Oh, just running away from things in Chicago."

"Brook, you didn't run from anything. You'd been talking for the better part of a year about wanting to start over someplace new. And don't even get me started on you wanting to leave Neal." I feel a nagging in my stomach at the mention of his name. "Speaking of Neal, have you heard from him since you left?"

I shake my head *no*, even though she can't see me. "No, I actually haven't heard from anyone."

"What do you mean?"

"Like our old friend groups that Neal and I shared. Apparently, they all chose his side in the breakup and I guess I don't blame them. It's . . . whatever." I try to shrug it off, but the bottom line is, it *does* bother me. I thought we were real friends, but clearly, I was just replaceable.

"Not even Becca?"

"Not really. She came over to see me off the day I moved, and I texted her when I got out here and even sent her pictures of the mountains, but she just responded with emojis. At first I blew it off, because I thought maybe she was just busy, but she hasn't responded to the last few texts I sent her."

"That bitch! You guys have been best friends since college—hell, you were roommates!"

"I know, Mal. It does hurt, and I'm not giving up on the relationship. Honestly, I've just put it out of my mind while I'm getting my bearings out here. I really love this job more than any other I've had, and while I know it's only been a few weeks, I feel like this is home out here. I have to make a good impression and do my best, ya know?"

I feel like I'm trying to convince myself of this so I don't do something stupid like fall in love with Tyler Slade and rip out my own heart.

"Well, I'll drive over to her apartment and confront her if you want."

I laugh. "No, that won't be necessary." That's Mallory, always a pit bull ready to instigate a fight to protect her older sister. "When are you coming out to visit me?" I ask, changing the subject.

"Soon, I hope. I should be able to take some time off in another month or so. I'm so excited to come out there and meet some sexy cowboys. What's that situation like? You gone on any yee-haw dates yet?"

"Yee-haw dates?" I laugh. "I don't think they'd like that. Honestly," I lower my voice and stand up to check down the hallway outside my office, "it's like a Hollywood cowboy movie out here—these men are *unreal*." She gasps. "Yeah, like everyone—including all their dads—is a smokeshow. You're going to lose your mind."

"Yeah, that guy you're using for the campaign is, like, seriously drop-dead delicious. What's his story?"

I panic internally at the mention of Tyler. "Yeah, he's a loner—kind of a brooding mountain-man type. There's, like, six more of him in the family, so you can certainly have your pick of the litter."

We both giggle and she jokes about running out of her clinic and jumping on a flight right now.

"Ugh, I hate that I have to wait a few weeks to come see you," she says. "I have to get back to work, but promise me you won't go radio silent on me again, okay?"

That Feeling

"I promise," I say, and we both end the call.

"Can you take your shirt off but leave the hat on for this one?"

"Gotta be fucking kidding me," Tyler mutters as he dismounts from Misty. "You know cowboys don't do this shit, right?" He unbuttons his shirt and rolls his shoulders to pull it down his arms.

I stare at my phone screen, watching the way his muscles flex with the movement. The sun glints off his tanned skin, hitting his belt buckle and bringing back images of that belt wrapped around my hands. That was by far the hottest thing I've ever experienced.

"You promised you were going to go with the flow more and not complain every time we film a TikTok or take photos," I tease him, knowing full well he hates every second of this. I'm just grateful he's being accommodating—especially after I decided to take some of my own photos after Kevin's photo shoot.

"Now what?" He hooks his thumb into the waistband of his jeans and leans his weight on one hip.

"Don't move," I say as I capture the image.

"Just stand here?"

"That's what 'don't move' means," I say as I squat down to get a better angle. I snap several photos. "Now get back up on Misty and ride past me."

I won't lie, this job is like a damn fantasy. Recording and photographing a sexy-as-hell shirtless cowboy as he rides a horse with the Rocky Mountains as the backdrop? Are you kidding me?

"So for the last one, I just need a quick clip of you in that other outfit you brought. Could you change really quick?"

He sighs and picks up his shirt from where he left it on the ground. He walks over to his truck, which is parked next to us in the field, and I follow behind him.

"After we're done here, I'm going to grab my things from the motel and start moving into the cabin." I stomp through the weeds and stand by the truck as he reaches for his belt.

"Turn around," he says, gesturing with his hand.

"Seriously? We've had sex, you know. I've seen you naked already." I let my eyes drop down his body.

"Yeah, but that doesn't mean I don't get privacy. We see each other naked when we fuck, but that's it. Otherwise, it gets complicated."

I roll my eyes and turn around, giving him his privacy. "Maybe I'll have you do some naked TikToks—just you wearing your boots and your hat strategically placed to cover things."

"Depends on if I'm hard or not . . . the hat might not cover it fully."

I laugh and turn back around to face him as he finishes buttoning his shirt. "Someone thinks highly of himself."

"You know I'm not full of shit," he says, taking a few steps toward me. "You've seen it."

"Yeah, and I think that hat," I point to where it's sitting on top of his head, "would be more than enough coverage. Don't ya think?" I bite my bottom lip seductively.

He puts his hands on the edge of the truck bed behind me and leans in. "You tell me, Brooklyn. You're the one who's had it down her throat." I clench my thighs together as his voice lowers a full octave. "Weren't you the one who said it was too big?" He presses against me and I can feel his erection digging into my hip. "Didn't you tell me it hurt—that it was too deep?"

He always wins when we play this game, but I'm a glutton for the punishment. I reach for his shirt and fist it—tugging it forward to bring his lips down to mine—but he pushes against the truck to resist me. I give him a confused look and pull again, but he reaches down and removes my hand from him.

"What the hell?"

"We're not doing this, Brooklyn. We can kiss when we fuck, but

That Feeling

not this. We're not a couple—we don't hold hands or kiss each other goodbye."

"Then fuck me."

"We need to finish this shoot so I can get back to work."

I feel my cheeks flush with embarrassment. I want to point out that we don't even kiss when we fuck, because when I tried the other night, he pushed me away again . . . but now isn't the time. He's right; we need to wrap this up.

I snap a few more photos and take another video before we call it a day. We jump in his truck and he starts to drive us back down to where my SUV is parked. I want to let go of what happened a moment ago, but I'm also frustrated.

"Hey, maybe you should write down the rules for this thing," I say, motioning between us. "That way, I won't inadvertently break another rule I didn't even know existed."

He looks over at me as he puts his truck in park. "Say what you really want to say."

"You're the one complicating things by making up these rules. I know you're doing it to protect yourself, but it takes the fun out of it. Just let things flow and happen naturally."

He shakes his head. "You want things to happen naturally? Meaning . . . ?"

"Meaning we can just act on feelings and desire rather than having all these stupid rules in place. Kind of takes the fun and spontaneity out of it."

"Sweetheart, if I acted on desire around you, I'd have you stuffed with my cock 24/7. I need to put boundaries in place. That's what I can offer. If you don't want it, then we don't have to continue doing it."

I want to slap him and tell him *fine! I don't need it*, but I don't want to stop sleeping with him. Just hearing him say he wants me nonstop has me ready to jump across this truck and say *fuck my feelings*.

I grab the door handle. "Fine, maybe send me a list of dates and times that work best for us to have sex so I don't make another mistake and attempt to touch or kiss you." I get out, slam the door, and walk to my own truck. I know I'm being childish, but my feelings are hurt and I'm embarrassed.

I haven't seen or spoken to Tyler since my little outburst at his ranch on Saturday. Between moving into the cabin and focusing my attention on work and tonight's bachelor auction, I haven't had time to worry about that situation.

I double-check my reflection in the floor-length mirror in my bedroom. The auction is black tie, which gave me the chance to pull out this stunning floor-length gold gown I've had in the back of my closet for the better part of a year.

The dress has a swooping neckline with very delicate straps. The back dips low, all the way down to the base of my spine. I pair it with simple, delicate jewelry and matching gold sandals. I grab my clutch and check in to see if Tyler has responded to the text I sent him almost an hour ago confirming he's showing up tonight.

I breathe a sigh of relief when I see he's finally responded.

Tyler: *Yup*

I find Trent when I get to the event and spend some time mingling.

"Milly, you look stunning!" I hold her at arm's length and take in the plum-colored gown she's wearing.

"Oh, thank you. This was my late mother's dress, actually."

"Brooklyn, this is Hudson's wife, Deven, and Clay's wife, Autumn."

"Hi!" I extend my hand but Deven pulls me in for a hug.

"We're huggers around here." She smiles and Autumn also gives me a hug.

"So lovely to meet both of you ladies. I have to say, Autumn, your son Logan looks so much like you, and Deven, Axle and Aiden are so

That Feeling

sweet. All of the Slade men have been so kind and welcoming at the brewery. You ladies raised some amazing men."

I've only met them a few times—once at the board meeting and here and there around the office—but I mean it when I say their sons are wonderful people.

"Oh, thank you so much, sweetheart. Truly, that means so much to us. Especially given how macho these cowboys can be."

Trent takes me around the room to meet several more people. The lights flicker a few times to get everyone's attention, and Milly takes the stage to introduce tonight's cause and thank everyone for attending. She highlights a few of the major donors who are present, then the auction begins.

"Oh my God," Trent laughs as Ranger is first on the chopping block. "Did you tell Tyler he had to wear *that* too before he agreed to participate?"

Ranger's wearing a pair of black Levi's that are practically painted on his body. His belt buckle is covered in rhinestones and he's wearing a bow tie and cuffs with a black cowboy hat.

I'm laughing so hard that I have to wipe tears from my eyes as I shake my head. "Nope."

In truth, I didn't tell Trent how I got Tyler to agree to this in the first place. He was beyond shocked—as were most people—but I couldn't exactly say I seduced him into agreeing.

The room fills with hoots and hollers as the bids start pouring in. Each man puts on a show, some more than others. Ranger and Decker both make sure to flex and strut around. Logan and Ethan do push-ups. The women are waving their paddles in the air, not able to shout their bets fast enough as each man enters and exits the stage.

Finally, the last bachelor takes the stage. The screams are the loudest when Tyler walks out. I'm trying my hardest to capture images and videos on my phone, but the moment his eyes meet mine, that's all I can focus on.

His gaze is direct and heated. I see Trent look at him then follow his gaze to me. "He's going to kill you."

"Oh, I hope so," I say, taking a sip of my champagne as butterflies fill my belly. Because I know that if he doesn't kill me, he's going to punish me... and I'm not sure my body can handle that.

The bids keep coming in, higher and higher. I hear a woman's voice keep shouting the higher bid every time someone else says one. I look around the room and finally see where it's coming from: a tall, slender redhead with her back to me.

"Who's that?" I lean in to ask Trent. He looks across the room until his eyes spot the woman.

"Selma, Tyler's ex."

A feeling of jealousy forms a pit in my stomach. I glance up at Tyler, whose eyes are on her. Without thinking, I grab a discarded paddle on a nearby table and shoot it into the air while shouting a counter bet.

"What are you doing?" Trent looks at me in confusion.

"Betting," I say as I see the same look in Tyler's eyes.

Selma fires back another bet, and so do I. After a few more rounds, it's only the two of us betting. The rest of the women have stopped now that the bet is more than double what anyone else's was.

I don't know what's come over me. Selma turns to see who keeps bidding against her, but I duck back a little in the crowd. Finally, she gives up.

"Sold! To the lady in the gold dress."

I slowly lower my paddle as the room cheers and Tyler exits the stage, his eyes still burning into mine—only now it's not lust or excitement... it looks like anger.

Chapter 11

Tyler

I stare in confusion at Brooklyn before leaving the stage.

What the hell is she doing?

I don't wait for her to find me after the auction. I change out of this ridiculous outfit and grab my bag, heading out to the parking lot.

"So when do I get to collect my date?"

Her voice stops me in my tracks and I turn around to see her batting her eyelashes at me. She has a curl wrapped around one finger and a hip cocked to the side.

Normally, I'd say something back about how nice her tits look, but right now I can feel my anger about to boil over.

"The fuck was that in there?"

She's clearly taken aback by my abrupt tone.

"Uh, it's for a charity, so doesn't really matter who won. The money is going to a good cause."

I shake my head. "Then why didn't you bid on anyone else?"

"What? I just thought—"

"Thought what? That this is how you'd get me?"

"*Get* you? What are you talking about?"

"Is this why you convinced me to do this? So you could bet on me and win so you could date me?"

She scoffs. "Seriously? You really do think highly of yourself, don't you?" She rolls her eyes. "You've made it abundantly clear that—"

"Then why didn't you bid on anyone else?" I say the words slowly and deliberately.

She stares at me, blinking a few times.

"That's what I thought. Like you said, I've made it clear, but I'm gonna make it crystal this time: I'm not your man, your boyfriend, or your friend."

"Why are you such a fucking dick?" she spits the words at me as a stray tear falls down her cheek.

"Because I'm not just some fun pastime for you. I won't be a cowboy fantasy you get out of your system before you run back to Chicago and act like I never existed. I told you from the jump that this was nothing—just fucking."

I turn and grab the handle of my truck door and yank it open harder than necessary.

"You're just scared. Who broke your heart, Tyler? Was it the redhead?"

I slowly turn back around to face her.

"Yeah, I know about her. Selma." She juts her chin out and crosses her arms like she's caught me in a lie.

"Yeah and . . . ? There's no secret there. I never hid her or anyone from you. It's none of your fucking business anyway."

"It's my business if you're still sleeping with her. Especially since we are."

"Well, we aren't anymore. I don't want a relationship with you and you need to stop trying to fix me or change my mind."

She crinkles the ticket she received for winning my auction and throws it at my feet, her eyes now swimming in tears.

"Oh, I'm aware you don't want anything with me. I was just your little—what'd you call it—fuck toy? Go to hell, Tyler."

That Feeling

My eyes follow her as she storms off, then they fall to the crinkled ball of paper at my feet. I bend down, pick it up, and smooth it before climbing in my truck and driving home.

I'm barely out of the parking lot before regret starts to take over. I know I was a dick—she's absolutely right. I didn't need to be cruel under the guise of being honest. There was no need for that.

"Fuck," I mutter.

I contemplate turning around and chasing after her, but I know she needs time, and I'm not about to make a scene in front of everyone left at the benefit.

When I get home, I grab a beer and walk up to my bathroom to start the shower. I pull the ticket from my pocket and smooth it out again. I can feel a smile pull at my lips when I see that she's draw two little hearts by my name.

Hearts . . . something that should scare me, but instead tugs at my own heart. I feel my chest warm at the thought of her.

I picture the way she lets herself get fully immersed in her feelings—the way she lets her head fall back as her full, throaty laugh bellows from her chest. It's not delicate or quiet and she doesn't care. She doesn't tamp down who she is, and that's one of the things I love about her.

Love? My throat constricts as a moment of panic grips me. It's not love, it just—respect, admiration, lust.

I strip out of my clothes and step into the steaming shower, letting my head fall forward as the water tumbles over my shoulders and cascades down my back. I feel old and tired. I know I'm only heading into my late 30s, but damn, I feel at least a decade older.

I keep replaying my words over and over in my head. My stomach sours as I hear myself telling Brooklyn *I'm not your friend*—a phrase I've heard myself say to her at least twice now.

I hate that I said it. The reality is, she's been nothing but friendly to me. She's been open and vulnerable—even allowed herself to be hurt by me—and I've been nothing but cruel.

She's right, I am scared. I'm scared of letting her in, even though she's already wormed her way into my heart. But what I'm more afraid of now is losing her.

I hate that I get excited every time I see her name pop up on my phone.

I hate that I get butterflies when I see her unexpectedly pull up at my ranch, even though I pretend she annoys me.

Mostly . . . I hate that I've hurt her for no fucking reason other than I'm too immature to recognize my own feelings for her.

I finish my shower and get dressed, walking downstairs to grab another beer. I pull back the curtain on the living room window and look across the field. There are no lights on in her cabin, so she must not be home yet.

"Fuck it." I pull on my boots and coat and grab my beer, making my way across the field to sit on her porch and wait.

AN HOUR LATER, I SEE HEADLIGHTS PAN ACROSS THE FIELD AS Brooklyn's SUV makes its way down the long, winding driveway. She pulls her coat tightly around her body as she slowly walks up the stairs of the porch.

The shadows must conceal me, because she jumps when I speak.

"The redhead, Selma, didn't break my heart." She looks over at me, her hand jumping to her throat. "I didn't mean to scare you. I'm sorry."

She stares at me, not speaking, so I continue.

"It was a mutual decision between the two of us. Just wasn't meant to be, is all." I hold out my hands and shrug. I'm doing a shit job of apologizing.

"You still have feelings for her?"

I shake my head slowly. "No."

"Is that all you came to say?"

I shake my head again. "No. Came to apologize."

That Feeling

She unlocks the door and turns the handle. "Want to come inside?"

I stand and follow behind her. It's my house and yet I feel so completely out of place. She flicks on a few lights and I look around the living space. I haven't seen it since she moved in. She hasn't decorated too much, but with what little she has done, it already feels and looks way homier than when I lived here.

"Beer?"

"Nah, already had two."

"I'm going to change; I'll be right back." She walks down the hallway toward the bedroom and I take a seat on the couch, trying to figure out what, exactly, I plan on saying.

A moment later, she walks back out in a matching baby blue pajama set that has dark blue hearts on it and dark blue piping around the edges. Her face is freshly washed. It's the first time I've seen her without makeup, and she looks even younger. I want to stare at her then pull her into my arms and never let her go.

"It goes without saying that I was a complete piece of shit earlier, and it wasn't the first time." She nods. "I'm sorry, Brooklyn. Nothing I can say will excuse my behavior. For what it's worth, I hated myself the moment I said those things to you. I don't want to hurt you and I never want to see that look on your face again."

She tucks her feet beneath her on the cushion where she's sitting. Her head rests against her hand that's propped against the back of the couch.

"You're right that I'm scared—I'm a coward, actually."

"Why?" she asks.

I look over at her and her expression is soft, her eyes big in the dim light of the side table lamp. I expected her to snap back and tell me I don't deserve a second or third or whatever chance I'm on, but she doesn't. She's warm and receptive, which somehow makes this harder.

"Because I don't want to get hurt. I—" I say, standing up and walking over to the fireplace, resting my hand against the mantle. Maybe if I'm not looking at her, it'll be easier to say. "I do like you. I do consider you a friend and I like talking to you and seeing you. I like spending time with you. I like touching you and feeling you."

She's silent, so I gingerly lift my eyes to meet hers . . . and she's smiling.

"What?"

"I didn't say anything."

"You don't have to. What are you smiling about?"

"Nothing, just go on."

"I'm scared of getting emotions involved with you, because I know there's a good chance you'll go back to Chicago—that you'll miss your family or you'll receive an even better job opportunity and I'll just get left behind. I've said it before, but life out here isn't for the faint of heart. It's tough."

"You don't think I can do it?"

"It's not that," my brow furrows, "I just don't want you convincing yourself that this is what you want because this is where I am. I thought if I pushed you away and was a dick, then you wouldn't let yourself develop feelings for me."

"It's too late for that."

I snap my head up and my eyes bug out. "Meaning?"

She slides off the couch and walks over to me slowly. She extends her arms and wraps them around my neck, pressing herself against me. I hesitate for a brief second before my hands come out and settle on her waist.

"Meaning that I already have feelings for you, and if I had to guess, I'd say you do for me as well."

I chuckle but I don't deny it. "How you figure that?"

"The fact that you're so worried about me settling and staying here for you tells me that you care more about my feelings than your own. If you didn't like me, you wouldn't try so hard to get rid of me. You wouldn't be so scared. It tells me that you see something between us. You see the potential for something you're scared to lose."

That Feeling

She put into words exactly what's been running through my head. Our eyes lock and I slowly lean in until our lips meet.

Fireworks explode behind my eyes as her soft, pillowy lips move against mine. I dart my tongue and taste her lips, coaxing them apart till I can slip inside. How did I ever deny myself this experience? This desire to devour her consumes me. I want to taste, touch, lick, and bite every possible inch of her while being inside her at the same time.

She lets out a soft whimper as my hands travel up her body and into her hair, tilting her head to deepen the kiss. Her hands pull on my neck to get closer to me and I can feel us both on the verge of losing control. Against every fiber of my being, I step back and break the kiss.

"No... *more*..." She pulls me back to her and just like that, I'm once again lost in her taste. Lost in the little mewls she makes as our tongues dance together.

This time when I step back, I grab her hand and lead her over to the couch. I sit down and pull her onto my lap, one thigh on either side of mine so she's straddling me.

"Let's talk about that date."

She smiles. "Oh, so it's back on? And which date would this be, exactly? Because I recall winning one on the bull and buying one tonight."

I grab her sides and she erupts into a fit of giggles.

"Which one do you want it to be?"

She squints one eye and taps her chin like she's thinking. "Well, if it's the date I bought, we should probably take sex off the table."

"The fuck we are!" This time I pinch her bottom and she yelps.

"I'm just saying it feels a little like prostitution. I did buy a date with you, so ya know, you okay with hoeing it out for a few dollars?"

We both laugh.

"Tell you what, let's just table those two options and this is me asking you out on a date. So, where would you like to go?"

"Camping."

"As in?"

"As in real camping: in a tent, in the forest with the animals, with a campfire and s'mores."

"Now *that* I did not see coming. I thought for sure you'd say renting a cabin up in Grand Lake or borrowing my dad's RV that's the size of a small house."

"No, I want the true experience."

"Bugs and snakes and all?"

She scrunches up her face. "Okay, don't ruin it for me."

"Okay, baby, it's a date." I pull her face toward me and plant a soft kiss on her forehead.

"Excellent. Now let's get to the good part."

"Good part?" I ask, confused.

She reaches down and grabs the hem of her shirt and pulls off her pajama top. Her breasts are bare beneath the shirt and they sway slightly with the movement. My attention instantly falls to them and I reach my hands up to cup them.

"Make-up sex."

I lean forward and gently bite each nipple before standing up and swinging her around and over my shoulder as I march toward her bedroom.

"Don't have to tell me twice."

I STARE AT THE CEILING, RUNNING MY HAND SOFTLY UP AND down the smooth skin of Brooklyn's exposed arm. The room is completely silent, with only the faint sounds of her soft breath coming out in puffs next to me.

I turn my head to look at her, and she's fast asleep, her blonde curls splayed across the pillowcase. My heart feels full and scared at the same time. I know I'm falling in love with this woman—hell, I might have fallen already.

That Feeling

I have to be up in just a few short hours and I don't want to disturb her, so I slowly slide my arm out from beneath her and exit the bed. I brush her hair away from her face and lean in to plant a kiss against her cheek.

"Sweet dreams, sweetheart."

Chapter 12

Brooklyn

"Wait, so we hike to the campground?" I tighten the straps on my pack as Tyler unloads a few more items from the truck.

"Yup. Second-guessing?"

"Not a chance, Slade." I put on a brave face, but I'm actually terrified. First, I grew up in the suburbs, where the only thing we were worried about was mosquitos. Second, while I've been here for many weeks, I still haven't acclimated to the altitude, so climbing up even further will be a serious test of my fitness.

"All right, let's do it. It's actually not a long hike—just about two miles—but with our packs and the ever-increasing altitude, it'll be a challenge."

He looks back at me and I smile. "Ready."

"Hey, come here." He gestures with his head and I walk up to him. He grabs me by my coat and pulls my mouth to his, kissing me furiously and taking my breath with it. "Now we're ready."

The hike isn't as bad as I thought it would be—for the most part. I dart my arms out to steady myself as we walk across a few slippery boulders in a creek.

That Feeling

There are a few parts where the trail seems like it almost turns back on itself in a hairpin turn. Every few minutes, Tyler looks back over his shoulder to check on me, sometimes asking if I'm okay.

"Yes, I'm okay, I promise."

It's nearing dusk when we make it to our campsite. If Tyler hadn't been with me, there's no way I'd have known this place was a campsite other than the small clearing among a few trees and the small fire pit.

"Wow, this is—" I look back down to where we started our hike. I don't finish the statement as Tyler walks up behind me and places his hands on my shoulders. "Thanks," I say, looking back over my shoulder at him.

"For?"

"Bringing me up here. I know this is your land and probably your solace—where you come to escape. It means a lot to me." He squeezes my shoulders before removing my pack from my arms.

"It's nice having you with me. I've never brought anyone up here. Never camped with anyone, actually—unless you count Trent and my dad when I was growing up."

I turn around and watch as he places our packs on the ground and unfolds the tent. A warmth spreads through my belly and I want to ask him, *Why me? What makes me special enough to bring up here?* But I'm also not sure I'm ready to pull at that thread. We've just admitted that we like each other, so trying to pull out more might put him back on his guard and ruin this intimate moment. Instead, I smile and walk over to help him.

"You ever pitched a tent before?"

"*Pitched?*" I laugh. "I didn't even know there was a technical term for it."

He gives me a knowing smile—like it's no shock I've never roughed it in the wilderness—and holds up a pile of metal rods. "These are the stakes. We'll put these into the ground through the loops on the corner of the tent itself. That keeps it in place. First, though," he stands up and kicks away a few rocks and bends down to pick up a stick by his feet, "we need to clear this area of debris."

"Sounds easy enough." I follow along and pick up any rocks and sticks I see.

"Now we lay out our footprint—where we're going to put the tent and assemble these." He bends down and produces several long poles. "We'll put these through the loops on the tent canvas then pop it up."

It's actually a lot easier than I expected. We follow his steps and pretty soon the tent is assembled and we're working on building a small fire in the stone fire pit. I gather kindling and Tyler grabs a few larger logs. Once it's crackling, I set up our chairs and pull out the sandwiches and chips I packed for us.

"This is so fun." I smile over at him between bites.

"Really? I thought for sure you'd hate something like this."

I give him a slightly annoyed look. "Why?"

"Well, ya know..."

I don't know.

"You're a city gal and I figured something that would get you dirty or feel unfamiliar like this would be a major turnoff... but you're extremely capable. I'm impressed."

"Gee, thanks." I roll my eyes.

"Sorry. That sounded really sexist and condescending, but I didn't mean it like that."

"I think you underestimate me." He nods in agreement. "I'm more than just my corporate job or my life back in Chicago. I feel like you have me painted into this box based some preconceived notions you have of me. Like, I can't be a city girl from Chicago who moves to the Rocky Mountains and enjoys a slower-paced life than what I had previously."

He sighs. "You're right. I'm sorry. I guess I feel like we don't know that much about each other, so I fill in the gaps based on what I *do* know about you."

"You can always ask." I see a bit of unease on his face. "For exam-

That Feeling

ple, you ever regret not following in your father's footsteps and taking over the business?"

He grabs a log and tosses it on the fire before settling back into his chair. I angle myself so my back and shoulder lean partially against him as I watch the flames dance in the fire.

"No, regret isn't the right word." I can feel his voice rumble in his chest where my shoulder is resting against him. "More like fear. I worried that I disappointed my dad. I know now that it isn't the case, but I struggled with it for years. Growing up, it was always a foregone conclusion: *When you take over* . . . Guess everyone just assumed I would—being the eldest son and all—but I never had the passion."

"Your heart was always in the land?"

"Yeah, I guess so. I just felt like I wasn't the outgoing person like Trent. Kind of seemed like I was in his shadow, which is ironic since I'm the oldest."

I can hear the sadness in his voice and I want to wrap my arms around him, but I know Tyler Slade isn't the kind of man who wants or needs pity. So I stay quiet and let him continue.

"Don't get me wrong, though. I'm no pushover and I sure as hell don't like being told what to do."

Images of him taking control in some of our more intimate moments flash through my mind and my cheeks redden at the memory. He must notice, because he shifts behind me and looks at me.

"What's going through that head of yours?"

I giggle. "Oh, just that I'm very aware that you like being in charge."

"Mmm, you certainly don't seem to mind it." He tips my chin upward and captures my mouth with his as my body immediately comes to life. I break away and settle back against him, hoping he keeps talking.

"Did your parents ever express disappointment toward you?" I ask.

"No, not at all. In fact, it's the opposite. My dad is really impressed with how I've grown our ranch. He tells me all the time how grateful he is, because now he can retire on it." He laughs. "I'm happy Trent was born with that drive to take over and grow the business, because if he'd wanted to move away or do something else, it would have fallen to me, and I absolutely would've stepped up and done it."

"You would've sacrificed your passion and the life you wanted for your father? For the business?"

He nods his head. "Without a second thought. Family means everything to me."

I curl against him tighter. Tyler Slade is an impressive man—one I hope and pray I don't lose, because every moment we're together, every moment he opens up to me, I fall a little bit more in love with him.

"So now for the hard questions." I turn to face him.

"Oh boy, whatcha got?"

"You said Selma didn't break your heart. Was there someone who did? Was there the one who got away?" I smile, hoping it conceals the fear I feel. No one wants to know they're someone's second choice—that if there is that *one* out there who could return, it might destroy you.

"No, Brook. I kno—"

"You called me Brook."

"Sorry, that okay? Guess I heard someone else call you that."

"No, I like it. All my close friends call me that."

He reaches out and brushes a stray hair out of my eye. "Well, *Brook*, nobody has broken my heart or gotten away. There's no big story about lost love that has turned me into a jaded asshole. I've dated and met several women over the years, and some were a stronger connection than others, but none were both the physical and emotional connection I've been looking for."

"Which was Selma?"

He lets out a strained laugh. "Physical. We ended things mutually. I think we both wanted more and couldn't offer it to each other."

That Feeling

"Did she or you ever regret it after?"

"I didn't. She did stop by a few weeks later and wanted to know if I was reconsidering at all. I don't think she really was, either. I think she was just lonely. Since then, though, neither of us has talked about getting back together."

My stomach clenches at that information. I get it. I know it took me several tries before I left Neal.

"So, what is it you're looking for in someone?"

"I guess what we all want."

"Elaborate."

He looks off in the distance as he pulls me in tighter. "What my parents have. Love with a partner who's supportive and meets me on my level. Attraction, obviously—like, undeniable attraction that feels visceral. I want someone I trust—someone who's a teammate with me. We push and challenge each other and won't allow the other to fall behind or be half-assed in the relationship. I want it all, I guess: wife, white picket fence, kids. What about you? What is Brooklyn Dyer looking for?" He kisses the top of my head.

"The same. I was in a long-term relationship before. We met in college and dated for just over five years. On paper, we were perfect together: liked the same things, had the same interests and goals. We both wanted to marry and have a family and careers. A mutual friend set us up, actually: my friend Becca. Funny thing is, after the first date with Neal, I felt like there wasn't a connection. That spark or electric moment I thought I'd feel never happened. So I didn't plan on seeing him again."

"So how do you go from that to five years?"

"I stupidly let Becca talk me into it," I laugh. "I remember telling her, and she told me I'd be crazy to pass up a guy like him, because he checked every box. She wasn't wrong. I honestly believe he will make an amazing husband and father someday, just not with me."

"Makes sense. I don't think there's anything wrong with not settling."

"Yeah, that's how I feel, but others didn't see it that way.

Honestly, I have no one to blame but myself. I remember asking my mom if that's what love is like, and she said that love is a choice, and that sometimes feelings fail and you have to *choose* to love someone."

He looks at me a little sideways. "I mean, yeah, you do choose to love your partner when times are tough, but I don't think it should be that way from the get-go."

"You're right . . . it shouldn't. I kept listening to everyone say, 'He's perfect, he's amazing, you guys look great together and will have an amazing life.' So I stuck it out and I did end up loving him, truly I did. We got along great, so it ended up being easy to love him, but eventually, it just felt like we were roommates, because while I did end up falling in love with him, I never felt that spark and pull toward him—like I craved him."

"So what was the catalyst? What made you finally leave?"

I sigh and think about all the different times I tried to end things.

"I actually tried to end things a bunch of times, but he would genuinely fall apart and cry and beg me to stay. He'd tell me how amazing we were together and how we fit so well, and I'd feel bad and second-guess things. I think I was scared to start over with someone else or be alone, so I'd stay. But one day I just realized I was wasting his time and mine, and it was so unfair for me to stay in the relationship when I had fallen out of love with him. So I just told him the truth—that I was done for good and I was so sorry I broke his heart."

Neither of says anything else as he pulls me against his chest and wraps both of his arms around me. We stare at the fire for several minutes before he speaks again.

"Seems like we're two lost souls looking for the same thing."

I let his words hang in the air. I want to say I think I've already found it, but I don't.

"It's getting late and cold. Let's go to bed," he murmurs in my ear.

"Okay." I stand and he grabs my hand, leading me toward the tent. I stop and pull against his hand and he turns to face me. "I don't want to sleep yet though."

That Feeling

He pulls me against him, cupping my cheek with his free hand as he looks down into my eyes. "You think I brought you all the way out here in the woods to go to sleep?" He leans down and gently nips at my bottom lip. "Baby, you don't know me as well as I thought."

He kisses me harder this time, moving his hand from my cheek to grip my throat as he forces his tongue inside my mouth.

"There's nobody for miles out here. Nobody to hear you scream while I wreck your tight little pussy."

I feel myself throb at his crass words and I only want more.

"Tell me more," I whisper as we tumble into the tent.

"More what, baby?" He rips my shirt from my body as I reach for his belt.

"Dirty talk."

"That right? My baby likes to hear all the filthy fucking things I'm going to do with you?"

I nod as he pulls my jeans down my thighs before removing his own. We're both naked. He grabs both of my ankles and jerks me across the sleeping bags on the ground.

"First, I'm going to devour your sweet little cunt like it's my last meal." He doesn't hesitate. He spreads my thighs wide open. I feel so exposed as he drags his tongue between my folds. "And then I'm going to stuff you with my cock till you're begging me to stop, but will I stop, baby?"

I moan as he slides a finger inside me, circling my clit. He pulls his finger out and slaps my pussy.

"What the—"

"Answer me. Am I going to stop when you're sore and think you can't take any more?" His eyes are dark as he looks down at me.

"No."

"Good girl. Now watch as you take my cock."

I prop myself up on my elbows and look down my body to where he's positioned at my entrance. I watch as he spits in his hand runs it over his cock before thrusting his hips forward. I let out a groan of pain.

"I know, baby. You're not fully ready, but I need to be inside you." His voice is strained as he holds my legs open. I can see the veins pulsing in his neck as he pulls back and slides in harder this time.

My mouth falls open as he repeats the process a few more times. He leans over and grabs a pillow, lifting me and sliding it beneath my hips as he tosses my legs over his shoulders.

He leans forward onto his hands, practically bending me in half and hitting me deep in my G-spot. I scream as he pistons his hips back and forth, his breath growing more rapid with each movement.

"Oh fuuuuck, yes," his voice is loud and deep as he grunts. "I can't get enough," he pants, "God, you were made to fuck, baby." I feel my orgasm seconds away, and his eyes fall to my tits, which bounce wildly with every thrust.

Seconds later, we're both coming undone. I claw at his back as he fists my hair, my scalp burning at the force.

I'm barely able to catch my breath before he's flipping me onto all fours and entering me again from behind. His hands grip my hips so tightly I'm sure I'll have bruises, but I don't care. The sounds of our slapping flesh fills the tent as I ride his cock.

"Ohhh, I'm so close," I moan as my release builds again, but just as I say the words, he stills. I turn around to look at him. "Why'd you stop?"

His grin is wicked. "Because I'll let you come when I want you to come."

I attempt to push myself back against him to resume the movement, but this time he completely pulls out of me then lands a heavy hand against my ass, the slap echoing around us.

"Ow!" I scream as I scramble to turn around, but he reaches forward and pushes me back down.

"Don't fucking move."

I look back over my shoulder and meet his gaze. He keeps eye contact with me as he slowly raises his hand again over his head and brings it back down against my flesh.

That Feeling

I cry out again.

"Do you want me to stop?" he asks, and I shake my head *no*.

I don't know why I'm enjoying this. It hurts like hell, but watching how turned on he is has me even more excited.

He spanks me several more times, landing his hand in different places while dragging his fingers between my folds. When he enters me again, my walls grip him so tightly that my body begins to convulse and shake as I fall apart beneath him.

Chapter 13
Tyler

I know I've pushed Brooklyn's limits tonight. Something inside me comes alive when we're intimate—like a wild beast that needs to dominate her, mark her.

"Are you okay?" I brush her hair away from her shoulder as she lies on her side next to me, my fingers tracing over the small bite mark I left on her skin. "Shit."

"Hmm?" She rolls onto her back to look at me, her eyes heavy with sleep and what I hope is satisfaction. Her lips are still swollen from kissing and her hair is a wild, sexy mess.

"I left a mark on you," I say.

"I'm sure there will be more in the morning." She smiles and curls into my chest.

"I feel so out of control with you. Like I'm scared to break you but I also can't seem to control this desire that just . . ." my voice trails off as her eyes meet mine.

"I get it," she whispers, her hand coming up to cradle my face as she lifts her head and softly touches my lips.

"It's different with you."

"What is?"

That Feeling

"Everything." I reach up and take her hand, intertwining our fingers before bringing them to my lips. "You make me think about things... *want* things."

"What things?"

I let my hand rest on her chest as I slowly drag it down between her breasts. I don't answer her—instead, I let my hand wander further until it settles on her lower belly. I have so many things I want to say and express to her, but I'm scared. Scared to admit them to myself. Scared she'll run for the hills if I dare give voice to what's running through my mind.

Instead, I kiss her. I take her in my arms and make love to her slowly. It's different from the experiences we've shared so far, and different from the experiences I've had with anyone else. Our bodies are speaking—saying all the things our hearts are too scared to express.

IN THE MORNING, WE DON'T TALK ABOUT HOW LAST NIGHT ended. I think we both have things we wanted to say, but in the end, we didn't.

We pack up the campsite at sunrise and make our way back down to the truck.

"You ready for this meeting at 3 today?" She looks over at me coyly and I shake my head.

"No. Not exactly looking forward to seeing my social media posts on a giant screen in front of the entire board."

She laughs and reaches for my hand. "It'll be fine, trust me. You're going to be impressed. The metrics are," she makes a pretend explosion sound and gestures with her hand, "mind-blowing."

"Yeah, well, I can just about bet Trent will never let me live it down. I'm actually shocked that Ranger and Decker haven't teased me much yet."

"Have you not looked at the posts?"

I shake my head *no* and check if there are any cars coming before I pull the truck out onto the road.

"Why not?"

I shrug. "Just weird, I guess. Seeing myself on the internet like that."

She reaches into her pocket and pulls out her phone, tapping around for a few seconds. "Well, you're going to love the comments then."

"Oh shit," I mutter as she giggles and starts to read a few to me.

"Holy hell, I never thought I'd wanna be a horse so bad."

"Nobody said that." I reach for her phone but she jerks it away and continues to read.

"Yes, I'm married . . . but it's not that serious."

That one makes me chuckle.

"Oh my God . . . this one just says: *'Daddy? I mean daddy?'*"

I shake my head and pray nobody reads these comments in our meeting later today.

"Mr. Slade, are you blushing?" She giggles and reaches over to poke me, but I grab her hand.

"Don't make me bend you over my lap while we're driving and repeat last night. Maybe this time I'll use my belt."

I spend the rest of the morning tending to the ranch while Brooklyn gets dressed and heads into the office. I have a lot I need to get done before the meeting later.

If there's one place I can let my guard down and my mind wander, it's on my ranch. There's no pressure to impress anyone or explain myself—just Misty and me and the land.

"Hey, old girl." I step up to where Misty's nose is protruding over her stall door and give her some pets. "You doing okay today?"

She whinnies at the sound of my voice and roots around my breast pockets. She knows that's where I keep the dried apricots she loves so much.

"Now, hold on," I laugh as I attempt to pull it free from the

That Feeling

pocket. It's barely out when she grabs it. I give her another before walking down the stable to our newest horses.

They're still pretty green, so it's going to take some time to gently break them in and get them used to not only being ridden but herding cattle and taking commands. I grab the reins of a young black mare that's barely three years old and lead her out to the training pen. Today we're just working on her being led with a bit in her mouth and getting used to the sound of my voice.

"Need a hand?"

I look up to see my cousin Ethan approaching.

"Hey, buddy, what brings you all the way out here?"

"We brought the baby down to see my parents and I wanted to check in on you. Feels like we haven't talked much these last few months."

I hook the mare up to a post and grab a brush. "Yeah, having a newborn is a lot of work. How's Krista doing? You guys sleeping at all?"

He shakes his head and props one foot on the fence as he leans his elbows on it. "Not really, but it's worth it. Krista's good—her delivery was really smooth and she's just so glad to not be pregnant anymore."

"I bet. I need to stop over and see your parents. I promised your dad I'd bring him a bottle of the new reserve whiskey that's coming out. Granted, I'll have to sneak it past your mom."

We both laugh. Destiny, Ethan's mom, has kept a tight leash on Wyatt after his stroke last fall. He's fully recovered, but she took it a serious sign that he needed to reduce stress and clean up his diet.

"Yeah she's got him eating pescatarian now or something. Bah!" He waves his hand. "I can't keep up with them half the time. Mom's always spouting off something about why everything is bad for me, which then gets Krista on my case. Just want to eat my burgers in peace. For Pete's sake, I'm not even 30 yet!"

"They just want us healthy. Besides, you've got a baby to take care of now. How's life up in Jackson? I hear the steakhouse is one of the busiest."

Several years ago, my dad and Uncle Colton opened a restaurant called the Loveland Maple. It turned out to be such a hit that they've since expanded and opened three others: one in Montana, one in downtown Denver, and the one Ethan manages up in Jackson Hole, Wyoming. It's where he met his wife eight years ago when she was hired on as a hostess and he was just a line cook at the time.

"It's insane but I love it. Looks like the ranch is doing well?"

"Yeah, we've bought about 6,000 more acres since you were here last. This is it, though—no plans for more land. Brought on a few more cowboys and a ranch hand or two. Keeps me busy."

"That's what I hear. Too busy for a family of your own?"

I knew this was coming. I narrow my eyes at him. "My mom sent you by, didn't she?"

He chuckles. "Nah, I just know you, Tyler. You're meant to have a family." I don't respond. "There's really nobody?"

"I didn't say there's nobody."

"Ohhh, so there *is* a somebody?"

I laugh. "Tell you what, the moment I've got it figured out, I'll let you know. Now come in here and see Misty. She misses you."

I FEEL GIDDY THE CLOSER I GET TO THE OFFICE.

Shit, did I just say giddy? Who the hell am I even?

I step on the gas a little harder, hoping to make it there a little early so I can stop by Brooklyn's office before the meeting.

This is the first time, I realize, that when I'm not with the person I'm dating—*are we dating? I'll pull at that thread later*—I miss them. I miss Brooklyn. Not because she's the hottest fuck I've ever had, but because being around her is comforting. It just feels right.

I push aside the fear I can already feel bubbling up and focus on the fact that in two minutes, I'll be seeing her smiling face again. I

That Feeling

pull into my parking spot and jog across the parking lot. By the time I make it through the front doors and up the three flights of stairs, I'm a little winded.

I'm five steps from her door when Trent rounds the corner and almost runs into me. "Whoa, bro, where's the fire?"

"I, uh," I try to think of something to say other than *I'm dying to see my sorta new girlfriend,* but my brain goes blank and he quickly catches on. He looks over his shoulder toward Brooklyn's half-open office door then back at me.

"I see," he smiles like an idiot. "Someone's got a little crush."

A crush? Is that what we're calling making her come six times in one night while being buried balls-deep inside her? Okay, no, can't say that.

"Don't be an idiot. Just wanted to ask her a question about the auction thing from the other night."

He raises an eyebrow, telling me he knows I'm full of shit, but then just pats me on the shoulder and steps aside. "See ya in the meeting."

I take a deep breath then knock softly on Brooklyn's door before opening it slowly.

"Come in," I hear her say in a muffled voice, but I don't see her.

"Brook?" I look around the office until her head pops up from behind her desk. "What the hell are you doing?" I laugh.

Her hair is a little out of place, and the exasperated expression on her face quickly morphs into a big smile as she pulls herself upright and walks boldly around her desk and right into my chest. She throws her arms around my neck and pulls me in for a kiss.

"That's one helluva greeting," I murmur against her lips as I cautiously try to look over my shoulder to see if anyone is in the hallway to witness her very public display of affection.

"Hey, yourself."

"What were you doing under your desk?"

"Oh, the stupid chair wheel keeps getting stuck on a cord and it's pissing me off."

I step around her and take a peek beneath the desk. I see the issue immediately. "You need to feed the cord," I say, bending down to reach for it, "through this hole in the desk. Keeps stuff like this from happening."

When I stand up, she's leaning against the desk. "I was just too lazy to do that."

I'm still on my knees looking up at her when her eyes glance down to my lips, her tongue darting out to wet her own.

"Don't look at me like that." My voice is instantly low and thick with desire.

"Like what?" She's teasing me again.

I glance over my shoulder and lower my voice. "Like you want me to—"

"Oh, hey, Mr. Slade!"

I whip my head around to see my dad standing in the doorway of the office as a flaming red blush grows across Brooklyn's cheeks.

"You two coming to the meeting?" He doesn't seem to have caught on to anything, or if he has, he's playing it off, very much something my father would do.

"Yeah, just helping her with a computer cord issue." I stand up and awkwardly shove my hands in my jeans. I feel like I'm 17 again, getting caught with Hannah Baxter in my bedroom with the door closed.

My dad just nods and glances between us one more time before walking down the hall.

"We should—" She points to the hall and grabs her laptop as I follow behind her down the hallway to our biggest conference room.

"What the fu—" I grab her elbow before we enter and whisper in her ear, "Why is everyone here?"

"Because this is huge stuff, Tyler. We're going over the results of the last eight weeks of this campaign."

I try to stay along the perimeter of the room with my hat down low, praying nobody notices it's me. The last thing I need is everyone

That Feeling

dissecting the shirtless social media posts and raunchy-ass comments from horned-up women online.

"There's the stud muffin!"

"Oooh-weee!"

Wishful fucking thinking.

While I'm incredibly proud of Brooklyn as she walks through the results of the first several weeks of the social media campaign, it's also like watching my nightmare unfold in real time. She clicks through a few images and I quickly avert my eyes, pulling the brim of my hat down a little lower to avoid anyone's eye contact.

"Here are some examples of the kind of posts we've been using, and you can see here . . ." She points with a laser at the hearts and comments at the bottom of the photo.

"Wow, that's a lot of likes and comments," someone says, and I can't help but lift my eyes and look at the photo of myself on the massive screen at the front of the room.

It's one of the photos Brooklyn took on her phone. I'm walking in the meadow by the lookout, leading Misty by her reins. My head is tilted down and the sun streams across the photo like it's been edited, but it hasn't.

I stare at the photo then glance to where Brooklyn is speaking. Her eyes are lit up as she talks about the success of her efforts. She's not bragging or cocky—she's confident, proud, and happy. I feel my stomach flutter as I watch her in her element.

Then I look down at the numbers at the bottom of the picture. I squint my eyes to make sure I'm seeing it correctly: *14,567 likes, 782 comments.* She's fucking amazing at this. Guilt instantly creeps in when I remember all the times I belittled social media and her job.

"Miss Dyer, I think I speak for all of us when I say how impressed we are with what you've done in just a few short months here at Slade. I don't know much about social media, but I do know that if all the likes and clicks and such don't translate to sales, it's not worth much . . . but seeing as how we're already up 15% from last quarter because of these efforts, it's impressive."

Pretty sure that's the most I've ever heard my father speak in one of these meetings, and he's not done yet.

"We—and I do mean all of us—hope that you plan to stay on with us for a long time. Maybe grow your team here at Slade and help us take over the industry." He gives her his smirk of approval. "Hopefully Colorado has been as warm and welcoming to you as you've been to us." I see his eyes look casually over to me as he readjusts himself in his seat.

"Thank you so much, Mr. Slade. Truly, that means so much, especially coming from you. I can't thank you all enough for giving me this opportunity." Her eyes travel around the room slowly before she settles them on me.

"And, yes, Colorado has been amazing and wonderful, and honestly, more than I could have hoped for. I'd even go so far as to say that I—" she hesitates, as her eyes look down at her hands then back up at me, "I'm in love with it."

Chapter 14

Brooklyn

I look around the room after the meeting concludes, trying to stay engaged in a conversation with Trent. Tyler is nowhere to be found. I worry my oh-so-obvious attempt to tell him I'm falling in love with him scared him off.

"Uh-huh." I nod my head, trying to stay focused on what Trent is saying. "I actually need to get back to my office. Got an email I need to send before I head back to my place."

"Hey," Trent's hand comes out and grabs my arm, "so you and Tyler?" He bounces his eyebrows and nudges me.

"Me and Tyler what?" I say, trying to sound confused.

"Riiiight." He laughs and pretends to zip his lips and throw away the key before turning and walking away.

I don't have time to try to explain anything to him, and honestly, I don't even know what I'd say.

Hey, so your brother and I flirted and I blew him then he seemed to hate me and be annoyed with me and now we're sleeping together and I'm in love with him but I don't know where he stands and I just confessed my feelings to him through your dad in a room full of people . . . Yeah, sounds about crazy.

I grab my purse from my office and take the stairs so nobody else can stop me to make small talk. I don't know what I'm going to say to Tyler when I get to the ranch; I just know I need to try to explain what just happened.

I don't see Tyler outside when I approach the house, so I get out of my truck and make my way over to the horse barn.

"Tyler?" I call out as I make my way inside. "Hey, girl." I stop to pet Misty's nose briefly as I follow the sounds I hear at the far end of the stables. "Hey, whatcha doing?" I lean against the doorway of the next-to-last stall. Tyler drags a brush along a smaller horse's body in a long, slow stroke.

"Brushing horses," he says without looking up.

"So the meeting went great. Wasn't too embarrassing, I hope, showing the photos and some of the comments and stuff."

"Yup."

Ah, so we're back to one- and two-word answers. Grumpy, taciturn Tyler is rearing his head again.

"What's wrong?" He doesn't respond, just keeps brushing the horse. "Hey! Look at me."

This time he stops. The brush falls from his hand and hits the ground with a thud as his eyes bore into me. He takes three long steps, grabbing my arm and spinning me so my back is flat against the wall behind me.

His hands are in my hair, his lips crashing against mine before I can even register what's happening. His lips are needy—hungry against mine. Just as quickly as he kissed me, he pulls back, his breath coming out in ragged puffs.

"That's not an answer."

"Are you playing with me?"

My brow furrows. "Playing with you? No. I, I want you Tyler. I —" I can feel the words threatening to break free, and it feels like there's nothing I can do to stop them. I don't want to stop them. "I'm in love with you."

His eyes search mine before he's pressing himself against me, his

That Feeling

mouth taking over once more. I'm lost in this erotic, passionate, demanding kiss. My hands are still pinned when he drops a hand to the front of my pants. His fingers slide straight down into my panties, where I'm already wet with need.

I don't even notice the sound of footsteps approaching, but Tyler does. He releases me and removes his hand from my panties just as Decker approaches with two younger men I've never met.

"Sorry, boss, just bringing Mikey and Dustin back to practice some roping skills."

Tyler doesn't say anything as he tips his hat and waits until the three men have grabbed the ropes and exited the stables.

"We'll finish this talk later." He tips my chin upward. "Be at the house at 7."

"Is it a date?"

"It's a date." He leans in, planting one more scorching hot kiss on my lips then smacking me on the ass as we walk back toward my truck.

"What should I wear?"

"Doesn't matter, baby," he says as he opens the door and helps me inside, "because the second you walk through that fucking door, I'm ripping it off of you."

I'm practically a melted puddle of goo by the time I pull my truck out onto the main road, a massive smile across my face so big I look like I slept with a hanger in my mouth.

I know Tyler honestly couldn't care less what I wear, but I want to look extra cute tonight, especially after just telling him my feelings for him. There's a chic boutique in town I've been wanting to check out, and if they're open at least until 5 p.m., I have just enough time to get over there.

I pull out my phone and decide to try Mallory.

"Hey, Brook, I was just about to text you."

"I told him I love him," I blurt out the words.

"Wait, what? Who?"

"Tyler, the hottie you've been seeing all over the Slade social media pages."

She gasps, "Oh my God, I didn't even know—"

"I know. I wanted to tell you but thought that maybe it was just a hot hookup and I didn't want to get my hopes up. Things have . . . escalated, and I'm on my way to find a cute outfit for our date tonight."

"I'm confused, though. Neal was just here and—"

"What?" Shock resonates throughout my body.

"Neal. He was just at Mom and Dad's house. He came by for lunch. I wasn't there for the lunch—just caught them as they were having coffee—but they were all laughing and acting like everything was normal."

I'm trying to process what she's saying, but I can't make sense of it. "I don't understand, Mal. What the hell was Neal doing at Mom and Dad's?"

"That's what I'm saying, Brook, I don't know. He said that you guys were just *on a break* and that you weren't officially broken up or were talking about getting back together."

I feel like I'm going to vomit. "Mallory I haven't spoken to him since I left Chicago. We are officially done—no breaks or getting back together. He's crazy!"

"That's what I thought, too," she says. "That's why I was so confused by what he was saying."

"And Mom and Dad? What did they say?"

"They were acting like they understood and knew. They said that love takes time and that you two will figure it out. It all felt so weird and *Twilight Zone*-like. I think you need to call them and set the record straight. I don't trust Neal."

"I will. I don't have time right now, but yeah." I feel so hurt that my parents would carry on with him behind my back like this. I'm trying to give them the benefit of the doubt that Neal's ability to charm absolutely anyone got the better of them.

"There's one more thing," my stomach drops even further as she

That Feeling

continues, "I found out why Becca fell off the face of the earth. Turns out she and Neal dated for a bit after you guys broke up. I guess it's over now. Makes me feel like this is why he popped back into our lives."

I rub my forehead because I seriously cannot comprehend what is happening.

"You okay?"

"Yeah," I finally say, "just a lot to process." Silence falls between us again.

Finally, Mallory lets out a small sigh. "This feels fast, Brook. Are you sure you're not just rebounding?"

The thought sends a gnawing feeling through my stomach. I'd be lying if I said I hadn't had the same thought flash through my head a few times, but I always push it away. I knew long before I left Chicago that I wasn't in love with Neal anymore; I'd emotionally moved on ages ago.

"No, it's different Mal. I—I can't explain it, but I just feel like he's the one. I feel like this is the life I'm meant to have."

"And he feels the same way?" I can hear concern in her voice.

"I dunno, honestly. I think so, but he didn't say it back."

"Oh, Brook." Her tone instantly makes me wish I hadn't said anything. I'd hoped she'd be excited for me, but at the same time . . . I get it. I've barely been here a few months, and already, I'm calling to tell her I've fallen in love and found the man I want to spend my life with. "I hope he wants the same things as you."

"I gotta go, Mal. The boutique closes in 15 minutes. I love you." I hang up the phone quickly. Tears prick my eyes, but I shake them away and push aside the information Mallory just shared with me.

Of course the moment I feel like things are coming together for me, something has to rear its ugly head and threaten to destroy it.

The bell above the door jingles. "Welcome to Dolly's Boutique!" I hear a voice coming from the back, but I don't see anyone. Then a petite brunette pops out from behind a wall. "What brings you in?"

"Hi, I'm Broo—"

"Brooklyn Dyer." She smiles as her full round cheeks threaten to take over her eyes. "I'm Dahlia, or Dolly. I've heard about you."

I laugh nervously. "Good things, I hope. I'm just looking for a nice dress. Something flirty and cute for a date."

"Oh, how fun! A date! We absolutely have some dresses that will fit the bill." She motions for me to follow her to a corner. "I think these three would look fabulous on you."

I run my fingers over a blush-colored one. It's fitted almost like a corset on the bodice with a long, flowy skirt. It's romantic and sexy, with long sleeves that sit off the shoulders.

"This one is beautiful. Can I try it on?"

I step into the small curtained dressing room to try on the dress.

"So, I hear you're from Chicago. I've been there once. It was summertime, though, so I avoided the cold."

"Smart move," I say as I step into the dress.

"I don't mean to pry, but small-town gossip always travels fast. I guess it's nice to hear when someone younger moves into town."

I slide the curtain open and step out to look in the floor-length mirror.

"You have to get that one. It looks stunning."

She stands next to me as we both look at my reflection, with everything my sister just told me sitting so close—just under the surface. I swallow down the lump in my throat, telling myself that tonight, none of that shit matters.

I decide to get the dress and change before heading up to the register.

"If you ever want a friend to get coffee with or even check out a spa—I know an amazing one down in Fort Collins, by the way—my cell is on my card." She holds it up to show me before putting it in the bag with the dress.

"Thanks! That's so sweet of you, and I'd absolutely love to hit up a spa. God knows, the dry air out here feels like it's sucked every bit of moisture from my skin."

That Feeling

I thank her and make my way back to my cabin to get changed and head over to Tyler's house for our date.

———

"Now I'd just feel bad ripping that off your body." Tyler runs his thumb over his bottom lip as his eyes slowly inch their way up my body. He reaches his hand out to my waist, running it over the material before snaking his arm around to settle his hand on my ass. He pulls me forward, my hands catching his biceps as his warm mouth lands on my exposed neck and shoulder. "But I *did* warn you." He bites softly at my neck, up to my earlobe.

"Are you going to invite me inside?" I giggle. We're still standing in his doorway. "Something smells amazing."

"Mmm, yes it does," he murmurs.

"I didn't realize you could cook." I follow him down the hallway and into the large chef's kitchen. The smell of fresh garlic and herbs makes my stomach rumble. "I'm starving."

"My mom taught us growing up. She said it shouldn't be up to a woman to feed us."

"I like Celeste. She's a smart lady."

I follow him over to the stove, where a pan of roasted green beans with slivered almonds sits ready to eat. He opens the oven and pulls out a cast-iron skillet with two mouthwatering steaks swimming in butter.

I help him plate up our dinner and we both take a seat at the table.

"You sure you don't want to be my appetizer?"

"If I'm the appetizer, we'll never even get to dinner."

"Probably right," he laughs and we dig in.

Dinner is amazing—the food, the conversation, the wine. Neither of us talks about my awkward confession at the meeting and again at the barn earlier. I push all thoughts of Neal and Becca from my mind and just get lost in Tyler's company.

After we've finished eating, I clean up our dinner mess as Tyler pours us each a generous tumbler of Slade whiskey.

"I turned on the fire pit and warmers on the back porch. Thought we could enjoy a nightcap out there?"

I nod and we make our way to the porch.

"It's so still out here—so peaceful." I stare out into the darkness that surrounds the house.

"That's what I like most."

I take a sip of the whiskey and it burns. "Wow, this is strong."

"It's straight whiskey, baby," he laughs. "Can I get you something different?"

I take another sip. "No, it's okay. I'll probably let you drink most of it though."

We sit on the back porch for close to an hour, sipping our drinks . . . well, I take another sip and then Tyler finishes off the rest.

He tells me stories of how he and Trent once got lost in the mountains for two days. He says his dad wasn't worried about it—that he knew he trained his sons well enough that they'd find their way home. His mother, on the other hand, was ready to call in the National Guard to find them.

We're settled into two massive chairs with our hands tangled together, but it's not close enough for Tyler. He pulls on my hand and I stand up as he leads me so I'm in front of him. He places his hands on my waist and pulls me down onto his lap.

"You like this position," I say as I situate my legs.

"Mm-hmm, I like feeling you on me. Plus I can kiss you." He leans forward, his tongue instantly demanding entrance and sweeping through my mouth. He tastes like whiskey. Need instantly pools between my thighs as I clench them against his hips.

My hips start to move on their own as I grind against his hardening cock. I run my fingers through his silky hair, tugging it gently.

"You needy, sweetheart?"

I nod and lean forward to kiss him again.

"What do you need?"

That Feeling

"You," I say as I try to pull him closer.

"Pull my cock out, baby. Let me see if you're ready." He slides his hand up my thigh beneath my dress as I try to focus on undoing his belt and jeans. I fumble as his fingers travel further, burning a path across my skin. He pushes my panties aside and runs his thumb back and forth over me.

"Goddamn, you're practically dripping." He pushes his thumb against my folds as my hand finally pulls his zipper down. He thrusts it into me and my lips form an inaudible sound as I fall forward. I rest my head against his shoulder, my hand finding his cock as I slowly pull him free and begin to stroke him. He replaces his thumb with two fingers, sliding them in and out of me as he presses his palm against my clit.

"I think you're ready to ride my cock." He pulls his fingers out and pops them straight into his mouth, his tongue snaking around and between them to lick off every drop of my arousal.

His movements are deliberate and sexy. He grabs the base of his cock with one hand as his other holds my panties to the side. I grip his shoulder with one hand, and the arm of the chair with the other as I slowly lower myself down onto him.

"Yesssss!" The word comes out in a hiss as my head falls back.

"Look at me," he grunts as I finally sink all the way down onto him.

His eyes are dark and glassy, the effects of lust and whiskey coursing through his veins.

"You're mine," he grits out as his hands grip my waist. He reaches forward and pulls the top of my dress down roughly, exposing my breasts. "These are mine." He cups them gently before squeezing hard. He presses them together, leaning forward to suck my nipples into his mouth. "I'm a possessive man, baby, and I won't be denied. I mark my territory." He bites me, hard.

"I want—I need . . ." I begin to move slowly, lifting my body up and then coming back down harder.

"Oh fuck, yes, baby, fuck me." His eyes roll back in his head as I repeat the process. Each time I come down, his eyes grow darker, heavier. They feel like they're going to burn through me. "Mine," he says again, "you're my woman, you understand that?"

I nod, but it's not good enough. He grabs the back of my neck, pulling me down hard and slamming himself inside me. "Say it!"

"I—I'm yours."

He's like an animal in these moments—a predator that has finally caught his prey but is consumed by the desire to devour it. He leans back in the chair, his eyes staring intently into mine as I continue to ride him.

My movements have slowed to a rhythm that's both driving me insane and building so much pressure that I know when I come, it's going to be explosive.

"Tell me again," he demands. I'm about to repeat what I just said when he adds on, "What you said in the barn."

I study his eyes for a moment when I realize what he wants to hear.

"I love you."

His eyes fall from mine down to my belly. He moves one hand from my hip, placing it against my stomach like he did that night in the tent.

"Are you on birth control?"

I nod my head *yes,* thinking he's asking if it's okay for him to not pull out. "Yes."

"You should stop taking it."

I'm so close that I can't understand what he's saying. I don't think he understands what he's saying. It's just the whiskey talking.

He holds up my dress as he watches himself slide in and out of me, his hips starting to come up as I come back down. He's entranced, holding my hips tightly as we both start to tremble.

"But I could get pre—"

"That's the point, darlin'," he grunts as he pulls me down and buries his face in my neck. I feel him twitch and spill himself inside

That Feeling

me just as my walls clench around him, my orgasm rolling through me, crashing in waves of pure ecstasy.

I stay in his arms, with only the sound of our labored breathing echoing around us. His hand is back to resting on my belly, his breath warm against my neck.

I know there's something we need to talk about, but right now, I don't want to ruin this moment. The fact that he's clearly not ready to say *I love you* back—yet previously hinted at wanting me pregnant and told me just now—is alarming. I love him without a doubt, and the thought of a life and a family with him sends butterflies dancing through my stomach, but the nagging feeling that he's scared and unsure hangs heavy over my head.

Did he make this confession because he wants those things with me too? Or is it because he's scared I'll leave like everyone else and this is a way to ensure I can't run away?

Chapter 15

Tyler

I groan and reach my arm behind me, expecting to feel Brooklyn's warm, naked body, but instead I'm met with a pile of cold sheets.

I roll over and squint at the sunlight streaming through the parted curtains. The smell of coffee hits my nostrils, and instinctively, I toss the covers off and pull on my pajama bottoms to walk down to the kitchen.

"Mornin'. Now that's a sight I could get used to."

Brooklyn's hair is piled high on her head, my T-shirt just covering her ass and the tops of her thighs.

"Morning to you too." She turns and looks at me over her shoulder, a coy little smirk on her face.

I stretch my arms overhead and come up to stand behind her, sliding my arms around her waist and burying my face in her neck.

"You smell so good," I murmur, nuzzling her. "How are you feeling?" I drop my hand from her waist down to her lower belly. "Hope I didn't work you over too hard."

"I'm okay . . . a little sore."

"Mmm, good. I like knowing you'll be feeling me all day."

That Feeling

I pour myself a cup of coffee and lean against the counter as she goes back to whipping the eggs in the bowl in front of her.

Watching her move around my kitchen does something to me. It's nothing grand—it's just a simple, everyday activity that I realize no other woman has done in this kitchen. I've also never gone camping with a woman or agreed to do anything remotely close to a bachelor auction. I smile into my cup when I think about how easy it was for her to talk me into anything.

"I love you."

I don't have to think twice about saying it. I know I've felt it for a while now and was just too scared to say it back. But this right here . . . waking up together and realizing that she makes me not want to get out of bed and start my day if she's lying next to me . . . makes me want to experience all the mundane things together that make up our days. She makes me want it all: the happily ever after I've been searching for.

She drops the whisk and it clangs against the ceramic bowl as her head whips around. "I love you too." She smiles and I nod my head slowly, taking another sip of my coffee.

"Glad we cleared the air on that."

She giggles at my comment.

"Get over here," I say, placing my cup on the counter just as she takes two big steps and jumps into my arms, her legs wrapping around my waist.

"Took you long enough."

I hold her in my arms for several minutes before placing her on the counter and stepping between her thighs.

"Hey." I know I owe her an explanation for last night, and while I'm tempted to just use the whiskey as a cop-out, I know that's unfair to her. "I, uh, about last night . . . I'm sorry if I scared you or pushed you toward something you're not ready for. I just—you're the first woman I've ever wanted those things with."

"It was a little shocking. It's not that I don't want those things with you—I do—I just don't think I'm ready."

"I understand completely." I try to hide my disappointment as best I can, but I know she can see it on my face. She places a hand on either side of my face.

"I'm in love with you, deeply. I want time to experience life with you. I promise you, Tyler, I'm not going to run away. I'm not going to break your heart. Colorado is my home now."

I feel relief, but it still feels so foreign to just jump in with both feet like this, especially after only a few short months. "Does this feel strange to you?"

She tilts her head. "Strange? No. Vulnerable? Yes. I realize we've only known each other a short time, but that doesn't mean it's not real. People always say *when you know, you know*. Maybe this is one of those times when we both just know."

I wrap my arms around her and hold her in my arms. Even if we get this all wrong and I end up brokenhearted, I can't see myself ever regretting loving her.

"You just gonna stand in the corner all night and leer at her?"

Trent sidles up beside me as I finish off my beer. Tonight is our annual board and executive dinner at the Loveland Maple.

"I'm not *leering*. I'm giving her some space and just admiring her."

"Well, that's a lot more than I thought you'd give me. Figured you two would still try to deny there's anything going on between you even though I'm pretty sure people up in Montana are aware by now."

I roll my eyes and place my empty glass on a passing waiter's tray.

"Wait, *we'd* still deny?"

"Yeah, after that last meeting we had with the board about the social media campaign, I tried getting some info out of Brooklyn, but

That Feeling

she acted confused like there was nothing." He raises his hands. "Hey, I get it, you want some privacy. I won't pry."

About 10 seconds of silence falls between us—enough time that my stomach does a little flip at the thought that Brooklyn might be hiding us.

"So, are you guys official or . . . ?"

I glare over at Trent. "So much for not prying." I let out an exasperated sigh. It's not like Trent and I are in the habit of sharing our most intimate feelings with each other, but what the hell, I'm turning over a new leaf and all that. "I thought we were but, uh, not sure she wants people to know, it seems."

"Well, she is new here, and new at the company. She probably wants to make a good impression and really solidify her place. You and I know things are laid back out here, but city folk do things a little differently. I'm sure if she dated the owner's son while she was employed anywhere back in Chicago, she could risk losing her job."

Trent is most likely right, though I can't say it doesn't sting a little to be a secret. I'll explain things to her so she doesn't feel weird about people finding out about us.

"Since when are you the type of guy who cares about that shit, anyway? I don't think you ever once introduced a woman to any of us as a girlfriend."

"Guess things are different this time."

Brook looks over at me, her eyes sparkling in the dim light of the room. It feels like there's nobody here but us. She smiles, waving her hand sweetly before being pulled away by someone else.

"That Brooklyn is something else." My mom appears to Trent's right. "She had nothing but amazing things to say about you, Tyler."

"Oh, I'm not surprised," Trent mutters as my mother raises an eyebrow.

"Oh?"

"I think our boy is in love, Mom." Trent lazily flings his arm over my shoulder and I quickly shrug it off.

"Jesus Christ, this is why I don't come to these things."

"Well, I think you two would be lovely together. You need someone like her. She's sweet and outgoing and loves to take charge."

If my mom wasn't standing here, I'd say something to the effect of *you should see how submissive she is when I pull off my belt*.

My mom gasps and places her hand on my arm, startling me as if I *did* say it out loud.

"You should invite her to our family Thanksgiving. I heard her saying she isn't going home for the holidays."

That's actually a good idea. I feel a little shitty knowing Thanksgiving is only a few days away and I haven't asked her what she's doing yet.

"I'm getting some air." I walk across the room and exit through the patio doors. There's a large outdoor dining area that's used in the warmer months. It overlooks a beautiful stream with a small waterfall. I lean my elbows on the railing and look up at the inky-black sky dotted with sparkling stars.

"Hey."

Brooklyn's voice interrupts my thoughts—thoughts about what Trent said. When Brooklyn and I spoke about this dinner, and the fact that it was an hour from the ranch, I told her we should make a weekend out of it and get a hotel in Loveland. She agreed but talked me into driving our own cars to this dinner so no one would catch on —an agreement I'm now regretting.

I've waited my whole damn life for this kind of love; I don't want us to be a secret.

"Are you hiding me?" I ask.

"Hiding you?"

I turn around to face her. "Yes, hiding me. You ashamed that we're together? *Are* we together?"

She nervously places her champagne flute down on a bar top table in the corner near the door.

"No, I'm not ashamed of you and I'm not hiding you."

I don't wait for her to add anything else. I grab her and pull her to me.

That Feeling

"You're mine, remember? I told you when you were riding my cock the other night that you're *my* woman." She glances over her shoulder as if she's checking to see if anyone's watching or can hear us. "Don't worry about what they're doing. Look at me."

Her gaze snaps back to mine as I slowly back her into the corner of the patio, out of view of the glass doors.

"Are you mine, Brooklyn?" I tip her chin upward, my mouth centimeters from hers.

"Yes," she whispers.

"So why the secrecy, hmm?" I grind my cock against her. "You afraid people will find out how naughty you are? How hard you liked to get fucked?"

I can see the effect my words are having on her. She tries to stay stoic, but she's ripe with desire.

"Tell me, baby girl."

"I just—"

I don't play fair. I slide my hand right up her skirt and settle it between her thighs. Her eyes flutter before she swallows and regains composure.

"I just want to be taken seriously at my job. I don't want people thinking I slept my way to the top."

"Of course not," I agree. I slide my hand up her neck and around the back, holding her head in place as the fingers of my other hand tease her. I run them softly over her sheer, damp panties.

"I promise you, honey, I will never attempt to negate your authority at work. You're the boss, remember? Nobody will know that when we're home, you're my little fuck toy. Nobody will know that you're mine to use and pleasure how I see fit." I lean in and drag my lips from hers across her cheek to her ear. "But they will know that you're my woman. They will know that you're the love of my life, and that someday, you're going to have my children."

I pull my head back and look her in the eyes. I swirl my thumb over her clit a few times and feel her panties growing wetter by the second.

"Is that clear?"

"Yes."

"That's my good girl." I plant a kiss on her forehead and slowly pull my hand away from her, allowing her dress to fall back into place.

"Now, go get in my truck. We're going to go back to our hotel and I'm going to remind you what kind of man I am."

THE 10-MINUTE RIDE BACK TO THE HOTEL IS SILENT.

There's a heavy energy that hangs between us. I feel like I'm grinding my teeth to keep from bending the steering wheel in half. My cock aches to break through my jeans.

The moment I get her in our room, I see the anticipation in her eyes. She loves not knowing what's coming next. Seeing her in the boardroom—in control, commanding—is sexy as hell. But this, this right here . . . her almost trembling with need, not knowing what I'm going to do to her, is pure fucking heaven.

She sits nervously on the end of the bed and I walk over to my suitcase, reaching inside to pull out a belt. I can see her watching my movements. I toss the belt on the bed next to her then bend down to remove my boots.

I slowly unbutton my shirt, removing it completely and tossing it on the chair next to the bed. Next, I undo my belt buckle and slowly pull the belt through the loops. Her eyes watch me intently.

"You curious why I brought two belts?"

She nods. Gone is that confident businesswoman. Right now, she's just Brooklyn, my little plaything, and she loves it.

"You see those two posts on the bed?" I nod toward the head of the bed and she swivels to look at them. "Saw those online when I booked the room and thought of how lovely it would be to see you strapped to the bed—spread-eagle for me to have some fun with."

Her mouth falls open.

That Feeling

"You ever been tied to a bed and fucked till you can't walk, Brooklyn?"

"No," she says, swallowing hard.

I step forward, my jeans hanging undone. I place my hand beneath her chin. "Do you need a safe word? I promise I won't hurt you, but I don't plan on being gentle, sweetheart."

"No safe word."

I lean down and kiss her softly. "I love you, baby. Don't ever question that in these situations, okay? Did you bring your vibrator like I asked?" She nods. "Go get it."

She scurries over to her suitcase and produces a pink vibrator, placing it on the bed as she comes to stand in front of me.

"Anything in particular you want me to do to you tonight, baby?"

I like watching how nervous she gets when I'm blunt with her. She was so flirty and confident with me the day we met. It's like a fun switch I can flip with her.

"What do you need?" I demand.

She chews her bottom lip nervously. "I want," she hesitates, "I want you to use me. I—I," she stutters.

"Shh, it's okay, baby, I'll give you what you need."

The time for talking is over. I spin her around and unzip her dress, allowing it to pool at her feet before kicking it to the side. I quickly remove her bra and panties and toss them on top of her dress.

"Mmm, those heels stay on."

I run my hand down her bare back then push against the center of it until she falls forward. Her hands come out to catch herself. She's bent over the bed, her arms outstretched. I kick my feet against each of hers so her legs are spread further apart.

Then I drop to my knees behind her and devour her. She's panting, arching her back like a cat in heat as she presses her pussy harder against my mouth. She starts to tremble, shouting my name, but I pull back, not allowing her to finish.

"Please don't stop," she begs as she presses harder against me, but

I stand up and slap her ass hard, the smacking sound bouncing off the walls.

"You need some discipline." I smack her again before grabbing her and flipping her to her back. I step off the side of the bed. "Scoot up the bed and spread your arms out."

She obeys as I grab the belts. I loop one around her wrist before tying the end to the bedpost, repeating with her other arm. She watches me as I finally remove my jeans and underwear and crawl up the bed toward her.

"This should be fun," I say, grabbing her vibrator and turning it on a low setting. I press it against her already-swollen clit and a low moan escapes her lips. She tries to lift her hips when I pull it away, but she can't reach it. I try a few more settings, edging her over and over until she's begging me to finish her. I put it inside her, slowly sliding it in and out before returning to her clit.

I finally can't take it any longer. I toss it to the side and slam my cock balls-deep inside her. I grip her ankles, spreading her legs as I thrust in and out of her.

"Don't fucking move," I grit as my orgasm takes over. My thrusts grow erratic as I spill myself inside her.

"I know you need to come, baby." I lean forward and undo one wrist so I can flip her on her stomach. I jerk her waist up so she's up on her knees, and then slide back inside her. "Ohhh, yes."

My voice is loud and I'm sure the neighbors can hear everything that's happening to Brooklyn right now, but I don't give a fuck. "Oh shit, look at that view." I grip her waist and pull her back hard and fast, her ass bouncing with every movement. Her hands are fists, gripping the sheet so hard that her knuckles are white. "You close, baby?"

"Yes!"

I slow my pace and she looks over her shoulder at me, now so frustrated I'm worried she might actually rip my dick off after this.

"Just hold on, baby." I reach for the vibrator again and spit on it before turning it to the lowest setting. I gently press it against her asshole as I move my hips in time with its movements.

That Feeling

"What the fu—" she turns around. "No way." She shakes her head, her eyes growing wide.

"It's either my cock or this vibrator, baby," I pull out of her completely and hold it next to me, "and it's by far the smaller option."

She looks concerned and I run my thumb over her pink rosette a few times, her hips involuntarily thrusting back, so I push against her harder. The tip of the vibrator slips inside.

"You like that?" She groans her approval and I slide it in deeper. "Just relax like you're doing, baby. I want to fuck you in both holes right now and you're going to like it, trust me." I grit my teeth to keep myself from coming already as I slide back into her and press the vibrator into her.

It's tight, so I go slowly, allowing her to acclimate. "Just relax and let it inside." I can barely get the words out myself, I'm so fucking turned on.

Soon, I'm sliding my cock in and out of her tight little pussy while I move the vibrator in and out of her asshole. The sounds she's making are driving me crazy.

She's begging—pleading for me not to stop—and then she's screaming my name as her body quivers and falls into a sweaty pile of orgasmic bliss.

Chapter 16

Brooklyn

"Have you always been so dominant in bed?"

I rest my back against Tyler in the deep soaker tub. The essential oils and lavender candle attempt to relax my worn-out body.

"No, I don't think so," his voice rumbles against my back. "I haven't been with someone who made me feel comfortable expressing that side of myself."

"Why me?"

He runs his fingertips up my bare arms, sending a tingle down my body.

"Something about you just lets me be free. I think because you're so strong and capable, it makes me want to do it more. It probably sounds toxic or completely fucked up. I can't explain it, but knowing you don't need me or any man is a turn-on. You're choosing *me*."

"You have no idea how good it feels to hear you say that in a positive way."

"What do you mean?"

"That was always an argument or an issue for me in the past. I've never wanted to feel like I'm an obligation to someone—like they're with me because they married me or we have a child or a house

That Feeling

together. I want to feel wanted, to be chosen. So I always figured my ex felt that way, too, but it actually made him feel incredibly insecure that I didn't need him for financial stability or anything like that."

"That can be hard for a man, I won't lie. We want to feel needed and wanted, like we're an asset."

I turn around to face him. "I do need you. And I want you more than anything, honestly."

"I know you do, baby, and I'm not worried about it. What we have is special—different from anything I've ever experienced with anyone else. I think that's why I'm so sure."

I feel the butterflies again, but they're mixed with unease because I have yet to deal with the Neal drama. I promised myself I would call my family and explain things, but I've just been too afraid to ruin this cloud of elation I've been floating around on with Tyler.

"Which is why I want you to come to my family Thanksgiving . . . as my girlfriend."

I smile but then the unease grows heavier. He must sense it.

"Is it too soon?"

"No, no, not too soon at all. I'm honored and would love to go with you." I smile, and this time, it's just the butterflies. "I'm excited but incredibly nervous," I laugh.

"Trust me, you have nothing to be nervous about. According to Trent, everyone from here to Montana can pick up on the chemistry between us, and my mom even chimed in about it."

"Celeste?" My hands come up and clamp over my mouth. "So your mom knows I'm sleeping with her son?" I try to submerge myself beneath the bubbles, but Tyler grabs my arms.

"Trust me, they have no idea about the things I do to you, and we're going to keep it that way."

My laughter is replaced with nervousness again. "You sure nobody will question me working for the brewery and dating you?"

"Well, I didn't hire you, and I didn't ask you to be the face of Slade Brewing. I guess we could tell them you seduced me into doing it." He laughs and I splash water at him. "Seriously, baby, nobody will think you're being unprofessional. Besides," he pulls me back against him and nips at my earlobe, "you're never getting away. You're mine. Forever."

———

I PACE MY BEDROOM NERVOUSLY AS THE PHONE RINGS FOR THE fifth time. Finally, my mom picks up.

"Hello?"

"Hey, Mom, it's me."

"Brooklyn, sweetie, how are you? Your father was just saying how it won't feel the same without you here this year."

"I know, Mom. I'll miss you guys."

"I just don't understand. If it's about the money, your father and I will gladly buy you a ticket home. I just hate thinking of you all alone on a holiday, eating mac and cheese in your apartment."

I let out a breath. "Well, that's kind of why I'm calling. I know I texted you guys a few days ago letting you know I won't be home, but, uh, I'm not going to be alone out here."

"Oh?"

"Mom, is Dad nearby? Can you put me on speaker?"

"Terry, our daughter's on the phone and she wants to speak to both of us." I hear my mom fumbling with the phone as she asks my dad how to put it on speaker.

"Hello? Brooklyn? This is Dad; we're both here, sweetie. How are you doing?"

"Hey, Dad, I'm good. Listen, this is uncomfortable, so I'm just going to come out and say it, because I feel like I honestly don't know what's going on back home. But Neal and I . . . we're not on a break." The phone is dead silent on the other end. "We're completely done and have been since before I moved out here. I don't understand why he's suddenly back in my life and telling people we're working things out when I haven't seen or spoken to him in months."

"Oh dear," my mother finally speaks.

That Feeling

"Sweetie, we had no idea," my dad adds.

"I know, I talked to Mallory and I don't have all the details, and honestly, I don't care about them. I just need you guys to know that he's lying. I've met someone else—someone who makes me incredibly happy. I'm trying to move forward with him, but I can't if Neal is still trying to lie and weasel his way back into my life."

"So he hasn't talked to you at all?" my dad asks.

"No. He hasn't even called or texted me, but for some reason, he's telling you guys all sorts of crazy things. My guess is the same as Mallory's: now that things didn't work out between him and Becca, he's trying to get back with me."

"Well, that is *not* okay," my dad says firmly. "I'll go have a talk with him if you want me to, and set this young man straight. You know Silas will come with me; he never liked that boy much."

I laugh at my dad's bravado. "Dad, no, please don't rope my brother into this."

"Speaking of your brother, you need to call him. I know he's busy with his job and his daughters, but he misses you."

"I know, Dad. I will." I do feel guilty that I haven't kept up with my family as much as I should have. I miss my nieces even though they lived four hours from me back home in Illinois and I didn't get to see them too often.

"Anyway, I'm going to call Neal and get to the bottom of all this, but in the meantime, can you guys please just have my back?"

"Absolutely! We had no idea, Brook. Now, more importantly, who is this man you're seeing?"

"He's someone really special to me. I promise to go into more detail soon when I come home for Christmas, but just know that he's wonderful and he loves me."

I hear my mom sniff and I know she's crying. That's one of the most amazing things about my family: If I ask them to have my back, they have it, no questions asked. I know Mal is worried things are moving too fast, and she might be right, but since the last time she and I talked, she's just been blowing up my phone with questions about when she can meet him.

"Hey, sis! Bought my ticket!" I hear Mallory chime in.

"Oh, that's your sister. Listen, she wanted to talk to you. Your mother and I have our casino night over at the country club, so we need to get going, but we love you so much. And don't worry, Neal is dead to us."

"Terry!" my mother chimes in. They hand the phone off to Mallory and head off to their game night.

"Hey, I'll keep it quick, but I just wanted to let you know that I got my ticket to come see you next week, and also, Neal has been texting and calling me begging me to get you to talk to him."

I rub my temples. *Fuck, this isn't going away.*

"Don't worry, though," she says. "I told him to suck my ass and blocked him."

"Ugh, I don't even know what to do. I'm going to call him; I have no other viable option. I'm afraid if I block him, he's going to show up out here or something crazy." I shudder at the thought. An awkward phone call is a much better option.

"I'll support whatever you choose. Just keep me posted. Let me know if I need to drive over to his apartment with Silas and a tire iron."

"What the hell is with you guys? Dad said something similar. Just let me handle it."

"Fine. So, what's been going on with Tyler?"

"He asked me to go to his family's Thanksgiving dinner . . . as his official girlfriend."

"And? Does that make you nervous or anything?"

"Yes and no. I'll feel better once I handle this thing with Neal."

She gives me a pep talk and we say our goodbyes.

I hold the phone in my hand, my thumb hesitating over Neal's name. I hit the call button then immediately hang up. My stomach is in my throat. I close my eyes and pinch the bridge of my nose trying

That Feeling

to muster up some courage when my phone vibrates in my hand. I look down and see Neal's name across the screen.

"Shit!" I hit the reject button. I thought I'd hung up before it connected earlier, but apparently not. The phone rings once more, and again, I hit the reject button.

I feel like a coward. Then a text comes through.

Neal: *Hey, beautiful. Saw you called me. Been wanting to talk. Got a few minutes?*

I debate on if I should just say everything in a text, but instead, I swipe across the chat and delete it, then go to the call log and do the same.

Guilt grips me as I realize I'm officially hiding this whole situation from Tyler, but right now, I just don't have it in me to deal with it.

"YOU GUYS ARE DATING?" TRENT FEIGNS SHOCK AS TYLER USES his free arm to smack his brother, since the other one is wrapped tightly around my waist.

"So this is the new social media genius who's kicking ass."

"Brook, this is my Uncle Hudson and his wife, Aunt Deven."

"Hi, Deven, so nice to see you again." I extend my hand but she pulls me in for a hug. Next, I turn to her husband. "Hudson, so nice to finally meet you."

"Pleasure. Sorry I couldn't make the last two meetings. I promise I've been keeping up with what you've been doing, though. Drake and Colton won't shut up about it." He lets out a loud, bellowing laugh.

"Brooklyn, I'm going to snatch you away for a few moments." I turn to my right and Celeste is looping her arm through mine and pulling me toward the kitchen.

"Sorry about that," she says, "but I figured you might need a moment to collect your thoughts. Lord knows, this family has no boundaries and I don't want them scaring you off after one holiday with us." She gives me a wink and hands me a much-needed glass of wine.

"Thank you." I glance over my shoulder and see Drake and Tyler heading out back with cigars and whiskey.

"They'll be out there for hours if we let them. Two peas in a pod, those two."

"Drake and Tyler?" I ask curiously.

"Oh yes. They're both so quiet sometimes I don't know how they communicate as much as they do. Tyler was always Drake's little shadow growing up. And they revert back to it when they're together."

I smile. It all makes sense now that Tyler worried as much as he did about disappointing his father.

"He's a good man. They both are."

I turn back around to see Celeste leaning against the counter with what looks like tears in her eyes.

"You make him so happy, Brooklyn." She's crossing the distance between us and throwing her arms around me before I realize what's happening.

"I never thought he'd find you."

"Brook, we need to go, don't we?" Mallory yells to me from down the hall.

"Just a second! Feel free to start the car," I yell as I swipe away the unread text from Neal and delete it.

I've lost count of how many calls and texts he's sent me over the last few days that have gone unread and now deleted. I feel awful—like I'm a liar who's hiding something from everyone.

After spending an amazing Thanksgiving with Tyler and his family, I promised myself I'd deal with this once and for all. I can't risk losing what I have now that I've found it.

That Feeling

I pull up Neal's contact info and scroll down to the bottom, hitting the "block contact" button. I slide the phone into my pocket and grab my overnight bag to head out to my car.

"Drive safe, baby. Text me when you get there." Tyler grabs my ass and plants a panty-melting kiss on my lips right in front of my sister.

I push against his chest, but it only makes him deepen it. If there's one thing I've learned from dating Tyler, it's that he won't be hidden, and if I do try to tamp down his antics, he only lays it on thicker.

"I will. Behave while I'm gone. No strippers." I wink and climb into the truck. "I love you."

"Love you too, darlin'." He kisses me again through the open window before waving us off as we drive away.

"How are you not pregnant yet? That man is like a damn fantasy."

Mallory and Tyler instantly hit it off. He picked up on her sarcastic wit and gave it back to her just as hard. Feels like two against one now.

"Trust me, if it were up to him, I would be. One thing at a time. For now, I'm ready to drink my weight in mimosas and enjoy our weekend in Grand Lake with Milly and Dolly."

By the time I pick up the other two and we make it to Grand Lake, my stomach hurts from laughing so much. We quickly settle into our hotel then change to head out to get drinks and dinner.

"So, we know Brook is wifed up with Tyler, and I haven't seen a penis since starting vet school, but what about you two? I feel like there's nothing but sexy-as-hell mountain men as far as the eye can see out here."

Milly laughs. "Yeah, I'm related to almost all of the men around here, so it's slim pickings for me. I basically have to go to Denver to find a man who isn't a Slade, and by that point, they're a bunch of boys with Peter Pan syndrome." She lets out a defeated sigh.

"And you, Dolly?" I give her a questioning look.

Her cheeks turn pink. "Well, I, uh . . ." She glances sideways at Milly.

"Oh God, what?" Milly's hand goes to her nonexistent pearls.

"I just have kind of always had a thing for Ranger."

Mallory looks around the table, confused.

"That's Milly's half-brother. He's one of the cowboys at the ranch," I explain.

"You have my blessing, Dolly, you know that. But girl, that man is a player and a half. Never seen him bring home the same girl twice . . . which is surprisingly weird considering we live in such a small town."

Dolly's smile falters a bit and I elbow Milly. "I'm sorry, I didn't mean to say he won't ever settle down," Milly says. "Dammit, I just meant—"

"No, I get it. Like I said, I've always known that about him—we all do. But for some reason, I can't seem to shake this damn crush." She giggles and it breaks my heart. Maybe the next time I see Ranger, I'll talk some sense into him, or at least get Tyler to do it.

"And things with Tyler?"

I down my drink and motion to the waiter for another. "Things are good—great, actually. He's amazing."

The table sighs in unison. "You guys are so in love," Dolly says.

"I'm calling it now: married by next January," Mallory adds on.

I blush and play it off, but secretly, I would love if that were the case. But the moment I start fantasizing about walking down the aisle, the feeling that I need to deal with the Neal situation and tell Tyler about it comes creeping back in.

I make a promise to myself that as soon as I get back home, I'm not only telling him about Neal, but I'm going to ask him to come home with me at Christmas.

Chapter 17

Tyler

I pull into the bar and see my dad's truck is already there.

Dad and I try to grab a beer at least once a month. We see each other more than that, obviously, but this is our night. No women around or Trent to distract us with work talk.

"Hey, Dad." I give his shoulder a squeeze as I take a seat on the empty barstool next to him. He lifts his beer to me and takes a swig.

"Just ordered you one."

Danelle, the bartender, places a stout down in front of me.

"So how are things, Dad?"

He looks over his shoulder at me. "Feel like I should be asking you that. I'm an old man these days, not much changing."

I smile. "Yeah, things are good." He doesn't have to elaborate for me to know he's referring to things with Brooklyn. He and I had a short chat about it on the porch at Thanksgiving. I wanted to go more deeply into things with him, but not with everyone around.

"The family loves her, your mom especially. She told me to tell you tonight not to screw the pooch with this one."

"With this one? What makes her think I'm the one who screwed up any of my other relationships?"

Dad gives me *the look*.

"For the record, Selma and I both agreed we weren't each other's person, and as for Alana, she was only looking for a distraction from her impending divorce."

"Look, I'm not saying you screwed anything up, but you also have a knack for walking away too quickly. Marriage is damn hard, son. You're gonna face more hardships than you realize, and you just gotta be willing to fight for it."

"Whoa, who said anything about marriage?" I give him a smirk and he just chuckles and shakes his head. "Actually, that's part of what I wanted to talk to you about tonight. Mom's ring."

He looks over at me briefly just as a young man I've never seen before walks into the bar.

"You think it's too early to ask?"

"It's not about what *I* think. I don't adhere to rules about stuff like that. You know that. Hell, your mom and I had one helluva trip finally making it down the aisle."

"Would you have changed anything? Like if you could go back?"

The young man walks up to the bar and smiles at Danelle while ordering a beer. Most likely a tourist down from Jackson, just passing through.

"No. I mean, hey, I probably wouldn't have been such a stubborn asshole, but it all worked out in the end. I tried not to fall for your mom."

That piques my interest. "You did? Why?"

"Same as you. I was hard-nosed and thought I had my life all figured out. I let the brewery consume my life and convinced myself I didn't have time for anyone or anything else. I wanted to keep things . . . *casual* with your mom."

I crook an eyebrow. "*Casual?*"

"Just sex," he says bluntly, and I shake my head.

"Jesus, Dad, maybe some tact?"

He just shrugs and I carry on. "Yeah, I tried that too, with Brook."

We both laugh—never thought I'd be sharing this with my dad.

That Feeling

"So you love her. I know that, and we can all see it. You think she's it?"

I nod as I slowly roll the bottle in my hand. "I really do. She's everything and so much more than I thought I could ever get."

"You know what that means though, right? You can't just focus on yourself anymore. You need to find a way to fit her into your life—into your sun-up to sundown ranching schedule."

I take a drink, mulling over his words. "Yeah, been thinking about that. Decker has been itching to take on more at the ranch since Ranger is already handling a lot. I think I can offload some stuff to him. I'll talk with him about it."

Dad looks at his watch then pulls out his phone. "Your mom will be calling me any second. Better get going. You have my blessing if that's what you're looking for, and I know your mom will be more than happy to give you that ring. Just talk to her." He pats me on the back and tips his hat to Danelle before heading out.

I pull out my phone to see if I have any texts from Brooklyn. She let me know when she got into town in Grand Lake the other night. She also sent me a selfie of her in a sexy little black dress she was wearing out with her friends. I made sure I put that image to good use in the shower later and then told her about it.

Sure enough, her name is on my screen.

Brooklyn: *Thinking about you. Miss you and can't wait to crawl into your arms tonight. Xoxo.*

I smile and put the phone back in my pocket. I don't want to bug her while she's out with friends, especially with her sister in town. She seems to be having a blast and I know she's heading back here later tonight.

Mallory is a pistol, just as much as Brooklyn. The two of them together can go from 0 to 100 instantly, but she's a good time. She teases me, so I assume that has to be a good sign. Brook has assured me she likes me, so I don't fret over it.

"I'm proposing too."

I look up and the stranger who came in earlier is talking to me, I think. I look over my shoulder to see if there's someone behind me, but it's just me.

"Pardon?"

"Sorry, didn't meant to eavesdrop. Just heard you talking to that man about a ring and marriage." He holds up something and it's only now that I see that it's a ring between his fingers.

"Oh, congrats," I say, raising my beer toward him before finishing it.

"Yeah, she's something else."

"You new in town then?"

He nods. "Yeah, first time here. Just passing through."

I turn in my stool back to the bar, trying to mind my own business. I lift my beer toward Danelle to signal another. Not sure I really want to go home and sit alone. The house feels so empty without Brooklyn in it.

She's still in the small house. We haven't had the talk about her officially moving in with me, but she's pretty much stayed in my bed every night since we made things official.

"I screwed up with her."

"Huh?" I turn back to the stranger.

"My fiancée—er, ex-fiancée, I guess." He lifts the ring up again and shakes his head.

I feel bad for the guy, but I really don't want to get involved in anyone else's business. I'm just trying to enjoy my beer and think about taking the next step with Brook.

"Well, good luck."

"Thanks, I'm gonna need it. Yeah, I'm the one who messed it up. Dragged my feet with the commitment. I'm an idiot."

Clearly this kid wants to talk to someone.

"She's my soulmate. You know when you meet someone and it's like a light comes on—like the universe put this person in your path for a reason and there's no denying that fate feeling?"

"Yeah, I get that." I nod, because I do know that feeling—now. I

That Feeling

feel like Brooklyn and I are just meant to be together. "So she gave that ring back to you?"

"Yeah." He shakes his head and places the ring on the bar top to reach for his beer. "She changed her mind or got cold feet or something. All I know is, I'm not going to let her get away this time. I'm going to make sure she knows what she means to me and remind her of what we had together."

I finish my beer. "That's all you can do." I toss a few bills on the bar top and pat it. "Thanks, Danelle. Have a good night." I tip my hat toward her and shrug into my jacket. "Hope things work out for you and your lady friend." I hold out my hand toward the kid, suddenly having a soft spot for him when I put myself in his shoes. I can't imagine losing Brooklyn like that.

"Thanks," he smiles and shoves his hand into mine.

I turn to walk away when he says something after me.

"Brooklyn."

A cold shiver runs down my spine and I slowly turn back to face him. "Excuse me?"

He smiles broadly. "My fiancée . . . her name is Brooklyn."

I stop dead in my tracks but keep my stoic expression in place. "She live out here?"

He nods. "Yeah, for now. She did live with me in Chicago, but, uh, she got a job out here and that's when she dumped me." He laughs but he's clearly in pain. "Yeah, she said she just wanted to start over someplace new and that was it. She left me and the ring and moved out here to Colorado to work for some brewery. I must be crazy, right? Chasing her all the way out here after she did that? Especially since she's been ignoring all my calls and texts, even though she called me first."

I nod slowly, though my head feels like it weighs a hundred pounds right now. The sound of rushing water fills my ears and I reach out to stabilize myself with the back of the stool. I look over at Danelle, who's busy drying glasses. Thankfully, she's not paying attention to what's unfolding right now.

"Guess we can't explain the dumb shit we do for love," I mutter as I tip my hat toward him again then fly out of the bar and into my truck.

I punch the steering wheel several times, the horn beeping in a staccato pace with my movements. I have no idea what to do.

I open my phone again and reread the last text from Brooklyn, trying to search it for some clue that she's been lying to me. *Is she lying?* I'm trying to recall all the things she told me about her past relationship. She never mentioned that she was engaged or lived with the guy, and she certainly never told me she was still dating him up until the day she moved out here. She did tell me she wasn't running from anything.

I type out a few messages, mostly variations of *go fuck yourself* or *don't bother coming over tonight,* but I don't hit send. I don't actually feel that way. I'm angry and hurt, but more than anything, I'm scared. What's going to stop her from doing the same thing to me?

Instead, I simply type out one message then hit send.

Me: *Neal is at the bar looking for you.*

She reads it immediately, because the screen lights up—she's calling me. I don't answer. Instead, I turn off the phone and toss it into the center console, peeling out of the parking lot of the bar to head home.

She'll be home in just a few hours and I have no idea what's going to happen.

I STAND IN THE SHOWER LONGER THAN NECESSARY—THE STEAM billowing around me as the hot water scorches my skin.

Tears threaten to fall and maybe they already are, but I pretend not to notice as the water pelts my face. I want to scream and punch the marble wall.

I feel like a fool. I ignored all those little voices in the back of my head that told me to limit this to what I'd promised myself it would

That Feeling

be: just sex. But the moment that thought manifests in my head, I push it aside, because I don't regret loving her. I want to love her, and I want to be with her, but I don't know how I can trust that she's not just young and naive, rebounding with me and thinking it's happily ever after.

I finish my shower and dry off. I start to head downstairs when I hear a pounding on the front door.

"Tyler, please open up! It's me," Brooklyn's voice is muffled.

I pull the door open to see her tear-stained, panicked face in the doorway.

"I'm sorry, I swear," she says, her lips trembling.

"For what?" I ask coldly.

"For everything. I didn't go to the bar—I came straight here. What did he say?" She reaches for me but I take a step back.

"You don't owe me an explanation." My words sting, and she steps back and drops her arms.

"What do you mean? Why don't I?"

"Because what's the point, Brooklyn? He already told me enough."

She reaches for me again, mascara-stained tears running down her cheeks. "Please tell me what he said. I can explain things . . . he's a liar!"

I scoff. "That's rich, coming from you."

She shakes her head furiously. "I—I didn't lie to you. What did he say? What did I lie about?"

"You lied to me. Did you live with him?"

"Yes, but I never said I didn't. We didn't even talk about that."

"Did you break up with him the day you moved out here?"

"No! I mean, I guess, technically," she fumbles. "I had broken up with him so many times before. I'd told him we weren't going to be together. I just—I wasn't going to get my own place in the short time before I moved, because I knew I wasn't staying in Chicago anymore."

"Those are lies of omission, Brook. You obviously felt the need to hide that shit from me. You also hid the fact that he's been calling and texting you." I point my finger at her. "But Neal told me."

"I can't believe this is happening." She shakes her head, her chin quivering, and I want to pull her into my arms and tell her it's all going to be okay, but I don't know if it is.

"I get that what happened in the past doesn't concern me, but when I told you over and over how scared I was of you deciding one day that you were done with life out here and leaving it all behind to start over someplace new, you could've told me about Neal. You were engaged to him and didn't even tell me that."

Her eyes snap up to mine, instantly growing angry. "I was *never* engaged to him," she says emphatically.

"Did you really break up with him the day you moved out here?"

"I had ended things with him weeks before," she says as she furiously wipes her tears away with the back of her hand. "Yes, I was still living in his apartment, but I slept in the guest room. We hadn't been intimate in months. I had broken up with him and he couldn't accept it. He thought if he proposed that it would somehow change things. So when he proposed the night before I left, I said a big NO. I told him there was no way we were ever getting back together or married or anything. It was done—final." She spreads her arms out like an umpire calling a play.

"Why didn't you tell me that he's been calling and texting you?"

She buries her face in her hands and shakes her head.

"I don't know. He went to my parents' house and they were acting like everything was okay with him. He'd told them we were just on a break and that we were going to work things out. I set things straight with them and I just—I don't know—I was so worried it would fuck things up with us . . . and I was right, it has!"

"No, it wouldn't have if you hadn't hid this shit," I spit the words out.

She recoils.

"I'm so sorry. I don't love him. I love *you*, more than anything. What we have can't compare to anything with anyone else, I promise.

That Feeling

I didn't go see him at the bar and I have no intention of speaking to him again. I deleted everything from him and blocked him." She fumbles in her purse and pulls out her phone, thrusting it toward me. "You can see for yourself."

I don't take the phone. I'm exhausted and I don't know what to believe or think at this point.

"The only reason I had that talk with Neal the night before I left Chicago is because he proposed. I wanted him to understand that there was no hope—there was no maybe."

"Well, clearly, he didn't get the message, because he showed me the ring tonight and said he's not leaving town without you. Honestly, Brooklyn, this thing between you two doesn't involve me. You need to talk to him and sort out your shit."

I go to close the door and she extends her arm, pushing it back open. "So that's it? What now?"

I shake my head. "I don't know!" I shout angrily. "I just need some fucking space. Please leave."

A sob breaks through her lips, "Tyler, please."

"Leave!" I shout, and this time I slam the door, marching back upstairs to go to bed—trying to pretend that this is all just a horrible nightmare that will be gone when I wake up tomorrow.

Chapter 18

Brooklyn

It feels like my entire world is collapsing around me. I jump when the door slams shut. I try to inhale, but it feels like I can't. My chest is tight and every breath burns. I fall to my knees on Tyler's front porch and sob.

When I finally gather my strength, I pull myself up and hug my arms around my body. It's only now that I register the cold night air biting at my exposed skin. I don't know what this means for Tyler and me.

Are we done?

I walk back to my cabin, the door flinging open before I can reach for the handle. Mallory takes one look at me and pulls me into her arms. She wraps them around me as I break down again.

"This isn't supposed to happen," I sniff between words, each one catching in my throat. "I'm the big sister! I'm supposed to comfort you."

She strokes my hair as I lie in a ball on the floor, my head in her lap.

"You can't always be the strong one, Brook." She wipes a tear

That Feeling

away from her own eye. I know seeing me like this—a complete emotional wreck—hurts her just as much.

We stay like that for the better part of an hour. She strokes my hair as I go through fits of crying and silence. My head feels like a lead weight. I don't think I can possibly cry anymore. I sit up and let out one long sigh.

"You just want to go to bed, or do you want to talk about it?"

I look over at Mal and shrug.

"Okay, well, here's what I'm going to do. I'm going to go start your shower and get you a glass of water. I think you're dehydrated after all that crying." She walks into the kitchen and fills up a glass then roots around in the cabinet before walking back over to me. "Here, take some Tylenol and drink this then get in the shower. Afterward, we'll see how you feel."

By the time I get out of the shower and into my pajamas, it's just after 10 p.m., but I know I won't be able to sleep. I walk back out to the living room, where I find Mallory flipping through Netflix with two glasses of wine on the coffee table.

"Thought you might need a little something to help you sleep." She motions toward the wine. "If not, I'll drink both since I'm on vacation."

I flop down on the couch and reach for the glass. "Thank you. Exactly what I need."

"So do you want to tell me what happened?" She puts down the remote and grabs her glass, tucking her feet beneath her as she turns to face me.

"I fucked up—like, catastrophically."

"Well, I gathered that. The fact that you told me on the way home that you never told Tyler about Neal popping back into your life, and that you never dealt with Neal, directly solidified that."

I nod and take several big gulps of the wine.

"Why didn't you, Brook? I don't mean to pile on here, because I know this is horrible, but why hide this from him? You told me early on you felt like he was the one."

I know she's trying her hardest to be sympathetic here, but from the outside looking in, yeah, it seems like such an obvious error on my part.

"I was scared and frustrated. I thought I'd taken care of the Neal situation before I left Chicago. I told him in every way I could think of that we were done—that there was no hope—and he seemed to get it, or so I thought. But then when you told me he was reaching out to you and our parents, it gave me anxiety. I know he was just doing it so I'd reach out to him and he'd have an "in" back into my life. It's just so exhausting, Mal."

I feel like I'm on the verge of tears again, so I take a deep breath and let it out slowly. I repeat the process a few more times.

"I feel like, for years, I tried to get out of this relationship. I tried to express how I felt to him, and he would constantly talk me back into staying with him. I know that's not an excuse, because I'm an adult and I'm responsible for my own actions. I think I just felt like it was easier to stay with him, because every time I left, it was so emotionally exhausting to constantly have the same talks with him and then the next day, he would turn around and act like I didn't just tell him I didn't love him anymore."

Mallory places her hand on my knee. "I'm sorry you suffered so much in silence. Truthfully, I never knew it was that bad. I mean, I know you had cold feet now and then, but I just thought it was one of those things you guys would work out. Like maybe you would take some time apart and realize he was the one you wanted to be with."

"I always had this internal battle with myself; I felt like I wasn't justified in leaving him. It felt like the fact that I didn't love him and didn't want to be with him meant there was something wrong with me, because according to everyone else, he was perfect on paper. We were perfect together. Like he always said, we had so much in common and never fought."

I feel my chest start to tighten again and take another few sips of wine.

"I guess I just convinced myself that hoping and dreaming for

That Feeling

some Disney fairy tale version of sparks and chemistry and happily ever after was bullshit and I was just kidding myself."

"So what now?"

I shake my head. "I dunno. I feel like I do need to reach out to Neal while he's here and sit down and have a conversation with him. But at the same time, I feel like what's the point? Because it's not gonna go anywhere."

"Maybe and maybe not. But that's not up to you. You do need to be firm with him and tell him how this has impacted your life. Tell him that you've met somebody else and that you're planning to spend your life with this person. Maybe that's the harsh reality he needs to hear to snap him out of his delusional fairy tale that you guys are going to end up together. Clearly nothing else seems to be working."

"Yeah, maybe you're right. At least Tyler knows now. Even if he never wants to talk to me again, at least he knows the truth about Neal. And if things *do* work out between us and Neal tries to come back into my life, he'll help me handle it."

Mallory smiles. "That's the spirit. And if Tyler doesn't handle it, Silas and I will." She winks. "Now, do you have any junk food to go with this wine?"

I laugh. "I think I have some Doritos. That work?"

"You get the chips and I'll cue up *Pretty Little Liars*."

I TAP MY FINGERS NERVOUSLY ON THE TABLE IN THE BACK OF the restaurant. The bell above the door jingles and I look over my shoulder. It's just an older man probably stopping in for lunch.

I glance down at my watch and it's 11:28. Neal agreed to meet me today at 11:30. After some serious doubt, I managed to talk myself into unblocking him last night and sent him a direct and curt message that we needed to meet and talk today.

I nervously pick at the skin around my fingernail when the door opens again. This time, I turn around and my eyes meet Neal's. A huge grin spreads across his face as he makes his way over to me.

"Hey, Brook."

He comes at me with open arms, but I don't reciprocate. I hug my arms tighter against my body and shake my head.

"Oookaay then," he says, taking a seat across from me.

"Thanks for meeting me."

"Yeah, of course." He darts his hand out to grab mine as I rest it on the table. "You look good."

I pull my hand back before he can touch me. "Please don't." I grab my water and take a sip as the waitress walks over.

"Hey there, can I get you something to drink or an appetizer?" She smiles sweetly.

"No thanks, nothing," I quickly say.

Neal looks at her and shrugs and she walks back to the kitchen.

"What the fuck are you doing here?" I ask him. I can't hold back my anger any longer and he looks genuinely surprised, which only pisses me off even more.

"I came out here to see you—to talk to you. You called me then started dodging all my return calls. You didn't respond to a single text, so I was worried." He feigns sincerity, and it makes me want to throw this glass of water at him.

"Worried? You went to my parents' house!" I'm starting to raise my voice, but as I glance around, I'm relieved to find nobody noticed. "You went to my parents' house and told them you and I were on a break when you know *damn well* that I told you we were done—for good."

"I was just upset is all. I'm sorry, babe, you know ho—"

"Don't you dare." I point my finger at him. "I'm not 'babe,' I'm Brooklyn. You completely fucked up my relationship, you know that? That guy you spilled your guts to in the bar?"

He looks at me, thoroughly confused. "Wait, what?"

I let out a sigh and try to calm my rapid heartbeat. "I'm seeing someone. I have been for some time now, and he's the man who was

That Feeling

in the bar the other night. The man you straight up *lied* to and said I was your fiancée? What the hell, Neal?"

"Whoa, okay, first of all, I didn't ruin anything. It's not my fault you didn't tell him about us."

"There is no us!" I shout, and this time the old man who came in earlier turns around to look at me. I smile and turn back to Neal. "You have no right to be here or at my parents' place or texting Mallory. Like, honestly, what is it going to take for you to get it through your head that *we*," I motion between us, "aren't a *we* anymore and haven't been for a very long time?"

"Okay, okay, I'm sorry. So I misspoke about the fiancée thing, Brook, but I was hurt. You just up and left without so much as a warning or anything."

"I didn't owe you an explanation or a warning, Neal. We weren't together and we hadn't been together for months. Just because we were still living in the same apartment didn't mean we were sharing a life together. And while we're on the subject of not telling each other everything, nice of you to tell me that you and Becca started dating."

He hangs his head when I bring up my best friend. "Yeah, that was . . . it was nothing. It meant nothing, Brook. I was just hurt and lonely and she was missing you too and it just kind of happened."

"Does *she* know that it meant nothing? Because that's really shitty if you just used her. Also, how strange that both of you missed me so much, yet neither one of you reached out to me."

He opens his mouth to say something, snaps it closed again, then opens it once more. "Damn. You don't have to be so hurtful about things."

I wring my hands in frustration. "That's the thing, though, Neal. I feel like I do have to be hurtful to you in order for you to actually listen to me. Our entire relationship is an example of that. How many times did I tell you I didn't feel like we were meant to be together? How many times did I tell you I felt like I was supposed to be alone and needed to focus on my career and myself? How many times did you hold my hands and tell me I just had cold feet and that you knew we were meant to be together? It just felt like you were constantly ignoring my feelings and gaslighting me into staying with you. Even now, when I'm trying to tell you how you fucked up my life here by following me to Colorado and continuing to try to get back with me, you still make it about you and your feelings. You just admitted that you used my best friend and slept with her then tossed her aside, and yet you're still making this about you?"

I see a dim light of recognition in his eyes and think that maybe, just maybe, I'm finally getting through to him.

"So what are you saying, Brook?"

"I'm saying what I said to you over six months ago when we broke up. I'm not in love with you, Neal, and I haven't been. I don't love you and I don't want a future with you. I'm in love with Tyler. He's the man I want to spend the rest of my life with if I haven't completely ruined it. I'm not saying this to be cruel. I truly want you to find your person and be happy. I just know that person isn't me."

He reaches into his pocket and pulls out the ring he offered me months ago, back when I turned him down the first time.

"Do you at least want to keep this? As, like, a token or memento of what we had together?"

"No," I shake my head, "you keep it. There's a woman out there who will wear it proudly as your fiancée."

He shakes his head and puts the ring back into his pocket.

"I'm sorry, Brook, for everything. I'll go now."

He squeezes my hand and gets up, walking out of the restaurant and out of my life for what I hope is forever.

IT'S BEEN TWO WEEKS SINCE I'VE SPOKEN TO TYLER.

Two weeks of crying myself to sleep almost every night.

Two weeks of having to look at his photos every damn day while I post to social media.

Two weeks of agonizing torture.

That Feeling

I make sure I'm not only at the office early in the morning, but I also stay late. Because if I'm at home, I find myself glued to one of the windows, hoping to spot him working the ranch.

It's pathetic.

I haven't heard from Neal since our last conversation. So far, he's kept his word. I wanted to reach out to Tyler to let him know that I resolved the issue, but I also wanted to respect his space. And honestly, I'm worried that if I do see him face-to-face, he'll tell me it's over for good.

But today, I'm sucking it up and walking over to his house to tell him that I bought him a plane ticket home before all this went down. I still want him to spend Christmas with my family and me, and I leave for home tomorrow.

I pull my coat tightly around my body as I walk across the field to his house. There's a car I don't recognize in the driveway. I'm about to walk up the porch steps when the door opens and Tyler steps out with Selma.

"Thanks again. I'll give you a call about it after Christmas."

Her back is to me as she leans in to plant a kiss on his cheek. "Sounds good, Ty. Have a Merry Christmas and tell your family I said as much." When she turns around and sees me, her eyes flash to me then Tyler. She offers me a tight-lipped smile before getting in her car and leaving.

"Are you guys back together now?" I try to keep my expression emotionless, but it's a losing battle.

"Hey, Brook, can I help you with something?" He doesn't answer my question and it pushes me over the edge. The floodgates open and big, fat tears tumble down my cheeks. I cover my face with my hands, hoping it'll help, but it doesn't.

"Hey," he says, walking down the stairs and pulling my hands from my face. "No, she and I aren't back together. She's an interior designer who decorated this house over two years ago. My mom sent her over to finish up some project."

I search his eyes, hoping to see some hint that he still loves me, but he turns and pulls me toward the porch, where we both take a seat.

"So?" he says, looking over at me.

"I, uh," I wipe away the snot and tears, "I wanted to stop by and apologize again for everything. I had a talk with Neal the next day. I told him about us—you," I correct myself, unsure if there's still an *us* to be had. "He's gone and he apologized for everything."

Tyler slowly nods like he's thinking over every word I say.

"I wish I could make things right. I wish I could apologize a billion times so you'd know I would never just up and leave you. I didn't just leave Neal, either—it was months, even years, in the making, because he wouldn't take 'no' for an answer and at that point, I wasn't brave enough to leave." I can feel myself start to hyperventilate and trip over my words. Tyler reaches his arms around me and pulls me into his side.

"Do you—" I hiccup, "do you still love me?"

He pulls me in even tighter then turns his face down to look at me. "I've never stopped loving you, Brooklyn, and I never will. That's not even a question."

The silence between us is deafening. I reach into my pocket and pull out the plane ticket as I stand up and remove myself from him. He stays sitting on the porch and I turn to face him.

"I had planned on surprising you with this," I look at the ticket in my hand, "the night I came back from Grand Lake. I was going to ask you to come home with me for Christmas. Anyway, the offer still stands, but I—I'll let you get back to your evening. I need to finish packing. Early flight."

I place the ticket next to him on the porch and walk back to my cabin.

THE NEXT MORNING, I'M UP WELL BEFORE SUNRISE TO MAKE IT to the airport in time for my flight. I leave the cabin and lock up,

That Feeling

looking over at Tyler's house to see if there are any lights on, but it's still dark.

Even as I make my way through the airport, past security, and all the way to my gate, I keep glancing over my shoulder, checking my phone, and searching every stranger's face—hoping and praying he'll show up, but he never does.

I sleep through the flight as best I can. I'm heartbroken, but I'm excited to be home to see my family. I grab my bag from the overhead bin and make my way down to ground transportation, where I'll take the train out to the suburbs.

I send a quick text to Mallory as I ride down the escalator.

Me: *Landed. Grabbing the train. See you soon!*

I put my phone in my pocket and look up just in time to see a gentleman holding a sign with my name on it. I stop and do a double take.

"Excuse me, I'm Brooklyn Dyer, but I—"

"Right this way, ma'am," he says, reaching for my bags.

"I don't understand. I didn't order a car."

The man doesn't respond as he leads me through the double sliding glass doors toward a shiny black SUV.

"Here we are, ma'am," he says, hitting a button that opens the back door, where he starts loading my bags.

I'm still so confused as I walk to the back passenger side door . . . just as it opens and Tyler slides out with a smirk on his face.

Chapter 19

Tyler

I watch as her face morphs from shock to confusion to full-on tears. "Baby, baby, what's wrong?" I grab her, holding her tightly as she buries her face in my chest. Finally, I pull her face back to look at her. "Hey, I'm sorry. I didn't mean to upset you."

"You asshole!" She hauls back and hits me with both fists in my chest. "What the hell?"

"I'm sorry." I brush her hair back from her face as the driver holds the door open for us. "Here, let's get inside."

"How did you . . . ?"

"Private plane," I shrug.

"Of course you own a private plane." She rolls her eyes and smacks my arm again. "I'm still mad."

I laugh and pull her into my lap.

"Listen, I needed time was all. I was never done with us. I never stopped loving you. I was scared and worried and just needed time to process my own feelings. So thank you for giving that to me."

Her lower lip starts to quiver and I reach forward and kiss it. "Don't cry, baby girl, I'm here now." I hold her in my arms for several

That Feeling

minutes, breathing in her scent and savoring the weight of her body against mine.

"I missed this so much."

"I did too. Thank you for inviting me to come to your family Christmas. That gesture was just what I needed."

"What do you mean?"

"I didn't know if you wanted to still be with *me*." I watch her brows knit together. "When I saw Neal that night, he still seemed so blissfully in love with you that I feared that's what you were running from. I thought that maybe you were scared of the feelings you had for him and just needed to run away from it, and that him coming back into your life was going to be this grand gesture that made you realize he was your person."

She shakes her head. "No, not even close. It just made me realize even more that *you* are my person. I felt absolutely nothing when I saw him. The only thing I felt was complete relief when he said he was done and walked out of the bar."

I cup her face with my hands and bring my forehead to rest against hers briefly as she whispers, "There's nothing I want more in life than you—nothing I've been more sure of than you and us."

She leans forward and kisses me softly. My hands snake their way into her hair as I thrust my tongue into her mouth.

"I was so scared of how intense things got with us so quickly, and the way I felt so comfortable and at ease with you like we'd know each other for a lifetime," I tell her. "I wanted things with you I've never wanted with anyone before, and I felt so confident about them that it was exciting but also fucking terrifying."

Her eyes study mine. "*Wanted?*" I can see the panic start to build.

"Want, baby—things I want with you. I want a life with you and I know I scared you talking about a baby," my hand goes to rest on her belly, "and I don't want that to trap you. I just love you so much that I want to share that bond with you."

"Still?"

I chuckle. "Yeah, that fantasy doesn't go away, trust me. I know it's probably a little kinky that I get off on thoughts of knocking you up, but it's not just sexual. It's like this barbaric caveman desire to see you pregnant with my baby."

"One thing at a time, big guy," she smiles and kisses me again.

"Why wait?" I murmur against her lips as I reach over and hit the button that slides the divider up between us and the driver. "We have time before we get there for me to put a baby in you?"

I slide my hand up her shirt and pull the cup of her bra down to roll her nipple between my thumb and forefinger. Her head lolls forward as she nips at my neck.

"Mmm, somebody is feeling feral." I laugh as she sinks her teeth into my flesh even harder. She peppers the spot with kisses, trailing them up my neck, across my cheek, then finally to my lips again.

"You haven't even asked me to marry you yet, and you're already trying to knock me up." She gives me that coy smirk I've come to love so much.

"Hmm, I haven't?" I say, shoving my hand into my jeans pocket and pulling out the ring my mother gave me. "Then what is this doing in here?"

Her face goes white. "Oh my God! Are you serious?" Her eyes go from mine to the ring then back to mine again.

"This was my great-grandmother's ring. It's been passed down from generation to generation. My dad actually proposed to my mom with it and she gave it to me when I told them both that I wanted to marry you."

Her eyes fill with tears.

"I know it's not the biggest, but the tradition in my family is that you upgrade to whatever ring your wife wants after you have your first baby, then the ring will go to our son or daughter when they get married."

"Are you proposing?"

I chuckle. "Well, not really."

She smacks my arm hard. "Then what the hell, Tyler?"

That Feeling

"I'm sorry," I laugh, "I will. I brought it because I wanted to ask your father for your hand in marriage, but I wanted to show you that I was serious. I'm not just toying with you. I wanted you to see this ring—to know how important it is to me and my family, because we all trust you. They want you in the family too."

Her shoulders drop in relief. "I know my parents will appreciate the gesture of asking for my hand, but I can just about guarantee you my dad will say I'm not his property or something like that."

"And that's perfectly okay; it's just about the gesture and respect. I want your family to know how much you mean to me and how much I love you."

We drive the rest of the way to her family home with her in my lap and my arms wrapped around her.

The car comes to a stop and she reaches over and takes my hand. "You sure you're ready to meet my family?"

I nod confidently. "Just one question," I say, and she stops and looks back at me. "What happens if tomorrow, TikTok calls you up and offers you $50 million a year to run their social media?"

"Well, first I'd tell them that their salary offering is absolutely insane, because not even the CEO makes that. Then I'd tell them I could only take the job if I could work fully remote in Colorado, where I live with my husband."

"Oh, so you'd leave Slade just like that, huh?" I tease, pinching her ass.

At that moment, the driver grabs our bags out of the back of the SUV and wheels them over to us. I tip him before turning back to her.

"Babe," she says, "if someone is offering me $50 million a year, you think I'm passing that up? But seriously," she grabs my hand and looks up at me, "I love my job and I'm not leaving. It's not about the money. It's about the fact that I'm working with and for people I respect and love. People who treat me like family. That's more important than any amount of money."

"Good answer," I say as I grab her hand and let out a deep breath as we make our way up the driveway to the front porch.

"Besides," she says with a snarky wink just as the front door opens, "I'm marrying into a billionaire family, so I'm not working much longer!"

Chapter 20

Brooklyn

"I'm gonna marry that man," I say to Mallory as we stand in the doorway of my parents' family room.

"I have no doubt about that, sis." She nudges me with her shoulder as we watch Tyler laugh hysterically at some photo my mom is showing of me when I was a kid.

From the moment he stepped foot into my childhood home two days ago, it's like he was instantly part of my family. My dad has already shown him not only his fancy fishing lure collection, but also pulled out the photo album of all of his "best catches" starting back in 1968.

"I hope he's ready to be constantly bombarded with texts of photos from Dad showcasing the fish he's caught and the random tools he's picked up at auctions. I think Silas will appreciate the break from it all." We both chuckle at the thought of our dad sending Tyler all the weird texts we receive from him.

"And this one is from her debate team championship. She not only took them to state, but nationals too."

"Okaaay," I say, walking over to where my mom is pulling out another giant stack of family photos. "I think Tyler probably needs a little break from Memory Lane."

He looks up at me from where he's seated on the floor next to my mom, who is surrounded by boxes of old photos and albums.

"I don't mind, sweetheart. Kind of nice getting to see this side of you." He tugs gently on my hand and I take a seat on the floor next to him.

"Now why am I not surprised that you were captain of the debate team?"

I snatch the photo from his hand and notice the serious look on my teenage face. I remember thinking back then that I wanted to be taken so seriously. I had my life all figured out at that point.

"Yeah, this was back when I was convinced I was going to be a WNBA star turned motivational speaker."

He laughs and look sideways at me. "All five foot three inches of you?"

"Hey, talk all you want, but if it wasn't snowing outside, I'd take you on the basketball court down the street."

He bumps my shoulder and we share a flirty little moment. I look up to see my parents looking at us with tears in their eyes.

"Okay, enough of that. Hey, isn't Silas supposed to be here?"

I barely get the words out when the front door bursts open and the sounds of my two nieces, Kendal and Tara, fill the room.

My brother and sister-in-law were already here the last two days and met Tyler. They're just staying at a hotel in town since there isn't enough room in the house for all of us.

My brother already looks exhausted as he carts in armfuls of presents.

"Hey, let me help you with that." Tyler hops up and grabs a few presents from Silas.

"Those two are already buddies, aren't they?" my mom says as the two guys are already laughing about something.

"Seems that way," I smile. "Hey, Jules, you ready for a cocktail?"

"Or three," she laughs while Kendal and Tara are buried in their

That Feeling

phones. We all three look at the girls, who are laughing and pointing at each other's screens.

"I fought the phones hard, but Silas convinced me and he was right. Worth it," she whispers to us dramatically.

"Hey, Dad, Tyler said he brought us some small batch reserve whiskey straight from the distillery," Silas says. "How about the three of us go pour a glass and let the ladies catch up?"

My dad jumps and runs over to where Tyler is showing the bottle.

"Looks like Dad found a bestie too," Mallory laughs.

"You girls okay in here?" Julie asks, and her daughters just wave her off. "They'll be entertained for hours. Let's go make a cocktail."

We follow her into the kitchen as the guys go to the back porch that my parents have turned into a four-season room.

"What do you think they're talking about out there?" Julie asks Mom, who doesn't skip a beat.

"Oh, probably about Tyler's intentions with Brook."

"Mom!" I blush.

"Oh, come on, sweetie, we both know he's going to propose soon. That man looks at you like the sun rises and sets in your eyes. You wouldn't be surprised by it, would you?"

I can't hide it. "No... actually, he already showed me the ring on the car ride here."

"Oh my God, what's it look like? Did he ask already?" Mallory can't conceal her excitement.

I explain the situation and they *ooh* and *aah* over his desire to show respect and ask for my hand in marriage.

"I told him Daddy would tell him it's not necessary."

"Oh, Brook, don't spoil Tyler's fun." Mom swats at me. "Your dad will think it's a wonderful gesture. He's very impressed with Tyler. We both are."

It feels like everything is finally falling into place, and I feel so blessed. I reach out and hold my mom's hand. "Thank you, Mom. I know you guys want me to be happy with someone who treats me right, and I promise you he does."

My mom gives me her sassy look with a devilish grin—the same one I give Tyler. "Trust me, sweetie, we're not worried about him treating you right. We're worried about whether that man knows what he's getting himself into."

THREE MONTHS LATER . . .

"YES, THAT ONE IS PERFECT, SO IS THIS ONE . . . AND THIS ONE . . ."

I pull the photos Kevin took of Tyler last week. This is our third photo shoot in as many months. Tyler's patience is wearing pretty thin with the number of shoots I booked, but with the launch of our new spring seltzer variety pack and two new spring beers, I don't have time to worry about that too much.

I stand back and look at the whiteboard in my office. I have my roadmap for this quarter pretty much mapped out, which is a great feeling considering I'm going out to a new winery in Fort Collins tonight.

I glance at my watch. "Shit." I was already supposed to be back at the house, bags in hand.

My phone buzzes and I don't even have to look at the screen to know that it's Milly or Dolly calling.

"Hey, I know I'm late. I'm on my way!" I say as I grab my keys and purse and run down the hall toward the elevator.

"Wouldn't be a girls' night if we weren't waiting on you to finish work," Milly teases.

"I know, I know. I promise I'll make it up to you ladies. First round's on me. See you soon!" I hang up the phone and toss it in my purse as I shift my SUV into drive and haul ass back home.

That Feeling

The last three months have been a complete whirlwind. Once Tyler and I came back home from my family Christmas, he insisted I move in with him—something he didn't need to actually insist on. And apparently, he has become best friends with my dad and brother, something I love even though it can also be annoying, especially when they get to talking on a group call and forget I exist.

Work has been stressful, but in the best way possible. I've even been able to hire two new team members who report to me and take some of the day-to-day stress off my plate. It's going to be a lifesaver once our new seltzer flavors and spring beers launch.

The best part is that Neal hasn't reached out to me or anyone in my family. Life is pretty damn perfect right now . . . except I still don't have a ring on my finger. It's something I've tried not to focus on, but it's starting to get to me.

"I'm here!" I shout as I jump out of the SUV and wave at Dolly, Milly, and Adrienne. "Two minutes," I say as I run up the stairs of my front porch to change my shoes and grab a snack for the road.

"Hey, sorry, can you do a little detour over to the barn so I can say bye to Tyler?" I say once I'm in the car.

Milly pulls over to the barn just as Tyler is walking out. I swing my door open and walk over to him, tossing my arms around his neck.

"Hey, sexy," I plant a quick kiss on his lips, "we're taking off for the night. I don't plan on being out too late, so wait up for me."

"Of course, baby." His hands settle on my waist. He pulls me in for another kiss, and this time his hands wander down to my ass. He grabs two handfuls and presses himself against me. "Just remember what's here waiting for you."

I whimper. "I'm sure we have time to duck into the barn for a few." I snake my tongue into his mouth, which elicits a low growl from his chest.

"After three rounds this morning? You're insatiable."

I giggle just as Milly lays on the horn and Adrienne shouts from the passenger window, "Let's go, you horndogs!"

We both laugh and Tyler picks me up, walks me back over to the car, and opens the back door for me as I slide down his body.

"You ladies have fun. If she gets wasted, I want videos of her dancing on the tables." He gives me a wink and another kiss and shuts the door.

"I FEEL LIKE I DON'T EVEN NEED TO ASK HOW THINGS ARE GOING with you two," Adrienne says as we dig into the charcuterie board on our table.

"No kidding. It would be hot if he wasn't our cousin." Milly scrunches her nose and everyone laughs.

"Things are amazing. I mean, obviously, our physical connection is off the charts, but we've settled into a nice life together. Crazy to think we're already living together but at the same time, it doesn't feel rushed or weird at all."

Dolly shrugs. "Hey, that phrase about just knowing when it's the right person is a phrase for a reason. My parents," she pops a cracker and cheese in her mouth and holds up her fingers, "five months."

"They what?"

"Married. Only knew each other five months when they got married. My mom said it was like fate, and she's not one to believe in stuff like that. My dad was actually engaged to someone else and had broken it off, like, one week before he met my mom. Then, bam, they got married and they've been happy ever since."

"Damn," Adrienne whistles, "I feel like it's rare to hear of people still being happy after—how long they been married?"

"Thirty-eight years this year," she nods.

I raise my glass, "Well, here's to Dolly's parents and all of us looking for that happily ever after."

We've each had three tastings, and I decide to settle on a crisp glass of rosé, even though my stomach feels a little off.

"Dolly, speaking of guys, any headway on things with Ranger?" I

That Feeling

bounce my eyebrows and give her a nudge, a blush flashing across her ivory cheeks.

"Not really. We hung out the other night, shot some pool, and just talked—same old, same old."

"Wait, I didn't realize you guys were friends. How'd I miss that?"

Silence settles over us and I glance around the table. Adrienne and Milly give each other a look.

"There's something you don't know about me, Brook. I was married before, briefly. We were high school sweethearts and he joined the military at 18. We got married five-and-a-half years ago."

I'm so confused but also worried I may haven unknowingly been insensitive.

"I found out I was pregnant on our one-year anniversary, and then I lost the baby three months later."

I gasp and reach out my hand to hold one of hers.

"Oh my God! I'm so sorry. I had no idea."

She shakes her head. "No, don't be. I appreciate it, but I'm okay now. Anyway, my husband, Dean, took it really hard. He started drinking more and staying out late. Anyway, he was coming home one night and lost control and hit a tree. He died on impact."

I don't know what to say, but my heart feels like it's breaking hearing her story.

"But all that to say," she laughs softly, "Dean's best friend was Ranger. They grew up together and were in the military together. So I don't think he would ever actually go for me."

"Ohhhh." Now I understand why she was sheepish about saying anything about her crush on him in the first place.

"For what it's worth, Dolly knows that we fully support her crush on Ranger. He was there for her when everything went down. He's an amazing guy; he just has his head so far up his ass he can't see straight." Adrienne shakes her head and Milly agrees.

"Well, damn," I pick up my glass again and take a sip, "don't give up on him yet, babe. I'm sure he's still healing too."

"Good afternoon, ladies. How are we doing today?" A tall, thin, dark-haired woman approaches our table and offers us a megawatt Hollywood smile.

"We're great, thank you."

"Wonderful. My name is Amelia Blanc, and I'm the owner of this new tasting room. I wanted to come over and personally say hello and wish you all a wonderful afternoon."

"Oh, so lovely to meet you, and thank you for creating this amazing place. It's gorgeous," Adrienne replies.

"Hey, are you at all related to the Blanc wineries on the West Coast?" I ask, and she instantly lights up.

"I am, yes. That's my family's winery business. I'm working on expanding us from California and the Pacific Northwest. This is kind of my launching pad. I decided a small tasting room would be a great way to get a feel for the market here before really diving in and expanding."

"That's so great to hear. We're actually—well, those two are Slades, as in Slade Brewery," I say, pointing to Adrienne and Milly, who both smile, "and I'm the director of social media at Slade Brewing International."

"What a small world!"

We invite her to take a seat with us for a moment, and she fills us in on how her family got started in the wine business and how they still have their original family winery back in France. She's extremely knowledgeable and tells us all about the different offerings on the menu and how they pair best.

I glance at the clock. We've been here for a few hours already, and while I'm having a good time, I haven't had a chance to pick the ladies' brains about something that's been weighing heavily on my mind.

Amelia tells us to enjoy the rest of our night and excuses herself to greet other patrons.

"You okay, Brook? You've barely touched your wine," Dolly says, motioning toward my still-full glass.

"Yeah, I just have such a headache today. I haven't been sleeping

That Feeling

great. I think I'm stressed and probably overworking myself. But I wanted to ask you three something."

All of them turn their heads turn toward me like they're on a swivel.

"When we were going to my parents' for Christmas, Tyler showed me his family ring. He had it with him and said he was going to ask my dad for my hand."

"Oh my God!" Adrienne claps. "How did you not tell us this?"

I smile. "Well here's the thing . . . that was three months ago now, and he still hasn't proposed. And I know," I say, holding up my finger, "that my dad gave his blessing, because Tyler, my brother Silas, and my dad are all besties now that they're in this group chat." I roll my eyes. "I hear Tyler laughing all the time looking at his phone, and when I ask what he's laughing at, he'll show me some football meme or whatever that Silas or my dad sent him."

"Aww, that's adorable, though," Dolly says with a smile.

"I know. Honestly, it makes me incredibly happy that they're so close, but where's the damn ring already?"

"Maybe he's planning something really specific, ya know? Like he's waiting until it's warmer out or a specific date or event?" Milly asks.

"Maybe," I say, trying to think if we have anything on the horizon, but I can't come up with anything. "I dunno. I'm sure it's nothing; I'm just impatient is all."

We thank Amelia again before heading out, and I give her my card so we can get in contact about possibly doing some cross-promotion someday.

As she drops me off at home, Dolly grabs my cheeks in her hands and gives me a tipsy pep talk. "Remember, you're a boss-ass bitch, and you are going to march in that house, put on some sexy-ass lingerie, climb that man like a tree, and tell him that he better propose or else!"

I giggle. "Thank you, Dolly. I'm going to do just that. Good night, ladies. Thanks so much for today. I needed it!"

I head into the house and most of the lights are already out. It's just past 9 p.m., but I figure I know where Tyler will be. I walk to the back porch, and sure enough, he has a fire going and a glass of whiskey in one hand, his feet kicked up on an ottoman.

He doesn't seem to hear me come in, so I quickly tiptoe upstairs to our bedroom to change into something sexy. I root around in my drawer and find what I'm looking for: a red lace teddy. I strip quickly and shimmy myself into the lingerie.

"Dammit," I suck in as I pull it over my hips and up my torso, "guess I need to start working out again." I hold my breath as I zip it up and give myself a once-over in the mirror. It's tight—tighter than usual—but it doesn't look bad. Just makes my tits look like they're about spill out of the top, but he'll love that. I grab my matching red silk robe and make my way back downstairs to Tyler.

"Hey, baby—oh, *fuck,* hi," he says as I walk around his chair and climb right into his lap to straddle him. "Someone come home horny again?" He runs his hands up my thighs to my waist and then straight to my breasts as his mouth trails hot kisses over my bare skin.

I run my hands over his chest and then into his hair. I tug it so his head falls back and I can kiss him. Within a few minutes, Tyler is already trying to take control, but I don't let him.

"No," I say, removing his hands from my wrists and placing them back on my waist. "I'm in control tonight."

His eyes darken. "Is that right?"

"Mm-hmm, and I've been doing some thinking," I keep my brave face on, "I'm going to call some shots around here."

He gives me a wicked grin. "And what kind of shots are you going to call, darlin'?"

"I've decided," I say, leaning in to run my tongue up his neck, "that we're getting married this summer. I'm not waiting around for you to propose." He laughs and I pull back. "That's funny to you?"

"No," he smiles, "I'll absolutely marry you this summer. What's funny is you thinking you're in control."

I narrow my gaze and reach for his hands, but he's too quick. He

That Feeling

grabs both of mine in one of his hands while standing up at the same time. He hoists me over his shoulder and smacks my ass hard.

"Hey!" I squeal as he walks inside and marches up the stairs, taking them two at a time. He tosses me onto the bed. I bounce against the mattress as he whips off his belt and winds it around one hand.

"Seems like you need to learn a fucking lesson about who's in charge here."

His pupils dilate as the vein in his neck flutters. My entire body is already quaking in anticipation of what he's going to do to me.

I bite my bottom lip. He slowly walks around the bed, grabbing my hands and looping his belt around them. He bends me over so I'm on my knees, my hands tied to the headboard.

"You know I love you, right?"

I nod and he leans down to kiss me softly. He drags his hand down my back slowly until he gets to my ass. I hear his hand pull back before it comes down against my flesh with a loud smack.

"Who's in charge?" he demands.

"You," I say softly just as his hand comes down again on the other cheek.

"Louder!" he shouts as he repeats the process.

"You!" This time *I* shout.

He rubs my ass where he just smacked the shit out of me and leans down, his mouth at my ear as his hand delves between my thighs—straight into my drenched folds. He toys with me, sliding his fingers up and down my slit.

"In the office, the boardroom, you're in charge. You can tell me what to do. But in our bedroom, I'm in fucking charge."

I fall forward as he plunges two fingers inside me. He pumps them vigorously, taking me just to the edge before pulling them back out.

I glance to my right and see him quickly removing his clothes before I feel him crawling back up the bed. He grabs the back of my teddy with both hands and rips it in half. The sound of the tearing lace startles me, but I'm too focused on him sliding into me and fucking me senseless to care.

By the time I wake to head to the office the next morning, Tyler is already at work on the ranch. I've been getting to work by 7 a.m. the last several weeks. Given how much I have going on with so many product launches coming up, I haven't had the luxury of taking it easy.

I've been at work an hour and I'm about to indulge in a second cup of coffee when I hear a soft knock on my office door. Tyler walks in, closing it behind him.

"Hey, baby, this is a pleasant surprise." I jump up and walk over to him. "Didn't get enough last night?" I press myself against him, our quick kiss starting to turn into something more.

"Not quite," he says as he pushes against me to break the kiss.

"You sure? We've never fooled around in my office before." I reach for his belt, but he just laughs and steps back.

"Have a seat." He motions to my chair and grabs the cup of coffee I just poured for myself and tosses it in the trash.

"Hey, I just made that!" I say in confusion.

He reaches into his jacket pocket and pulls out a box and places it on my desk.

I look at it. "What's this?" I lean forward to grab it. "A pregnancy test?" I'm so confused.

"You're pregnant."

My mouth falls open and then I laugh. "What? No, I'm not. How the hell would you even know before me anyway?"

He holds up his fingers as he starts ticking off reasons. "I haven't seen any tampons on the counter in weeks, I'm pretty sure you've missed close to a dozen pills in the last few months, and baby, I can't keep you satisfied."

I shake my head. "I've just been stressed. I've lost my period due to stress before, back in college." I feel my cheeks grow a little warm with embarrassment. "Thought you liked how much we had sex."

He chuckles and rubs his jaw. "Trust me, sweetheart, I love how

That Feeling

much you enjoy riding my cock, but baby, I've been giving it to you three times a night for weeks and it's not enough. You just tried to get me to fuck you in your office."

"Sex is also a stress reliever," I say.

He shakes his head. "Don't get your feelings hurt here, but when I bought you that red lingerie piece a few months back, it fit you just fine. Last night you were bursting out of that thing."

My mouth drops open. "Are you calling me fat?"

"Baby, just take the test." He grabs the box and starts to open it.

"Fine, but you'll owe me a serious apology when it turns out to be negative." I stand and straighten out my blouse as he hands me the test.

I go into my private restroom and pee on the end of the stick, putting the lid on and washing my hands. I open the door and step back into my office as Tyler goes into the restroom to look at the test.

"Takes three minutes," I say as he picks it up and holds it.

I sit back down and click through my email and calendar, completely preoccupied with the dozens of things I have to get done today. I'm replying to an email when out of the corner of my eye, I see Tyler approach my desk.

I look up at him and his hand is outstretched with the test. I reach for it with a smirk on my face.

"I told yo—" My voice falters as I do a double take at the single word staring me in the face.

Pregnant.

Chapter 21

Tyler

"I'm gonna be a dad." I can't stop smiling.

"What? No, no. It has to be wrong. It's a false positive." Brooklyn grabs the test from my hand and stares at it.

"Baby, I think it's pretty rare have a false positive when it comes to a pregnancy test."

She fumbles with the box, trying to get the second test out of it. I reach for the instructions that fall from the box to show her. "See, I think it measures the pregnancy hormone, HCG, so if it's not there, it won't show as positive."

"Oh, what the hell do you know? You're not a woman," she snaps, grabbing the test she dropped on the floor and marching back into the restroom. She shuts the door behind her. A moment later, she's back with the second test in her hand. She paces the floor as she stares at the screen.

The seconds tick by and it feels like the longest three minutes of my life. She stops dead in her tracks, staring at the test.

"No, no, no, this can't be happening," she mutters as she tosses it onto her desk and grabs the empty box. "Did it only come with two?"

I nod and reach for the second test. Again, pregnant.

That Feeling

"What the fuck?" she shouts and raises her hands over her head as she paces again.

"Baby, it's going to be okay."

"Tyler, do you realize how busy I am right now? I feel like I'm already running on fumes and we still have a few more weeks before this launch. Not to mention I'm still training my new employees. I love this job. I need this job."

Her eyes are pleading and I reach for her. "I know this was unplanned and not the best timing, but your job is safe. You know that. There's nothing to worry about in that regard, because you'll always have a job here."

She pushes my hands off her arms. "That's not the point, Tyler. I love my job, and I don't want to stop doing it to raise a baby right now. I'm not ready."

"Nobody is ever ready, Brook, but I know we're going to make amazing parents. We've got this."

"Stop it!" she shouts tearfully. "Just stop. You're doing the same thing Neal did. You're invalidating what I'm feeling right now. Just let me feel."

"Okay," I say, taking a step back to give her some space, "what can I do to make things better?"

She glares at me. "Haven't you done enough already?" she says, pointing to her belly, and it stings.

"What about what I'm feeling, Brook? Does that even matter to you?"

She shakes her head and covers her face with her hands. "I'm not ready to be a mom yet, Tyler. I'm not."

I'm trying my hardest to be understanding, but I don't know how to be in this moment. I'm elated, excited, happy—all of the above—finding out that I'm going to be a dad. I realize she's the one who has to carry the baby, but for fuck's sake, it wouldn't kill her to pretend to care about what I want.

I toss the pamphlet onto the desk. "Well, you're pregnant, Brook, so we need to figure it out." I open her office door and slam it behind me.

I speed back to the ranch, slamming my truck door when I get there and marching my sulking ass into the stables.

"Hey, boss, I've got those fence post diggers loaded up on the ATV for you," Carl says as I approach him.

"Well, what the fuck you waiting for? Grab Teller or one of the other hands and get up to the pasture and get to work."

"Oh, okay, I just thought," he stutters a bit, "you said—"

"Seriously, can't anyone do anything right around here?" I kick a shovel that was left leaning against the barn wall and it clatters down the walkway.

"Jesus, what crawled up your ass today?" Decker leans down and picks up the shovel.

"Not in the fuckin' mood, Deck," I say as I keep walking.

I spend the next hour doing stuff my ranch hands normally do, but I need a way to release my anger—one that doesn't involve punching a wall. I bale hay until I'm sweating bullets, my chest heaving as I toss the hay fork on the ground and walk outside.

Trent's shiny black SUV pulls up and he slowly walks over to me.

"What are you doing here?"

"Decker called. Said I might want to get out here and talk to you."

I roll my eyes. "What a snitch."

"So what's going on?"

I shake my head. "Hard to explain," I say.

"All right, saddle up Misty. I'll grab Fitz."

"You're in a suit."

He shrugs. "Wouldn't be the first time." I give him a questioning look and he laughs. "Senior prom, Jenna O'Toole and I saddled up my old horse, Boots. Let's just say nature got her going and I got her to the finish line."

We ride up to our lookout point, the same place our dad took us whenever we were fighting as kids or when he had something serious

That Feeling

to talk to us about like girls or sex or us taking over the brewery someday.

We dismount and spend a few moments taking in the scenery. Brook is right, it really is breathtaking up here. Sometimes I don't take the time to enjoy it; I take it for granted.

"So how bad is it?" Trent asks. I look over at him and he's propped his foot up on a boulder and leaning on one knee.

"You look just like Dad doin' that," I say, and we both chuckle.

"Brooklyn's pregnant." I shove my hands in my jeans but my shoulders stay up by my ears.

"Holy shit, man." Trent walks over and pulls me in for a hug. "Dude, that's amazing. I don't understand, though. Why aren't you happy? This is happy news."

I nod. "I'm very happy. It's just that she's not. She said she's not ready to be a mom—not ready to give up her job. I tried telling her that her job isn't going anywhere. I don't understand why she thought it would. Just sucks. I was so happy to see the test, then I felt like I couldn't be happy because she was upset."

"How long have you known?"

"Today."

His head whips around. "Today? You *both* just found out today or *you* just found out today?"

"Both. I took a test to her at work this morning because all the signs were there. She thought I was crazy, but she took two and both were positive. She just had this meltdown and I guess it took me by surprise. I thought she'd be shocked—sure, the timing isn't great—but I thought she'd show at least a little excitement."

Trent laughs. "You're more of an idiot than I give you credit for."

"Excuse me?"

"She's in shock, bro. She's not worried about losing her job, it's that she's at the height of this huge new adventure in her life. She's just brought on two new people and has three massive campaigns kicking off, so it's already stressful, and now she's about to grow a baby inside her? Not to mention her body is about to go through hell."

I feel like an asshole. I mean, I already did with how I reacted knowing all those things, but I let my emotions take over in that moment.

"Well, I think I made things a lot worse."

"Oh no, what'd you do?"

"I just reacted poorly. Kind of yelled at her and slammed her office door and stormed off back to the ranch."

He waves off my concern. "That's an easy fix. Make her a nice dinner, draw a relaxing bath, and apologize. Grovel. Tell her you're an idiot and you won't do it again. Just talk to her, Ty. Tell her that you're scared too, and don't shame her for not being happy yet. She'll get there."

I look over at my little brother. "Sometimes you really surprise me with your wisdom, you know that?"

He laughs. "Yeah, I'm good at giving it, but not so good at coming up with my own." He picks up a rock and tosses it over the ledge.

"Something bothering you?"

"A woman." He sighs. "Amelia Blanc of Blanc Wineries."

"I know the Blancs, though I'm not familiar with Amelia."

"She's a royal pain in my ass right now. Get this shit, she wants to bring her winery out here. Apparently, she's set up a tasting room in Fort Collins but plans to expand to open more full-scale wineries in Colorado."

I look at him, confused. "And? What's that got to do with us?"

"Are you kidding me? First of all, this is our territory. She knows that we've talked about getting into the wine scene."

"Our territory?" I laugh. "Aren't you being a little dramatic? We don't do wine. Yes, it's been talked about, but it's always been voted against in the board meetings, and for good reason. We don't need to diversify that much."

"Yeah, but I'd like to keep that option open for future endeavors. And also, her family are a bunch of fucking sellouts! They sold their

That Feeling

name to some parent company that owns strip mall wineries and shit. We keep our name in the family; we source everything locally and build relationships in the community. The last thing we need is some money-hungry company from the West Coast coming in here and pissing everyone off again and causing problems."

He's heated and it makes me chuckle. "Sounds like this Amelia lady is really under your skin."

"Don't do that. Don't act like it's a crush. This is serious shit, and even Dad is concerned."

I raise my hands. "I didn't say it. We'll talk about it with him, so don't worry, I'm not trying to brush off your concerns. I don't love the idea of chain wineries around here either, but we also can't control what comes in and out of this town." He gives me a sideways glance. "No, Trent, we're not going to do that. We're not going to be a family that runs others out of town, especially after what happened with our ancestors."

Brooklyn will be home in a few minutes. I let the filet mignon rest as I plate up the roasted potatoes and side salad. The chocolate cheesecake she loves is in the fridge. I step back and give the table a once-over. Lit candles, check. Her favorite meal, check. I grab the remote for the stereo and turn on a soft jazz playlist just as I hear the front door open.

I made sure to sprinkle rose petals from the front door all the way up the stairs to our master bedroom.

I hear her heels clicking as she walks toward the kitchen. I nervously lean against the doorway. She rounds the corner, and the moment she sees me, her face softens and her bottom lip begins to quiver.

"Sweetie." I open my arms and she steps into them and starts to cry. "It's okay." I rub her back for a few minutes.

"I'm sorry," she says through her tears.

"No, you don't need to be. I'm the one who needs to apologize. I was selfish and didn't think about the change this means for you and your body and your work schedule."

I hold her face in my hands. "Is that steak I smell?" she asks.

I laugh. "It is. I made your favorite dinner and there's even chocolate cheesecake in the fridge."

"You're about to make this baby and me very happy."

I feel a flutter when she mentions our baby, but I don't want to draw too much attention to it just yet. I know she's probably still in shock, and I have a happy surprise for her later.

"I'm so full." She walks slowly up the stairs to our bedroom.

"Here," I say, scooping her up and carrying her the rest of the way. I place her on her feet and guide her into our master bathroom. I've lit about two dozen candles and placed them around the room. The tub is filled with water and more rose petals.

"Oh my God, that looks so amazing."

"And I double-checked that this water temperature is fine while you're pregnant."

We strip down and gently lower ourselves into the warm water. I keep my jeans close by so I can reach into the pocket once I'm settled behind her.

"This is so wonderful. Thank you, baby." She leans back against my chest.

"I have something I want to say to you. I'm sorry again about how I acted earlier. You have every right to be scared and feel like you're not ready. I should have supported you better."

I grab the ring from my jeans without her noticing and slowly bring it around in front of her. I reach into the water and pull her hand out, sliding the ring onto her finger.

"I'm not doing this because of the baby. I waited too damn long to

That Feeling

do it in the first place, but I want you to know that I promise to be by your side every single day for the rest of our lives—loving and supporting you no matter what life throws our way."

The room is dead silent for a few seconds. Brooklyn's shoulders begin to tremble and I hear her let out a shaky breath. She spins around, water sloshing with the movement as she throws her arms around my neck and begins to cry.

"Are they happy tears?"

She nods her head against my neck. "Yes and no." She wipes at her eyes furiously before saying, "I feel like such an asshole."

"What? Why, baby? I was the asshole, not you."

"It's just that I finally have my dream job and my dream man, and then I'm blessed with a baby and I just ruin it. All I was focused on was the fear. I'm just worried that it'll put so much stress on us that you'll resent me."

I lift her chin up. "Look at me, Brooklyn. I will never resent you. You and this baby are my entire world. No matter what happens, we've got each other. Forever."

Chapter 22

Brooklyn

"Yes!" I feel like I have a flood of emotions taking over me, crashing down in one glorious wave after another.

"How did I wake up this morning and in the span of less than 24 hours, I find out I'm not only going to be a mom but a wife too?"

The floodgates open again the moment I say the words out loud. I spend the next 10 minutes going back and forth between crying and kissing Tyler to staring at my ring.

"How are you feeling?"

He places his hand protectively against my stomach and it's suddenly so different than all the times before. It feels so real. I look down at where his hand is resting and place mine on top of his.

"Scared. Terrified. Still in shock." I shake my head as I try to wrap my head around the fact that there's life inside me. "Is it okay if it takes me some time?" I look up at him nervously, hoping he understands, and I can see that he does.

"Of course. This is huge—a major life change we obviously weren't expecting yet. I know it won't be easy, but I do know that you

That Feeling

have a huge network of support out here with my family. There's like . . . close to 300,000 Slades now, I think."

I laugh. "Yeah, I don't doubt I'll have that support with your family. I know mine will also fly out and want to spend probably too much time with us and the baby. When should we tell people?"

"That's your call, sweetheart." He kisses my temple. "I know people often wait after the first trimester, but I have no issue if you want to tell your family sooner." He scratches his head nervously. "Speaking of, I may have really fucked up today. I told Trent. I was angry when I left your office, and Decker called him and told him he needed to come out and talk to me. Please don't hate me."

"I'm not upset, honestly. This morning was kind of a shit show, and if Mallory had been here, I probably would've run and done the same thing. But he better keep his mouth shut or I'll come after him. Trust me, you don't want an angry pregnant woman after you."

"You mentioned wanting to get married this summer. Is that still your desire, or has that changed with the baby?"

I think about it briefly. "No, it hasn't changed. I want to be your wife and I don't want to wait until I've had the baby. Plus, I feel like I want to wait to tell everyone else about the pregnancy. Maybe we could tell them at the reception?"

"That's an idea." He brushes my hair behind my ear. I've noticed all the little touches of endearment Tyler has given me in just a few moments. His protective instincts are already kicking in.

"I'm thinking something small and intimate—just our friends and family—so I guess not *too* small with the Slade brood. But yeah, something small on the ranch."

"Here?"

"Yes, this is my home now. You're my home and I want to make every memory I can here with our little family."

Tyler holds me in his arms, our hands resting against my belly.

"I think Trent has a crush on this wine lady."

"Oh my God, Amelia?" I spin around to face him.

"Yeah, how do you know her?"

"That's where we went yesterday in Fort Collins: her wine tasting room. She came over and introduced herself to us. She's so amazing and I gave her my card. We're going to connect and talk about maybe doing some cross-promotion together—her winery and the brewery."

Tyler winces. "I don't know if that will be a good idea."

"Why not? Just because Trent has a crush? Which, by the way, she's way out of his league. She's like an old Hollywood glamazon. So classy."

"There's a little more to it. I guess her family winery sold to some bigger conglomerate. They're a parent company that does those chain brewhouses and wineries in strip malls. Trent doesn't like the idea of a big chain establishment moving in here."

"Oh, I didn't realize that."

"Yeah, and my guess is if they do plan to build any sort of major chain out here, the other ranchers aren't going to like it either. It could really start a turf war situation. Don't worry, though. I told him we're not going to get involved—no underhanded shenanigans. My family has some really bad history with land rights and such, and it took my dad years to get back into the good graces of these people."

I turn back around and lie against him again. A small knot forms in my stomach at the thought of something arising between us and the Blancs. They're a powerful family—maybe not as much as the Slades, but right now, all I can focus on is my job and my baby.

"I should make a doctor's appointment this week."

"Yeah, good point. Any idea on how far along you might be?"

I do some mental calculations. "Maybe a month? My period math isn't perfect, but I'd say maybe four or five weeks, max. I'll call and get in this week."

The water has gone tepid and we both step out and grab our towels.

"When should we tell your parents?" I ask, holding up my ring finger.

"How about we get in bed? No need to get dressed, by the way,"

That Feeling

he motions to my towel around my body. "Then we'll send them a selfie of our faces with the ring. After that, we'll turn off our phones and let them all go crazy while I try to satisfy all those naughty little pregnancy hormone needs you have."

I bite my lip and drop the towel. "You don't have to tell me twice."

"Wow, a party this weekend? Already? Your parents move fast."

"That's Celeste Slade for you: Type A and on top of everything." He reaches over and grabs my hand. "They're just beyond excited for us. My mom has been wanting me to not only get married but give her a grandchild for the better part of a decade."

"Well, she's going to really freak out once she finds out about this one." I point to my belly.

I called the only obstetrician in town and was able to get in for my first appointment today. I'm nervous, partly because I want to make sure our baby is healthy—although I'm not sure they can tell much of anything this soon—but also because this makes it all so real. I think I'm still in disbelief at this point. I've had pretty much zero symptoms of pregnancy other than a little weight gain and a missed period. And I guess if you count being tired and headaches, those symptoms could be added to the list, though they could also be chalked up to stress due to my work schedule.

"What's going through that head of yours?" Tyler glances over at me and gives my hand a quick squeeze as we pull into the doctor's office.

"Just nervous. Are you nervous at all?"

He shuts off the truck and turns to grab both of my hands. "I am. Probably not for the same reasons as you, but I also want you to know that I'm your rock, baby. I can handle any fears that might arise on my end. If you need to freak out, don't hold back."

I smile. Just hearing him say those words sends a feeling of relief through me.

"Okay, we've got this," I say as I squeeze his hands and look him in the eye. "Let's go find out how long we have to wait until we meet this little bean."

"Hmm, okay," the doctor says. I glance nervously at Tyler as the doctor looks at his screen. "So your last period was in January, and we're about to head into April. You're most likely not very far along, as you've pointed out, so we'll be doing a transvaginal ultrasound today."

"Uh, what?" All this baby stuff is brand new to me, and while I've never even heard of that kind of ultrasound, I can just about guess that it means. "Don't you normally squirt the goo on the belly and use the camera that way?"

"We do when you're a little further along. Okay, I'll step out and you can change into this gown. We're just a country office here, so my nurse will assist, but I don't have an ultrasound tech."

He smiles and walks out of the room. I quickly change and take a seat back up on the table, chewing on the edge of my thumb as I tap my fingers.

"You okay?" Tyler comes over and pulls my hands away from my body. He intertwines his fingers with mine. "It's okay." He kisses my forehead as the doctor knocks on the door and enters with his nurse.

The procedure is uncomfortable, but I focus my attention on the screen to my left. The doctor is talking about something with his nurse when he suddenly points to a small blip on the screen. "There's your baby."

I don't know what I was expecting, but it wasn't this. There on the screen is the tiniest little outline of a baby. The image is clearer than I expected. I feel myself welling up as the sound of its rapid heartbeat fills the room.

That Feeling

"And that's the baby's heartbeat. Sounds strong and healthy, in a perfect range."

"Oh my God." Tears tumble down my cheeks. Emotion overflows and I begin to sob as I reach for Tyler's hand.

He grips my hand, and as I look up at him, I notice he's crying just as hard as I am.

"Look at us," I laugh as we both stare in complete disbelief at our unborn baby.

"Going by the measurements we see here and the stage of development, I'd estimate you to be just over nine weeks."

"What? I'm that far along already? I'm almost done with my first trimester!" Suddenly that thought sends me over the edge and I start to cry again. "I missed the entire first two months."

"Well, the fact that you haven't had morning sickness and cramping and any major symptoms is a nice relief for you. Don't worry, Mama, you've got about 31 more weeks to experience."

"We'll have some pictures printed out at the front desk when you check out and schedule your next appointment," Betty, his nurse, informs us.

The doctor smiles and removes the instrument, stepping out with Betty to let me get dressed.

"Nine weeks," I repeat in disbelief as Tyler helps me sit up.

"And to think you had no idea. Crazy."

I nod. "I also think we need to get this wedding planned ASAP, or I'll be waddling down the aisle." I glance at the clock on the wall. "Oh shit, I need to get over to the office right away. Can you drop me off? I don't want to have to go all the way home to get my car."

Tyler helps me off the table, continuing to hold my elbow as I walk over to the chair where my clothes are.

"What's going on? What is this?" I say, looking down at his hand.

"Nothing, just assisting you. Yeah, I'll take you to the office now. You need anything? You sure you'll be okay all day?"

I let out a long breath. "Babe, you're not starting in on the overprotective worry stuff this early. We had a deal."

"To Brooklyn and Tyler! I still can't believe we're blessed to call this amazing young woman our future daughter-in-law."

Everyone cheers and raises a glass in a toast to us. I smile sweetly at Celeste as she gives a toast and I will myself not to cry. Even though I didn't have many initial pregnancy symptoms, it's like as soon as I got the official confirmation from the doctor, I've been a horny, hungry emotional wreck. God bless Tyler for dealing with it, because we've got a long way to go.

"I gotta say, I like that she put my name first in that toast," I lean toward Tyler and whisper in his ear. "She recognizes the power dynamic here." I motion between us.

Tyler's eyes instantly grow dark as he listens to me, and his eyes find mine as he leans in closer. "Should I tell her that I had you begging me to fuck you not two hours ago?" He tips my chin to face him, his lips a centimeter from mine. "Or how you're so eager to fall on your knees and part those cherry red lips every time my cock's out?"

One thing about Tyler is whenever I try to play fun, flirty games with him, he always wins. I don't let him see that I'm quivering in my seat. Instead, I shrug and play coy. "Don't be gross, Tyler. That's your mom. You really think it's appropriate to share that kind of info with her?"

He laughs. "Sweetheart, you clearly must not remember who I am, because I'll grab that microphone out of my mom's hands so fast and tell every motherfucker in this place that I can make you come by fucking your ass. Or do you need a reminder?"

My face feels like it's on fire. I smack his arm and look around to make sure nobody heard. "Behave!"

"Why? Frustrated?" He reaches beneath the table and runs his hand up my dress to my upper thigh, the warmth of his hand threatening to burn through my flesh.

That Feeling

I'm about to grab his shirt and haul his sexy ass to the bathroom when I hear someone say my name. I look up and see Dolly heading toward me with Amelia.

"Oh, good! Dolly came and she brought Amelia."

Tyler looks up. "This should be fun. Better hope Trent doesn't see her."

"Oh shit! Must be pregnancy brain. I completely forgot he doesn't like her." I glance around the room trying to spot him, but he's nowhere to be found.

"Don't worry about it, baby. I'll go distract him. He's probably already drunk out back with Ranger and Decker." He gives me a quick kiss and heads out to find Trent while I socialize with my friends.

The party is a blast. Celeste threw it in an empty barn they tend to use for events like this. It's tastefully decorated with flowers and candles—exactly how I'd want it to be decorated for our wedding.

"Celeste, thank you so much," I say, pulling her in for a hug. "Honesty, this is just wonderful. My parents were sad they couldn't make it, but they will be out here for the wedding."

"Oh, no thanks necessary. We're just so happy Tyler found you. He mentioned you two are thinking of June?"

"Yes, I know, it's only three months away, but we both want something small and simple anyway. Just family and a few close friends."

"I think that's best. That's what Drake and I did, you know."

I open my mouth to respond when I hear shouting. Confused, Celeste and I both turn around to see a very tipsy Trent pointing a finger in Amelia's face.

"The fuck are you doing here?" he shouts.

I can't hear what Amelia says since she isn't shouting back. I scurry over and Tyler is grabbing Trent by the shoulders, trying to redirect him outside, but he jerks his arms away.

"No! This bitch has no business being here. Tell them what you're planning to do," he shouts louder this time.

I feel mortified. "Amelia, I'm so sorry," I try to apologize, but she just holds up her hand.

"I'm not trying to do anything, Trent. I'm simply here to celebrate Brooklyn's engagement. I'm happy to discuss business matters another time, in a professional setting."

She keeps her calm, which only seems to enrage Trent more.

"*Bravo,*" he claps dramatically. "So professional. You might think you're going to prove something here by taking the high road, but my family sees right through your bullshit. We know what you're going to do. We know what you've done throughout Idaho and California."

Chapter 23

Tyler

"Trent, stop, man! This isn't you."

"I said *no*," he snaps at me and I take a step back. Truthfully, I've never seen him this angry before, and I feel like there's something else going on here. "You." He points at Amelia and takes another step toward her. "Your sellout family sold their winery rights to Treymore Food and Bev. We all know the shady shit they're involved in—how they drive out small and locally-owned family businesses and replace them with strip mall wineries and shitty chain bars."

Amelia crosses her arms and leans back a little, clearly not impressed with the knowledge Trent thinks he's dropping on everyone.

"Yeah, look what they did in Idaho. They drove out more than 15 businesses so they could open up a fucking ski resort and ruin that town. You're in bed with some really fucking sleazy people, and I know what they've done."

"If you'd finished your research, then you'd have seen that I took all of my inheritance and every single penny I have to my name and bought back my family business. That's right, I own Blanc Wineries.

I'm not opening chain wineries; I'm trying to build back what my family once was."

Brooklyn steps up and grabs Amelia's hand. She pulls her away and tries to comfort her as Amelia apologizes profusely for ruining the party.

"Time to go, buddy." I grab Trent by the shoulders and spin him around to lead him outside. He shouts a few things as we leave the barn. He suddenly jerks away from me and starts to walk back toward my parents' house, but I follow him.

"Hey!" I follow after him. "What the fuck was that shit?" I shout as we walk up to the porch.

"I told you, Tyler, this shit is way more serious than you think. You're always out at the ranch, but you don't know the stuff I know. You don't see the shady back-door deals that go on in this business world."

I shake my head. Trent has a knack for being overdramatic, but this takes the cake. "You're drunk."

"I'm not drunk, I'm tipsy, but I still know what I'm talking about."

"Enlighten me, then." I take a seat in one of the rocking chairs while he paces.

"There's been a lot of talk around town about these land vultures swooping in here, buying massive amounts of acreage, and nobody knows why or what for."

"That's been going on for years. We both know it's only a matter of time before one of those huge hedge funds that has their hands deep in the government's pockets tries to swoop in with eminent domain and take the ranch for a resort."

"Yeah, well, what the fuck are we going to do about it? Money doesn't talk to these people. I've heard there have been a couple goons with guns spotted over on Gelson's Ranch, Tyler. They've got powerful people in their back pockets—politicians, the cops."

"What does it have to do with us, though? We aren't vigilantes and we're not just some small mom-and-pop brewery anymore, Trent.

That Feeling

We're a billion-dollar empire with power and a reputation. They're not the only people with long arms, you know that."

Trent takes a seat next to me and shakes his head.

"Amelia is just wanting to expand her winery business," I say. "Let her open up a winery in Fort Collins. It has nothing to do with us."

"What about Slade Wines?"

I laugh. "What about it? That's a pipe dream you came up with and have never done shit to make it happen. Like Dad said before, we're stretched thin enough. We need to stay in our lane. Business is great—better than it's ever been—so don't get fucking greedy."

I stand up and walk to the edge of the porch to head back over to the party and check on Brooklyn. "And for the record, you owe Brooklyn an apology. You could have picked any other time to have a meltdown over this."

"I'm sorry," he mutters, "but I still think you're being naive about all this."

I shake my head and walk back over to the barn to try to calm down Brook.

"What the absolute hell?" Her eyes are huge as she meets me outside.

"He's being dramatic is all. You okay? Did Amelia leave?"

"Yeah," she steps closer to me and rests her head against my chest. "She was upset, but she'll be okay. You promise he's just being dramatic? Is there something I should be worried about?"

I look down at her and poke the tip of her nose, then follow it up with a kiss. "I promise. We just need to focus on keeping you and our baby healthy, and getting your cute little ass down the aisle."

IT'S BEEN TWO WEEKS OF NONSTOP FIRE DRILLS.

Brooklyn woke up two days after our engagement party sobbing, convinced she'd lost the baby. When I asked her if she was bleeding, she said no, she just had horrible cramps, so we rushed to the doctor only to find out it was gas.

She's been on an emotional roller coaster with work and the pregnancy and planning the wedding. I tried taking the reins on a few things, but she chewed me out and told me it would stress her out to have a man planning her wedding, so I backed off.

"You okay? Seem awful quiet," Trent says as we work on a tractor together.

"Just feeling sorry for myself is all. Feels like I can't do anything right lately."

He hands me a wrench. "How so?"

"With Brook. Poor girl is emotional with the pregnancy, and work is just so busy I feel like she's not taking care of herself properly. I tried stopping by her office a few times to bring her lunch or check in on her, but she told me she knew what she was doing and she can take care of herself."

Trent chuckles. "Glad it's not just me."

I roll out from under the tractor and give him a questioning look.

"She's been on one at work lately with me too. She can be bossy, so you've got your work cut out for you."

"Yeah, it'll pass, though. She's overworked right now, so I'm just trying to give her space while also being there for her. It's a mindfuck, I won't lie."

"I was scared she was going to rip my head off when I went to apologize to her for the engagement party, but she was actually really understanding. She did say I had to apologize to Amelia before the wedding. Not looking forward to that."

Brooklyn and I actually had a bit of a fight this morning. Nothing major—she just felt frustrated once again that I was being overprotective. She said I made her feel like I thought she was incompetent and not taking care of herself or the baby. It wasn't my intention at all, but this is so new to me too. It just feels like we aren't working together, and we're both drowning a little.

That Feeling

"We got poachers!" Ranger shouts down the long hallway of the barn.

Trent and I whip our heads around and walk toward him.

"You saw them?" I ask, and Ranger nods.

"Saw their truck. It was pulled off the road with some brush thrown over it. They're up by pasture six."

"I'll mount up," I say, walking toward the stables to get Misty.

"I'm coming with you. I bet you anything it's these fucking land vultures swooping in."

We saddle up our horses and I grab my shotgun. You can't be too careful out here in the wilderness. People like to think the Wild West days are gone, but to Trent's credit, some of these folk out here are downright dirty and they'll make damn sure you won't tell anyone about it.

This isn't the first time I've dealt with poachers, and I know it won't be the last. Usually, it's just a hunter who didn't realize the land was private, but every once in a while, you get some rich schmuck who thinks the rules don't apply to him. Most of the time, I can handle it, but we never go alone when we run into one.

Trent grabs his pistol and slides it in his holster.

"Don't do anything stupid with that," I say, saddling Misty. "Keep it holstered unless I say, you understand?"

Trent isn't an idiot, but he can act on impulse, as he displayed at the engagement party. The last thing I need right now is him getting hyped up and running his mouth to some poor father and son who unknowingly crossed onto our land.

"I'm not stu—"

I stop Misty in her tracks and reach over to grab his saddle.

"This isn't a negotiation, Trent. You listen to me out there. This is my ranch and my land. When we're at the office and in the boardroom, I listen to you and I don't try to cowboy your meetings. But I'm the one in charge here."

He nods and we both take off to follow Ranger up to pasture six. I hate to pull rank on him like this, but Trent doesn't realize just how quickly these situations can turn from dangerous to deadly, and I'm not leaving behind a pregnant widow.

Ranger takes us right to where he found the truck. Decker is still there.

"You see 'em yet, Deck?" I ask as we ride up.

"Nope. Nothin' yet."

I dismount and look at the truck.

"Texas plates. Could be a rental. You boys strapped up?"

They both nod and show me their guns.

"All right, let's find these poachers. Trent, you stay with me. Ranger and Decker, you guys go to the south end of the pasture. If you see them, call out."

We break up and start to scour the pasture and surrounding tree line.

"You seeing anything?" Trent rides up next to me.

"I see some shoe prints here in this mud. I doubt that would be from our guys, since they wouldn't have a need to be on the ground over here."

We spend the next two hours searching, but there's no sign of them. It's nearly dusk and it's dangerous to be out here with potential poachers.

Ranger and Decker approach. "Hey guys, we gotta call it. Too dangerous to be out here once the sun's gone down."

"They probably spotted us and they're just waiting it out," Ranger says when I see what I think is movement across the pasture.

"Hold it," I say. "I think I might have spotted something."

Trent narrows his eyes. "Yup, that's someone. Let's go."

"Trent!" I yell after him, but he's already in a gallop. "Trent, it's not safe!" I shout as I heel Misty to take off after him.

I barely get her up to speed when I hear a shot ring out and feel a white-hot heat in my chest. I grip the saddle, but it's no use. I fall backward off Misty, who takes off in a startled sprint.

I stare up at the orangey-pink sky, struggling to catch my breath with the force of hitting the ground.

That Feeling

"Tyler! Tyler!" I hear someone screaming my name.

I try to sit up, but the pain is blinding. I reach my hand up to my upper shoulder and it hits something warm and wet. I pull my hand away, confused, and that's when I see it's covered in blood.

My head is getting heavier, swimming in confusion as I blink. It feels like my eyelids weigh a thousand pounds each, and no matter how hard I try, I can't keep them open.

"Tyler, stay with me." Trent's blurry face appears over me as his hands press down hard on my chest.

I try to push him off, still so confused about what's going on.

"What happ—happ?" My teeth clatter together and I can't get the words out as a cold chill takes over my body.

The last thing I remember is hearing Trent yell, "Call 911! He's been shot!"

Chapter 24

Brooklyn

I feel like a complete asshole.

I've been a little more than moody and short-tempered with Tyler lately, and I want to show him tonight that deep down, amidst all the stress and hormones, the sweet Brooklyn he fell in love with is still in here.

I dip out of work a little early to head to the grocery store. Something I've learned about Tyler is that one of his love languages is acts of kindness. He loves to cook for me and I want to return the favor, so I called up Celeste to find out what his absolute favorite meal was growing up.

It's nothing fancy, which doesn't surprise me: broccoli cheese bake. It consists of broccoli, rice, some sort of chipped ham, and Velveeta cheese. Easy enough. I can make it without too much preparation, and it sounds extremely delicious after this long day.

Normally, I'd pick up a bottle of wine or champagne, but that's out of the picture now.

"How can I make this sexy?" I stare down at the ingredients. "Candles, maybe some mood lighting and soft jazz."

That Feeling

I light a few candles and dim the lights, putting on a sexy playlist I found on Spotify, and get to cooking.

I decide to send him a text to hint that something special is happening tonight.

Me: *What's warm, gooey, and edible? I'll give you a hint: It's not me.*

I don't want to give away what I'm making for him, because I don't think he'd ever guess it would be his favorite childhood meal.

I finish assembling the dish, place it in the oven to bake, and check my phone. No response from Tyler. He's most likely busy, so I decide to up the spice a little. I run upstairs and put on a sexy lingerie set I can just barely still squeeze myself into. My boobs have certainly grown with pregnancy, which he has been very vocally appreciative of.

I slide on a pair of cute heels and my robe and go back down to the kitchen. I pull the robe down over my shoulders and squeeze my breasts together while I angle the camera. I take a few selfies, find the best one, and shoot it over to him.

The two other times I've done this, he loved it. The first time, he was just downstairs and I was already in bed. I heard the back door slam and his footsteps come up the stairs at breakneck speed. The second time, he was driving and said he almost drove through the garage.

Both times ended with me worn out and satisfied, followed by the best night's sleep of my life—something that sounds like heaven right now. I've been beyond exhausted and beyond turned on. If all goes according to plan, I'll scratch both of those itches tonight.

I pull the casserole out of the oven and check my phone. Still no response from Tyler. I look outside to see if his truck is gone, but it's still here. The sun is just starting to set.

I don't want to bug him since I know he's busy, but I decide a quick call can't hurt. It rings several times then goes to voicemail.

I kill some time putting laundry away and figuring out what I'm going to wear tomorrow. I pull my shirt up in the closet mirror and run my hand down my still-mostly-flat belly. I haven't popped yet at all and, really, the only weight gain has been in my breasts and hips. I do feel like my face is getting a little fuller as well.

I grab my phone and snap a picture from the side, figuring someday I'll be able to show my child their bump progress. Plus I know once we tell everyone, my mom will want pictures so she can put together a scrapbook, or as she likes to call it, *a Midwest Bible.*

Tyler still hasn't called, and weirdly, I start to get a little nervous. Trent's warnings about how dangerous some of these land developers are ring in my ears, so I decide one more call can't hurt. But as soon as my thumb hovers over his name, Trent calls me.

"Hey, I was just about ca—"

"Brook, listen to me," I can hear the panic in Trent's voice, "I need you to sit down."

"What?" I say, tears already gathering in my eyes. "What happened?"

"Tyler . . . he's been shot."

The room starts to spin and my ears begin to ring. This isn't real. This can't be happening.

"Brooklyn, are you there? Brook, I need you to breathe."

"I'm here, I—I don't understand." My voice begins to hitch and I sink down on the floor, all feeling leaving my body.

"I'm getting in the Flight for Life helicopter with him now."

The words *Flight for Life* make my stomach flip and I run to the bathroom to empty the contents into the toilet. "My dad is almost to you. He's picking you up and taking you to meet us at UCHealth in Fort Collins."

I can't process what's being said to me right now. I turn on the faucet and splash cold water on my face. Trent's voice is drowned out as I put down the phone.

"Brooklyn, I gotta go." The line disconnects.

Something takes over me and I run to the closet to throw on sweatpants, a hoodie, and shoes. I grab my purse and phone charger and run to the front porch to wait for Drake. Thankfully, it's not a

That Feeling

long wait. I'm barely out the door when I see a cloud of dust behind his truck as he flies down the driveway.

I hardly wait for him to stop as I pull the door open and climb inside. Neither of us speaks. Drake reaches over and grabs my hand.

Finally, after a few moments, he calmly says, "He's gonna be okay, kid. He's a fighter."

We make it to the hospital in record time.

The helicopter carrying Tyler has already arrived. We race inside just as Trent comes walking toward us.

A sound I've never heard myself make erupts from my chest when I see Trent. He's covered in blood—Tyler's blood. It looks like too much—like there's no way he could possibly still be alive.

Trent runs toward me, catching me just in time. He pulls me into his arms as I sob.

"Shh, he's okay. He's going to be okay. He's alive, Brooklyn."

We both fall to the ground and I cry until my eyes burn and my head feels like it's going to explode. He pulls my hair out of my face, and I can feel how swollen my cheeks and eyes are.

"Look at me. He's going to make it, I promise you that. He will fight for you and this baby."

I don't care if anyone can hear him. Celeste is still on her way and Drake is speaking to the doctor with Ranger and Decker.

Trent walks me to a chair and grabs a glass of water for me. I drink it down and finally compose myself enough to talk.

"What happened?" I ask as Ranger and Decker walk over with Drake and I stand up to meet them.

"Ranger reported some poachers, and I was back down at the barn with Tyler. We rode up there together and found their truck, but we couldn't find them anywhere. It was dusk and Tyler told us to leave, but we saw them at the last second. I—" He covers his face and starts to cry.

"It wasn't your fault, son," Drake says.

"I didn't listen to him. I rode toward them and that's when we heard the shot." He can't keep his composure. Drake grabs him by the back of the neck and pulls him to his chest. His body shakes as he cries.

Ranger and Decker walk me over to the chairs again.

"It wasn't his fault. He's blaming himself, but that shot would've been worse if Tyler hadn't moved to chase after him."

Even hearing the story from Trent, I don't blame him. I don't know the full story and I don't even have to. I know that Trent would never intentionally put Tyler's life at risk.

Celeste finally arrives, her face white as a ghost as Drake explains everything to her. She, Trent, and Drake hold each other for a moment before she walks over to me. We all sit together in silence, waiting on pins and needles for the doctor to come out and give us an update. All we know is that they took him into surgery immediately upon arrival.

Finally, a tall, thin man walks out. "I'm Dr. Jarmel Fink. We successfully removed the bullet that was lodged in Tyler's upper chest and shoulder area. Somehow, it barely missed any major arteries. He's stable now and resting, and we expect him to make a full recovery. You guys acted fast and it saved his life."

"Thanks, Doc." Drake shakes the man's hand.

"Any idea how long until we can see him?" I ask.

"Not tonight. I'd say come back in the morning."

Drake steps forward and places his hand on the doctor's shoulder. "I can't thank you enough for what you did to save my boy tonight, but that's his soon-to-be wife, and she's going to stay with him tonight. I'm sorry if this is against protocol, but we Slades aren't going to take 'no' for an answer."

The doctor nods. This is the first time I've ever seen Drake Slade use his family name to lay down the law and even break the rules.

"Okay, sir, let me see what I can do."

I step away to give my parents a call. They're both shocked and I tell them that while we don't have answers on who did this, I'm sure they'll find out.

"Sweetie, you need to fly home right now. You're not safe."

That Feeling

"Mom, I'm not leaving him. I'm safe. Trust me, being surrounded by the Slades is the safest place I can be."

I finally talk them both down from flying out here and my dad says he'll give Silas a call and fill him in along with Mallory. I don't have the emotional bandwidth to explain things to anyone else tonight, especially when I still have a million unanswered questions myself.

I hang up and see two police offers walk through the emergency room doors. They spot Ranger and Decker and walk over to them. Trent motions for us to gather around.

"Sheriff," Drake says to one man, "Deputy," to the other. Clearly, they all know each other.

"We're going to need to take statements from you three, standard protocol. But I wanted to come down here first and see how Tyler's doing and let you know we found them."

"And?" Drake says.

"They're two known poachers. They've had arrests and outstanding warrants in Montana, Wyoming, and Colorado. They claim they had no idea that Tyler was a man on a horse. They said he looked like an elk."

"Oh, bullshit!" Trent snaps.

"Hey, I think that's a crock, too, but I'm just relaying his statement. The guy mentioned that he didn't see any neon orange—"

"Why the hell would he?" Ranger shakes his head. "We aren't hunters. That's our fucking land and we were working."

"I understand. You guys aren't in the wrong here at all. They've both been arrested on poaching and trespassing charges, plus the unlawful use of a weapon."

"That's it?" Trent is practically up on the cop's nose.

"For now. I'm pushing to charge them with attempted murder, but we'll have to see what the judge comes back with. I gotta tell you, it could be attempted manslaughter or even criminal negligence."

Ranger pulls his hat off and walks away. Trent's face is so red it looks like it's about to pop, and Decker just laughs.

"Fucking joke," he mutters.

"You men need to go outside and calm down; you're making a scene. I'll talk to the sheriff and deputy," Drake says.

By the time the police leave, it's almost 1 a.m. Visiting hours are long over, but the doctor has given us special dispensation.

"We'll see him tomorrow. We want you to stay with him." Drake squeezes my shoulders as Celeste embraces me. I say good night to everyone and Trent stops on the way out.

"Hey, here's a few bucks. Please go over there get something from the vending machine just to humor me. I know you're wrecked and not hungry, but you have to take care of yourself right now."

I thank him, promising I will. I grab a pack of Cheez-Its and some juice and follow a nurse back to where Tyler is.

I hold my breath as her shoes squeak down the quiet hallway. I'm terrified of what I'm about to see. I stop just outside his door and brace myself. The nurse can clearly see my apprehension and she grabs my hand.

"He's okay. He's strong. Just go in there and talk to him. He can hear you."

I let out a breath and walk inside the room. The soft beep of the machines around him is all I hear. There are tubes coming out of him, and he looks so alone and helpless, I almost lose it again.

I pull up a chair next to him and grab his limp hand, bringing it to my lips. I plant tear-soaked kisses on it as I silently pray.

"You have to make it, please," I whisper. "I need you. Our baby needs you. I can't do this alone."

Chapter 25

Tyler

My eyes flutter, opening briefly to register daylight and then closing again. I can hear the soft hum of a machine and what sounds like beeping, but I can't figure out what it is.

I try to lift my hand, but it feels so heavy that I attempt to kick my leg instead. It feels like something is holding me down.

My eyes feel heavy. I try to open them again, but I feel myself being pulled back into a deep sleep I can't fight.

I HAVE NO IDEA HOW LONG I'VE BEEN ASLEEP, BUT FINALLY, MY eyelids shoot open today. I blink several times, glancing around the room and realizing I'm in a hospital bed.

Memories come flooding back to me: Trent bent over me, screaming my name. Someone yelling to call 911 as my body grew colder, and then, finally, the sound of a helicopter approaching in the distance.

I stir, moving my legs. I feel a warm pressure on my hand. I look down my body and there's Brooklyn, hunched over my bed, her face pressed against my hand as she's fast asleep. My heart aches to see her like this. It's evident she's been here as long as I have. I reach my other hand across my body, twisting and wincing in pain as I glance over to my left shoulder where heavy bandages hide the bullet wound.

"Baby?" I run my fingers over her hair. "Baby, you need to eat and sleep in a proper bed."

Her eyes open, shifting to look up at me, then they close again. A second later, her head shoots upward. She's clearly in disbelief.

"You're awake!" She stands up, her chair scooting back with the movement. "Oh my God, you're awake," she says as tears take over.

I can't help but laugh at how disheveled she is. "I'm okay, sweetheart. Why are you crying?"

She doesn't answer me; her emotions are running too high. She climbs into the bed with me and softly lays her body against mine.

"Well, look who's awake this morning." A tall doctor walks into my room, his glasses perched on the end of his nose as he grabs the chart off the bed. "How are you feeling today, Tyler? You aware of what happened to you?"

"I am." I wince a little as Brooklyn removes herself from my bed and takes a seat in the chair. "I mean, I guess I'm aware I got shot."

The doc nods, not looking up from his chart. "Seems that way. So we were able to remove the bullet fairly easily. No major arteries were hit, and it barely missed your clavicle, which is always preferred . . . no bone fragments."

"They catch the son of a bitch?" I laugh.

"That's a question for the sheriff." The doc doesn't seem amused. He makes a few notes on the chart then clips it back to the bed. "We'll keep you for one more night, then you'll be on your way, Mr. Slade." He walks to the door and turns back around. "You've got a good wife there. She never left your side."

I thank him then turn to Brook. "Hey, wife."

"Hey," she smiles, but her eyes are still sad. "How are you feeling?"

That Feeling

"Can't complain, especially after taking a bullet to the chest. But more importantly, how are *you* feeling? Are you okay? Have you eaten?"

"I'm okay. Yes, I ate. Trent has brought me food and has been texting me nonstop."

"So what happened? I know we were looking for those poachers, and next thing I know, I'm down on my back."

Brook starts to speak, then stops, looking up to the ceiling to blink away tears. "Um, yeah, it was—" She can't fight the tears and they begin to fall. "I'm so sorry, I thought you were dead. I thought—"

"Shhh, come here."

She crawls back up into my bed and lies beside me.

I'm almost asleep again when I hear rustling in the hallway outside my room and my mother's voice. "He's awake? Is he talking?"

I crack one eye open just as my mom, dad, and Trent come into the room. My mom's hands are covering her mouth as she also begins to cry.

My mom and Brooklyn spend the next 30 minutes crying over what *could* have happened, while my dad and Trent try unsuccessfully to get them to stop fixating on that and focus on the fact that I'll be damn near perfect in a week.

"The sheriff been here yet?" my dad asks.

"No. What's he going to tell me?"

"Well, it was two known poachers. They've got a record for doing shit like this in Wyoming, Montana, and here."

"And they weren't locked up why?" I roll my eyes at the amount of shit poachers get away with around here. It's not just about hunting animals illegally, it's shit like this. People get killed over mistakes because they're hunting on land they have no business being on.

"They will be now, son, you can guarantee that. Sheriff tried saying they were arresting them for trespassing and some criminal negligence bullshit, but I drove to his office yesterday and we had a little chat."

My dad has that look in his eye—the one my entire family has come to know as the *don't fuck with the Slades unless you plan on going to war* look.

"Yeah? How'd that go?"

"I reminded him of how I know he's looked the other way a time or two over the years for some unsavory people, and how if anyone found out, his career would be over real quick."

I know my dad, and the last thing he likes doing is throwing his name and knowledge around to get what he wants, but I also know the thing he hates more than that is when someone hurts or attempts to hurt his family.

"So what's that mean? I don't want them bringing unfounded charges against someone just because I got shot."

"That's not what it is, son. These two men knew the dangers and they've had several chances. This isn't the only time they've shot at someone, but it's the first time they've hit someone. The sheriff is aware of that and he's making sure justice will be served here and they won't just be let off with a slap on the wrist. Not this time."

A bit of relief washes over me. "Thanks, Dad. I'm glad they're locked up for now. I have no doubt it wasn't some targeted attack on me—just reckless behavior—but still, this is how people end up dead."

"Doc said you're going home tomorrow?"

"Yup, looks like it."

He looks over at Brooklyn then back at me. "Don't be giving her a hard time with all this. You better take it easy and listen to what the doc tells you. Take it easy for a while, son."

I wave off his concern. "I'll be fine, Dad, don't worry. I'm sure I'll be back to work by the end of the week."

"The hell you will!" Brooklyn snaps, overhearing my comments.

Dad laughs and motions for Trent and Celeste to leave the room. "Come on, let's get going so he can rest. I have no doubt he's in good hands with this one." He pats Brooklyn on the shoulder as they leave.

That Feeling

I'VE BEEN HOME FOR A WEEK AND BROOKLYN'S BEEN ON MY ASS every damn day. I love that woman more than life itself, but man, can she be annoying.

"You know our kids won't be able to get away with shit," I laugh as she takes the shovel out of my hand. She replaces it with a glass of lemonade.

"If they're anything like you, I'm going to have my hands full. Come on, sit on the porch with me."

"Speaking of kids, you ready for the 12-week appointment tomorrow?" I place my hand over her belly.

"I am. I can't wait for the 16-week one when we find out the sex."

"How are you feeling about the wedding stuff?"

She glances over at me with an annoyed look. "No, we're not putting it off. Things are going really smoothly and everything is already booked."

I chuckle. "Okay, okay, I just know with work and the pregnancy and me getting myself in this situation, you've got a lot on your plate right now, baby. I just want you to be able to enjoy our special day and not feel so stressed about it."

"I know, but I'll be even more stressed if we push it off. I'll barely fit into my dress two months from now, and everyone will be pretty suspicious when it looks like I have a basketball under my dress."

"You think we'll be able to pull off the surprise?"

She looks down at her belly. "I think so. Just have to make sure I don't cave to the constant donut temptation around the office."

We both look off into the distance as Trent's SUV comes down the driveway.

"You two look like Mom and Dad sitting on the porch drinking lemonade," he says when he pulls up. "Brook, you sure you're ready to settle down and be this old man's wife?" He laughs and walks up the porch with a basket of muffins. "Milly sent these with me."

"Oh, what flavors?" Brooklyn grabs the basket and pops half a muffin in her mouth, moaning in pleasure. She looks over at me. "Don't say a word."

"Wasn't gonna," I laugh. She's been playing this constant game of trying to deny her pregnancy cravings, only to give in later then get mad at me for not stopping her.

"So, you apologized to Amelia yet?"

Trent looks at Brooklyn. "No, but I'm going to, in my own time."

She sighs. "Please don't wait till the wedding. We're going to tell everyone about the baby, so I want it to be a very stress-free, happy occasion. No fights."

"I know, I promise I won't . . . unless she starts it first."

"Trent!"

"I'm kidding." He enunciates the words with his hands raised in surrender. "She just gets on my fuckin' nerves."

"Sounds like somebody has a crush," I tease, and he makes a mocking face back at me.

"This isn't high school, Tyler. Adults don't have crushes. I genuinely can't stand the woman, because even if she is right and she bought back her family's name, she's just so entitled and uppity."

I look over at Brook, who's smiling at me. "Yeah, definitely a crush."

"You have no reason to be mad at her now, so you're just making up stuff. It's okay, though. I did the same thing with Brook."

"Hey!"

"Why do you think I made fun of your little tourist getup that first day we met?"

She smiles. "Yeah, you were pretty obvious."

"And you were pretty fucking hot."

"Hey, Tyler, can I talk to you for a minute?"

I glance over at Brook, who grabs the basket of muffins. "I'll take these inside so you two can talk."

I wait until she's indoors. "Don't even start, Trent. I already know what you're going to say."

He looks a little surprised. His shoulders drop. "It was my fault,

That Feeling

though, Tyler. We both know it, and pretending it wasn't doesn't fix anything. Just let me speak. 'I'm sorry' is all I want to say. I'm sorry I didn't listen to you and I'm sorry I put your life in danger."

I fold my hands in my lap and think for a minute. "Trent, you remember when we were just boys and we'd play down by that pond behind our house? I remember Dad telling us to stay off the ice because it was too early in the season. We did; we knew the danger. But then Ritchie Millner showed up with Phil and Charlie and started taunting us. I remember how red your little face got when they started talking shit about our parents, and you flew across that pond faster than a fox with his tail on fire."

I laugh, remembering the scene, and it makes Trent start laughing too.

"You fell through the ice that day and I had to run out there and save your ass. Nobody blamed you for that. Nobody blamed you after I also got soaked. You stood up for your family and it was justified. You were ready to put it all on the line to defend us. That's who you are, Trent. You're a protector. I don't expect you to change now."

"Thanks." He gives me a single nod and comes to sit in the chair beside me.

"These are the moments that matter. These are the memories I want to share with my child someday, and I have that opportunity because of you. Now, will you shut up about it and be my best man?"

"Of course."

"Good. Now, your first task as my best man is to come inside and be my human shield when I tell Brook I'm going back to work next week. I can't stand to sit around another second, and she's going to throw a fit."

Chapter 26

Brooklyn

Three Months Later . . .

"Oh, sweetie," my mom breaks down into her third crying fit of the day.

"Mom, stahhhhhppp," Mallory says as I fan my face, trying to keep myself from crying.

"It's just such a big day and I'm so happy for you, Brook, sweetie." She grabs my hands in hers. "He's a wonderful man. Your father is so impressed with him and your brother just thinks he's the coolest *dude.*" She says the last word attempting to sound hip, and it makes Mal and me laugh.

"Thank you, Mom. Do I look okay?" I smooth down the front of my dress, pausing briefly on my bump, which has finally started to show. I explained it away as stress weight between work and Tyler being shot.

"Your boobs look massive," Mallory says, eyeing them.

"Well, that comes with weight gain sometimes. Way to make me feel confident on my big day."

"No, in a good way! Trust me, I'd pay top dollar to have those."

The dress I chose has plenty of room. It has a very flowy, bohemian feel that matches the crown of wildflowers my veil is

That Feeling

attached to. Since our wedding is outdoors beneath a flower arch, and our reception is in a barn, I'm also wearing the first pair of real cowboy boots I've owned. They were a gift from Tyler, complete with our names engraved on the inside.

"Isn't it crazy that just 10 months ago, you showed up to this town not knowing a single person and taking on this amazing new job . . . and now you're marrying the love of your life and creating this new journey for yourself?"

"Mal, now you're going to make me cry."

"I'm just so proud of you, sis. I hope you know that. I know you were so unhappy back in Chicago for so long, and I'm just glad you're finally getting everything you deserve." She gives me a hug and hands me my bouquet. "Now, are you ready to go marry this dude and have sex with one man for the rest of your life?"

"What the hell?" I laugh. "Although, trust me, it's almost like a different person every few days with that man. He's got so many fun sides." I wriggle my eyebrows at her and she leans in.

"Is he still doing that thing with his belt?"

I blush and shush her. "Hey, Mom is right there!"

She giggles and we exit the room to make our way downstairs, where my dad is waiting to walk me down the aisle.

Tears stand on the brim of his eyes as he waits patiently for me at the bottom of the stairs. He holds out his arm and I loop mine through it as Mallory lines up with Trent to walk down the aisle.

"You ready for this, honey?" My dad squeezes my hand that's looped through his arm.

"More than ready."

I slowly exhale and drop my shoulders back as a huge grin spreads across my face.

"Okay, then. Let's do this," my dad says as I take the first step toward the rest of my life.

THE WEDDING IS STUNNING: SIMPLE, ELEGANT, EVERYTHING WE wanted.

We each wrote our own vows that we read aloud to each other. We both promised to choose each other through everything in life—that no matter what happened, our love would keep us strong during storms.

A few weeks back, when we had our 16-week ultrasound, we both decided that we wanted to be surprised with everyone else at the wedding reception regarding the sex. The doctor wrote it down and put it in an envelope that's been taunting us ever since.

We make our way into the barn for the reception, where strings of twinkling lights create a canopy above us and wildflower petals are scattered on the floor beneath us.

Tyler holds my hand tightly in his as he leads me out onto the dance floor. The soft sounds of Shania Twain's "From This Moment On" begin to play through the speakers.

"So, Mrs. Slade, how does it feel to be a married woman?" The deep timbre of Tyler's voice resonates through my body, which is pressed firmly up against him.

"It feels good, unreal. How am I married to you?"

He smiles. "What do you mean?"

"I was just supposed to flirt with you to get you to agree to being the model for the big campaign, and here I am, your pregnant wife."

"So you *did* have an agenda?" He howls with laughter as I tell him that my plan worked.

"Truthfully, I didn't. I mean, I was incredibly attracted to you. Who wouldn't be? The only time I tried to get you to do what I wanted was when I stopped by your house to show you my plan, and then you got all annoyed when I had you try on different outfits, so I said I'd get Trent to do it."

"You think I didn't know that?" He has that devilish grin on his face, the one that tells me if we weren't dancing in a room full of people we know right now, he'd have me bent in all sorts of different positions.

That Feeling

"Is that why you agreed to do it?"

He smooths my hair out of my face and brings us to a stop on the dance floor. "Sweetheart, I agreed to all of it just so I could spend time around you. That's the bottom line: I was head over heels the moment I saw those cherry red lips at the Fall Fest."

"Makes you think that maybe we could've saved ourselves some heartache and headaches if we'd just said that from day one."

"Nah, it was all part of the fun to chase after you. You ready to go see what's inside that envelope with everyone else?"

I rest my forehead against his chest for a brief moment. "Yes, but I want to savor these last few seconds of just the three of us in our tiny little bubble."

The moment Tyler was shot, it was like a light went off in my head. I realized just how much I wanted this baby—how excited I was to raise a little piece of Tyler and me together in this world. All those made-up scenarios and fears I was fixated on went out the window when my maternal instincts kicked in along with this insatiable desire to protect my family.

We walk back to our table and Tyler grabs the microphone as we take a seat.

"I know this is a little unconventional to have the groom give a toast at his own wedding, but I first want to thank everyone for being here and celebrating our love today. I also want to say that I never want to take any of you for granted. Mr. and Mrs. Dyer, you raised an incredible woman. She should be the blueprint. She's the epitome of kindness and selflessness, of love and goodness. So thank you for raising such an amazing woman and for allowing me to be her husband."

He raises his glass toward my parents and everyone claps.

"I do have one more thing, and this is something I want to tell my wife. It's something I've been dying to tell her, because while we made a promise that we were going to be surprised by this . . . babe, I opened the envelope that night we got home. I just didn't tell you."

Everyone is looking at each other in confusion. I feel my jaw go slack at Tyler's confession, and it makes me burst into laughter.

"What the hell are you talking about?" Ranger mumbles to Tyler's right.

"It's a girl," Tyler says, looking at me.

The room is dead silent.

"It's a—we're having a girl?" I repeat, and he nods.

"There's an envelope in the center of each table. Go ahead and open them up," Tyler says, referring to the sonogram picture we secretly placed at each table.

He drops the microphone and picks me up. I throw my arms around his neck and bury my face in him as I repeat over and over again, "We're having a girl!"

Chapter 27

Tyler

Three Months Later...

"What do you mean her water broke?" I climb down from the loft of the barn and motion toward Ranger.

"She said it broke, but she had a change of clothes in her office, so she just changed. She won't listen to me." Trent sounds exasperated on the other end of the phone.

"I'll be right there. And Trent? Don't tell anyone yet." I hang up the phone just as Ranger approaches.

"Looks like I'm having a daughter today, buddy." I smack his arm. "Need you to hold down the fort today. Tell Decker and Carl they can handle moving the cattle to pasture four with Teller."

"Holy shit, man. Congrats! Why are you so weirdly calm?"

"Because I'm actually about two seconds from losing my shit. That was Trent," I hold up my phone, "who said Brook's water broke but she refuses to go to the hospital."

"Go meet your little girl, man!"

I jog over to my truck and head to the office.

"I already know why you're here," Brook says as I approach her office. She has several folders in her hands that she's placing into different piles with her two assistants.

"Jackie, this one goes to you," she says, continuing to work.

"Any particular reason you decided, of all times, that now isn't the time to go to the hospital?" I take a seat in one of the chairs that's been pushed to the edge of the room, kicking one foot over my knee as I lean back.

"Because I called my doctor, and since I'm past 37 weeks and I've had no contractions yet, he said not to rush."

I shrug and fold my hands behind my head. "Okay."

She eyes me suspiciously. "Why are you being so nonchalant?"

"Well, if you're not worried and you're the one about to give birth, then why should I be worried?"

"Then why'd you come down here?" She pops her hand onto her hip.

"Trent called me all panicked. I knew you were fine, but he sounded like he needed to be talked off a ledge. I told him, 'She's fully prepared to push this baby out. She's not scared; she's got this. She will deliver that baby in record time then probably take a meeting.'" I watch as her eyes shift back and forth. She's begun to nervously chew on her bottom lip. "Anyway, I should get over to his office before he has a coronary."

I stand up and give her a quick peck before walking back toward the doorway.

"I can't do this!"

I pause and turn around. She's wringing her hands as Jackie and Nilsa look at her then at me.

"I'm freaking out, Tyler. I can't do this! What do I do?" Tears tumble down her cheeks, one falling onto the desk.

"Hey, hey, it's okay," I walk over to her and rub her back. This is exactly why I pretended like I was okay. I knew that if she saw me freaking out, she would pretend she was fine. I guess I learned a lesson from her about reverse psychology.

"Baby, it's okay to be scared. You should be—not because you

That Feeling

can't do this, but because this is new territory for both of us. I'm right here. You can squeeze my hand, kick me, punch me, call me every name in the damn book if you have to. I just want you to express yourself and feel everything right now, because holding it inside and pretending you're okay isn't going to help anyone."

She nods her head. I gently place my thumbs below her eyes and wipe away more tears.

"You really think I can do this?"

I look over at the two young women staring at us with big eyes. "You ladies think she's got this?"

"Are you kidding me? Brooklyn, you're the fiercest, strongest, most badass woman we know. You are going to kill it in that delivery room."

"Yeah," Nilsa echoes Jackie's praise, "you are incredible. You're a woman! There's nothing you can't do."

"Yeah, yeah, you're right," Brooklyn says as she hypes herself up. "I am a badass woman, and I'm going to go in there and give birth to our beautiful, healthy baby girl!"

"There's my girl," I smile. "Now let's go to the house and get your hospital bags then make our way over there."

"But I don't have contractions yet," she rubs her lower left belly, "just this annoying gas cramp."

I crook an eyebrow. "How long have you had that cramp?"

"On and off for the last hour or so. Shit, feels like it's getting a little worse. The weird thing, though, is my lower back is killing me today, more than normal." She winces. "Guess I shouldn't have had that spicy breakfast burrito."

"Okay, baby, I think you're in labor. Those are probably your early contractions."

"You think I wouldn't know a contraction?" She glares. "This is gas pain; it's different. I just fee—ah, see, it's passing." She doubles over a little.

"Baby."

She sniffs and starts to cry again.

"How did I not know? I feel so stupid." She grips my hand as we walk down the hall toward the elevator. "I read all the same books as you."

"Honey, you've been so focused on work and nesting that you just got distracted, so don't be upset. You've had so much going on with your body these last nine months, it's hard to know what's what."

"I'm such an idiot, though." She's fully crying now. "I didn't know I was pregnant, and I just now didn't realize I was in labor."

I can't help but laugh, which certainly doesn't help the situation, but it is comical. Her emotions are so tapped right now—she's barely been sleeping and she's constantly having weird pains and new bodily experiences.

"I know this isn't going to help right now, but in just a short while, it'll all be over and you'll be holding our little girl."

By the time we get to the house to grab her bags and get to the hospital, the contractions are closer and stronger.

"You say they're about eight minutes apart now?" Her doctor makes a note. "Brooklyn, you're going to be fine. Let's get you set up in a room so we can start monitoring the vitals for the two of you, okay?"

It pains me to see her hurting like this. She scrunches her face and grips the bed railing so tightly, her knuckles turn white. I'd give anything to bear the burden of this pain for her right now.

"That one was the worst yet," she says, gently lying back on the bed.

The nurses get her hooked up to all the machines and both she and baby's vitals are measuring strong.

"Okay, you're at almost seven centimeters, Brooklyn, over halfway there. If you want to get an epidural, now is the time."

I glance over at her and squeeze her hand. "What do you think, sweetheart?" We've discussed it several times over the last few months, and while she was always leaning toward getting one, the cons do scare her.

That Feeling

"Do I have to decide right now?" She looks nervously at the doctor.

"No, but we can't give it once you're fully dilated. I'll give you a few minutes and see how you handle these next few contractions."

She makes it through two more contractions, but when the third hits, she screams for the epidural. Twenty minutes later, she's smiling from ear to ear.

"I literally feel nothing; it's insane."

"How are you doing? Still nervous?"

She nods. "A little. I just want to meet her already."

"Me too, mama. Have we fully decided on the name then? No going back?"

"No going back."

We debated for a while about the name. I never had any baby names picked out in my head and just figured we'd settle on what sounded natural. Then Mallory sent me a text one night with a picture she'd taken from an old diary of Brooklyn's that she'd found. It had a list of baby names with two of them circled several times with the word "favorite" in pink highlighter. So I took the picture and framed it. I gave it to her as part of her push present, and the moment she saw it, she burst into tears. That's when we knew we had the name.

"Why don't you try to get a little nap in?"

She closes her eyes and attempts to sleep. I can't help but smile at her as I cherish these final moments of just us before our entire world changes.

"Okay, Brooklyn, let's check you again." She stirs awake as the doctor comes back in. "Looks like we are pretty much there. You ready to push?"

Panic flashes across her face briefly before her eyes catch mine and I mouth the words *badass woman*. She smiles and nods. "Yes, yes, I'm ready."

One hour and three minutes later, our baby girl is here. We're both sobbing as the doctor pulls her from Brooklyn, cleaning her off and placing her on Brooklyn's chest.

"She's here . . . she's really here," she whispers as we both stare in disbelief.

"She looks exactly like you, thank God," I laugh through tears as I stroke her tiny red hand.

My heart feels so full, like at any moment it might explode. I never understood when people said they didn't realize they could love somebody so much, but I do now.

After examining Brooklyn while she has skin-to-skin contact with our daughter, the doctor does a physical assessment of the baby before handing her back to us. I unbutton my shirt and place her against my chest. I close my eyes, breathing in this moment. I know the second we tell our family she's here, it's going to be a circus with all of them wanting to meet her and check on Brooklyn.

Finally, after everything, we have a few moments alone.

"Hey, daddy." Brooklyn stares at me in awe as I hold our baby. "How does it feel?"

"Unreal. I feel like I still can't believe you were pregnant, and now we have an entire baby." We both laugh, because it really does feel like only yesterday we were flirting and trying to convince ourselves that this was just a hookup. Or at least . . . I was.

"I assume Trent told everyone at work after we left for the hospital?" she asks.

"Actually, I threatened to kill him if he did. And who knows if Ranger or Jackie or Nilsa said anything. I haven't checked my phone."

I place her back in Brooklyn's arms and pull my phone out. I have 11 texts and six missed calls from Trent. I open my camera and take a photo of Brooklyn holding her and send it to Trent.

Me: *You can sound the alarm now. Baby girl is here.*

"Can you send it to my family too? I know they're going to want to catch the next flight, but I'll call them tomorrow and convince them to wait a few weeks so I can breathe."

That Feeling

Not even 20 minutes after I hit send, the Slade brood descends on the hospital.

"Hey, guys, please just be very quiet and calm. Brooklyn is exhausted, so try not to stay too long in there. Only a few at a time, okay?"

"You sure you don't want to present her *Lion King*-style? You know, Pride Rock?" Trent pretends to hold a baby up over his head and Logan and Decker burst into laughter.

"Please don't reproduce," I say as he follows me down the hallway with my parents.

We open the door and my mom instantly bursts into tears.

"Mom, Dad, Trent . . . meet Cecilia Roxanne Slade."

Chapter 28

Brooklyn

I can't believe our baby girl is almost nine weeks old already. I watch my mom coo at her as she gently rocks her back and forth.

"She looks just like you when you were a baby, it's unreal." She looks up at me, tears in her eyes.

"That's what Dad said earlier. He said the only difference is I was already trying to boss everyone around while she's so peaceful."

Mom chuckles, "Yeah, that sounds about right. She must get that from her daddy, huh?"

She must. Tyler is the calming force in our lives—my rock when I freak out and let stress get the best of me.

"Where'd they run off to?" Mallory asks as she walks up behind me and wraps her arms around my shoulders.

"Silas and Dad wanted to go horseback riding one last time before you guys leave."

"I don't want to leave," Mallory says as she tightens her squeeze.

I lean my head against her. "I don't want you to leave either." I swallow, not wanting her to see me cry, because it will only turn into a chain reaction of her crying, my mother crying, and most likely, Cecilia will start crying.

That Feeling

"Oh, good news!" I say, changing the subject. "The sheriff called this morning and those two poachers are facing felony charges: second-degree attempted murder. Tyler said he was going to tell Dad and Silas on their ride this morning. I know they've both been worried about it."

"And you're sure they acted alone?" My mom still looks worried.

"Yes. I mean, obviously, the police are investigating further, but these guys have a history of poaching and causing problems because of it. They've never been associated with any other groups or criminals. But the bottom line is, they're both going to go away for a few years at least."

A look of relief washes over my mom's face. I've had several sleepless nights since the shooting, but Tyler and I both talked to a therapist to help us process things, and the sheriff has kept us very informed about the investigation. We're both ready to put it behind us.

My family has been amazing during their visit these last two weeks. My parents have spent every spare second soaking up little moments with their granddaughter while Silas and Mallory have kept me laughing so hard, I've almost peed myself a dozen times. Mallory has only been here for four days because of her residency, but she'll be back out soon. Silas' family came out for the first few days, but had to head back so the girls could get ready to start school soon.

"Mom," I walk over to her and crouch down at her feet, "thank you so much for everything. I've only been a mom for two months and it feels like I've already been so overwhelmed, and at times, I feel like I can't do it. I hate that it took me becoming a mom to realize just how much work you put into us and how much you sacrificed."

"Sweetie, it's all worth it, trust me. I look at you girls and Silas and I'm just blown away and so damn proud of my kids that I can barely contain it sometimes. Your father and I couldn't have asked for better kids."

"I don't know how you guys did it at 19 with Silas. I feel like even in my late 20s, I'm still not equipped," I laugh.

"Oh, trust me, there were times when your father and I felt like we were drowning, but at the end of the day, we had each other. You have such an amazing support system here with Tyler and his family, and the love that man has for this little girl . . ." She tears up again. "I just see his entire world melt when he looks at her."

By the time the men are back, all three of us are a blubbering mess fawning over Cecilia.

"Everything okay in here?" Tyler bends down and kisses the top of my head as I wipe my face with the back of my hand.

"Yes, just happy tears. You guys have a good ride?"

"Oh my God, you're not wearing those on the flight, are you?" Mallory gives my dad and Silas a look.

"Why not? Tyler gave them to us."

I turn around to see my dad and Silas both wearing cowboy hats along with cowboy boots. "We look official now." Dad slaps Silas' shoulder and they both proudly model their new outfits.

"I think they look pretty damn good myself." Tyler tips his hat.

"*You* look really damn good because you're a legit cowboy, but these two will look like dorks getting off a flight in Chicago."

"Mallory, leave your father and brother alone. I think they look handsome," my mom says as she gently places Cecilia into my arms. "Now, we have to get going to catch our flight."

"Truck's already loaded," Tyler says, thumbing over his shoulder. "You going to be okay here alone while I drive them?"

I nod and say my goodbyes to my family. I give my dad a final hug. "And don't listen to Mal. You two do look very handsome in your boots and hats."

They file out of the nursery to head outside. Tyler stays behind and leans down, planting a soft but tempting kiss on my lips.

"They certainly don't look as good as you did, *little miss tourist.*"

Tyler and I haven't had sex since Cecilia was born. The doctor actually cleared me over two weeks ago, but Tyler's been resistant. While I appreciate that he's scared it's *too soon* and he doesn't want

That Feeling

to hurt me, I'm about 10 seconds away from becoming a feral animal and tearing off his clothes.

Not only are the postpartum hormones driving me crazy, but I swear he's gone out of his way to be extra sexy lately. Watching him wash bottles, clean my breast pump, change diapers . . . it's like a new version of sexy has entered my world.

I feed Cecilia and put her down for a nap. I check the time and figure Tyler will be back in about 30 minutes. I sprint to our bedroom and take a quick shower, shaving every inch of my body and slathering myself with lotion.

I root around in my closet, pulling out the little jean shorts and flannel shirt I was wearing the first day I met Tyler.

"Please fit," I say as I tug the shorts up my thighs. I jump up and down, shimmying my hips back and forth until I squeeze them on. They can't button, so I fold down the top. I don't bother with a bra, and I leave the bottom three buttons of the shirt undone and pull them up, tying them in a knot right under my breasts. My body is certainly not back to what it was before pregnancy, but I'm not letting that stop me.

I find the boots and hat and put them on, looking myself over in the mirror. My gaze drops down to my now-soft belly and I run my hand over it. My brain immediately wants to overanalyze things, to focus on the fact that I don't look like I used to anymore, but I push those thoughts aside.

"Something's missing—oh!" I go to the bathroom and pull out the red lipstick I wore. I flip my head over and spray my hair with dry shampoo to give it some oomph since I didn't wash it.

The front door opens and I hear Tyler's footsteps slowly coming up the stairs. I let out a nervous breath and run to the closet to grab one more thing. I place it on the bed then casually lean against the doorway of the bathroom as Tyler enters the room.

"Hey baby, I—holy fuck." His eyes drag down my body before reaching down to adjust himself in his jeans. "Goddamn, you look good." He walks over to me, his hands settling on my hips as he leans in and presses his lips to my neck.

"So do you," I murmur, my fingers lacing through his hair as I pull him closer.

"You need something, sweetheart?" His voice is a low rumble in my ear as his hands slide up my body to my breasts.

"Mm-hmm," I moan.

"Tell me," he says as he pinches my nipples softly through my shirt.

"Look on the bed."

He pulls his head back and turns around, his gaze falling to the belt I've placed on it.

"You sure you're ready for that?"

I nod and step around him, my hand fisting his shirt as I lead him toward the bed.

"I'm done asking nicely, Tyler." I sit on the edge of the bed and lean back on my hands. "I'm *telling* this time."

His eyes darken as he rubs the scruff on his chin. He slowly nods once as he leans forward and grabs the belt. He wraps it slowly around his hand, the tension continuing to build between us.

He steps closer to me, his belt buckle at eye level. Finally, he reaches down, hooking his finger under my chin and forcing me to look up at him.

"Remember what I said about who's in charge in the bedroom?"

I drag my teeth across my bottom lip and shrug. "I guess I forgot."

"Well then, looks like I need to give you a reminder so you don't forget again."

I stand up and run my hand softly down his chest.

"Undress me," he demands.

I obey immediately. I unbutton his shirt and pull it open to press my palms flat against his taut, warm skin. My eyes go to the scar on his upper left chest and shoulder area, my fingers softly running over the rough edge of the scars. My eyes go to his.

"Don't go there," he whispers, knowing that my mind has

That Feeling

instantly started to spin around what life would've been like if he hadn't made it. "Not right now."

He grabs my hands, bringing my attention back to the moment, and loops the belt tightly around my wrists.

"It's been a while since you've ridden a bull, baby. Think you can last the full eight seconds?"

I smile. "What do I get if I win?"

He grabs my hair and kisses me, shoving his tongue in my mouth and swirling it with mine. It leaves me breathless when he pulls back and presses his forehead against mine.

"What do you want, baby?"

"The moment I met you, I already won."

Tyler spends the next hour worshipping my body. It's not the same roughness he's displayed in the past. Now it's more tender—passionate.

We've never had a problem expressing ourselves physically with each other. And honestly, I never thought it could get better between us, but every day it feels like we grow closer, stronger, and more in love with each other. I felt so lost for so long and now I feel like I finally have it all.

That Look SNEAK PEEK

COMING SOON!

Get ready to dive into the steamy, small town story of Trent Slade and Amelia Blanc as they try to navigate when hate turns to scorching hot love.

Keep reading for a little tast of what's to come...

Chapter 1

Trent

Amelia Blanc.

Sophisticated, stunning, successful, comes from a prominent family—the kind of woman men fight wars over.

But that's not all she is. She's sexy and tempting, a delicate flower who makes me want to forget being a gentleman and show her how a real man could make her feel.

She wants it. I can see it in the way she holds herself so professionally. The uptight facade that's just begging to be unraveled. The way her eyes search mine like she's begging me to read her mind—to do all the things to her that she's too scared to admit she wants.

She's also . . . the bane of my fucking existence and a pain in my ass.

I lean against the back wall of the tasting room in her winery as I watch her float around the room, stopping at each table to welcome guests personally with a genuine smile. Her dress lies softly against her long, lean body, and I can't help but take a peek at the way it accentuates her subtle curves—the curves I haven't stopped fantasizing about since the moment I saw her at my brother Tyler's engagement party.

Amelia stands out in small-town Colorado, no way around it. It's not that she's unapproachable or over the top, she's the exact opposite—subtle and down to earth. The kind of woman who casually mentions summers on the French Riviera but then downplays it so you don't feel like you're missing out.

I roll my eyes as the couple she's speaking to bursts into laughter at whatever she just said.

They can't all possibly buy this act.

All three of them toss their heads back dramatically, really laying it on thick.

Okay, now I know they're full of shit. Nobody is that funny.

Not only is she knock-you-on-your-ass beautiful, but she's gracious. Even when I drunkenly raised my voice at her several months back at my brother's engagement party, she remained calm and poised. Which is why I'm here now: to apologize and do penance for my outburst.

She lifts her head as she approaches another table near me, her eyes catching mine. We stay locked in on each other for several seconds before she reaches out her hand to touch the shoulder of an older white-haired woman at the table.

"Bonjour, Madame Aubert. C'est tellement agréable de vous revoir."

Of course she speaks French.

I cross my arms over my chest a little tighter. Why does this damn woman have to get under my skin so much? Yes, she's beautiful. Everyone can see that by looking at her . . . but why the fuck does she have to be perfect too?

Maybe she secretly hates kittens or puppies or something.

I know that if my brother Tyler were here right now and could hear my thoughts, he'd tell me it's because I have a *crush* on her. What am I, 12?

That old adage about boys being mean to girls they like is a bunch of horseshit, and I'm not being mean to her, I'm simply keeping my guard up because I don't trust her or her family.

That Feeling

"Is there a reason you're leering at me and my customers from the back of the room?"

Amelia's question interrupts my thoughts and I turn to face her, completely unaware that she'd snuck up beside me.

"I wasn't leering, tha—" I stop myself from making some rude-ass remark back and plaster on a big smile, reminding myself why I came here. "You have a minute?"

She motions toward a back door that she pushes open and we both step through to a deck that's lit by strings of lights. A few people are sitting at a table in the far corner, so we move to the other corner.

"So, what can I do for you, Mr. Slade? Would you like a glass of wine?" She smiles sweetly at me, which only annoys me further.

"'Mr. Slade'?" I chuckle. I can think of a few positions I'd like to get her in and have her call me that. "No, no wine for me. I'm here because I owe you an apology."

"An apology for . . . ?" She plays coy, crooking an eyebrow upward as she brings her hand to her chest. She knows damn well what for; she just wants me to say it.

"For raising my voice at you at the engagement party a few months back."

"Oh, you mean almost nine months ago, when you accused me and my family of being involved in illegal activities and running dozens of businesses out of town?"

I let out an exasperated sigh and remind myself to keep my cool. "Yeah, that."

"If you think I care or need an apology about you raising your voice to me, I don't. What you do owe me is an apology for your baseless and hurtful accusations."

"Hey, if the shoe fits." I shrug, flashing my boyish grin.

"But it doesn't fit and you know that. My family sold our winery years ago, and the company that took it over did those things. Given your background, you know just as well as I do that once a company's sold, you have no say or rights. So why was it my family's fault? My parents believed they were doing the right thing."

"Look, I don't know anything about all that. I can still have my opinion about your family selling out the business, but you're right, I shouldn't have made those accusations and I'm sorry."

"So why now, Trent? What made you decide I deserve an apology after all this time? Let me guess, your family is breathing down your neck about it? Or did you just finally come to the conclusion out of the goodness of your nonexistent heart?" She slowly lifts a finger as she speaks and pokes me in the chest.

"Dammit, woman." I throw my hands in the air then take a deep breath to calm myself. "I came to apologize and I mean it. Why the hell can't you take it so we can move on?"

She stares at me, her eyes narrowing, when someone pops their head out the nearby door. She drops her finger from my chest, where it feels like it's about to burn through my shirt.

"Sorry to interrupt, Miss Blanc, but there's a Mr. Gregory inside asking for you."

She turns her head to face the young waiter, her hair following the movement and sending her floral perfume straight to my nostrils and a bolt of electricity straight to my dick.

"I'll be right in, Nick, thank you." She smiles at him then turns back to face me. I'm completely distracted by the exposed skin of her shoulder as the shawl she's wrapped around herself slips down.

When the fuck did she get such lickable skin? Fuck, shit, no!

I quickly avert my gaze back to her face when I notice a slight pink blush on her cheeks that wasn't there before.

"You're right, Trent. I accept your apology and let's just agree to move on from this and put it behind us." She smiles and I wait for a *but,* but it never comes.

"Just like that?" I ask suspiciously.

"Just like that." She smiles wider and extends her delicate hand toward me. "Truce?"

I slowly extend my hand toward hers, clasping it in my own. Her skin is warm and soft and I have the sudden urge to pull her toward

That Feeling

me and taste her full, plump lips. I drop her hand like it's burned me, jerking my own back and shoving it in my pocket.

"You okay?" she questions.

"Great."

"Okay, well, I really should get inside. Mr. Gregory is waiting for me," she says as if I have any clue who this man is . . . or care.

"Better not keep Mr. Gregory waiting any longer." I hate the way the words sound on my tongue, like I'm weirdly jealous or spiteful of someone I've never met and have no actual idea why they're asking for her.

"Have a good night, Mr. Slade." Her words are breathy as she spins on her heel and heads back into the building just as she drops the shawl completely, giving me a glimpse of her sexy back.

I shake my head and walk down the deck stairs and around the building toward my truck, a laugh erupting from my chest as I swing the driver's side door open and slide behind the wheel. I flip on the radio just as Luke Bryan's "One Margarita" starts and I sing along, relieved to have finally put this thing with Amelia Blanc to rest.

With any luck, once her winery in Fort Collins is running smoothly, she'll haul her fancy—albeit tight—little ass back to California where she belongs.

***

"Morning, Charlotte." I place my assistant's favorite pastry on her desk and duck into my office before she can hand it back to me. We play this same game every Monday morning.

"Mr. Slade are you trying to get me in trouble with my doctor?" She holds out the Danish toward me. "He told me no more sweets. Gotta bring my cholesterol down."

"One a week won't hurt you, Charlotte. Besides, they had your favorite today: blackberry." Her eyes fall from mine down to the pastry and she brings it to her nose to smell it. "You can always take it home to Bill if you really don't want it."

"Well, maybe a bite or two won't hurt." She giggles and winks at me before heading back to her desk.

Charlotte has worked for Slade Brewing for over two decades now, and so has her husband, Bill. He's one of the chief brewmasters, and we're all dreading the day he finally retires.

Work has been stressful, but in a good way. Since bringing on Brooklyn Dyer—my now sister-in-law—to take over our social media, our numbers have increased quarter over quarter for a year straight.

Our most recent product launch, Slade Seltzers, has been an even bigger hit than any of our seasonal beers or small-batch whiskey. It's all thanks in large part to Brooklyn, who spearheaded a kick-ass social media campaign to not only introduce the seltzers but also get our beer on tap into some of the biggest sports arenas around the country.

I open my bottom drawer to look for the mini bottle of champagne Brooklyn gave me when we finished last year with the highest-posted revenue Slade has ever seen, but something else catches my eye. I reach for the folder and pull it out, placing it on my desk without opening it.

Slade Wines.

This has been my pipe dream for a while now, the legacy I hope to leave with Slade Brewing. My great-grandfather had only two beers when he started this company, and his son, my grandfather, introduced a dozen-plus more beer styles that became our staple line. My dad, Drake Slade, brought our whiskey line to life, and I want to leave a legacy behind now that I'm CEO.

But that's where Amelia Blanc comes in. The Blanc family has been one of the premier winemakers in the world for three decades. When her family finally sold their business over five years ago and her parents retired back to France, the business faced problems.

Treymore Food and Beverage was a long-standing company for decades before they sold out as well. When they did, they turned from small family-owned businesses to major corporations that cut quality, raised prices, and padded their bottom line so they could fight any legal issues that came their way.

They've since claimed bankruptcy, and according to Amelia, she spent every last dime of her family money to buy back Blanc Wines,

That Feeling

and she's on a mission to reestablish them as they once were. I've got no problem with that. Coming from a generational family business, I get it, but I say they should keep their wine in California and the Pacific Northwest, because Colorado is Slade country.

I stare at the folder. Every time I bring up the idea of launching a wine brand under the Slade umbrella, I'm practically laughed out of the boardroom. So I gave up on the dream for a while, and now it just feels like a slap in the face that this ethereal woman—who can do no wrong in everyone else's eyes—can come along and rain all over my parade.

"You okay, bro?" I look up and see my older brother, Tyler, standing in my doorway. "Looks like you're arguing with yourself."

"Nah, I'm good," I say, waving away his concern as he steps inside and takes a seat across from my desk.

Even though Tyler is the oldest in the Slade family, and was expected to take over Slade Brewing as CEO, he passed it off to me in favor of devoting his time to being a rancher. He's still an active board member, and now that his wife works for the company, he's here at the office more than usual. Growing up, he always loved hanging with the cowboys—we both did, actually—but numbers and boardrooms were never his dream like they were mine. Still, you can't take the mountain life out of me. I'll always be a cowboy at heart and never plan to leave this place.

"Came in a little early for the meeting Dad set up, and figured I'd stop in and see how things are going with you." He crosses his foot over his knee and picks at a loose string on his jeans.

"Why? What are you really worried about?"

"Hmm? Nothing," he frowns, "just curious if, uh, you and Amelia ever made up?"

"Made up? It's not like we were fighting this whole time; I just said some shitty things. But yeah, I apologized to her on Friday night, actually. What made you ask?"

He shrugs again and I'm starting to pick up on the fact that there's something he's not telling me.

"Brooklyn ask you to ask me?"

"No. I mean, she asks now and then, but mostly I think it's because she's friends with Amelia and she's always worried that if she invites her to something at our house and you show up, there will be drama."

"Drama? Seriously? Are we in high school or something? It was one time that I said something."

He holds up his hands. "Hey, you asked and I answered." He lets out a dramatic yawn and rubs his eyes.

"Baby keeping you up?" I ask. Tyler and Brooklyn recently welcomed their first daughter, Cecilia, to the family. She's a perfect little ball of chunky baby rolls.

"You think you're ready for the sleepless nights, but holy shit. You know I almost fell asleep on my horse the other day?" We both laugh. "Ranger and Decker have both had to tell me at times to go take a nap, because I'm not making any sense out in the pastures." He drags his hands down over his face and lets them fall to his lap.

"You boys coming?" Our dad, Drake, pokes his head in my office briefly before making a circle motion with his fingers as if to say, *let's move it*. That's my dad: gruff, few words, and straight to the point.

We stand and follow behind him until we reach the main conference room.

"Hey, Uncle Colton, didn't realize you were going to be here." I walk over and hug my uncle.

"Got the call from your dad with a meeting date and no question about availability, which means *be there, no excuses*." He laughs.

"Yeah, sounds like Dad," I laugh as I take a seat next to him.

"All right, let's get down to business," Dad says, tugging on his belt. He's still wearing the same cowboy hat, belt, and boots he's worn for the past 20-odd years. He's finally getting to that age where I'm starting to notice the physical changes in him. Growing up, my dad was my hero. He's tall and commanding, always in control and knowing exactly what to do in any situation. He's led our family

That Feeling

through hell and back over the years, and I can't imagine where we'd all be without him.

"You both know why I've called this meeting. This isn't an official board meeting, but that will follow soon enough."

I furrow my brows and look from Uncle Colton to Tyler, who quickly averts his gaze from mine. *What the fuck is going on here?*

"We've had a tremendous year—best we've ever had—and from the way things are going, we fully expect to outperform ourselves in the coming year. With that being said, we have an opportunity right now to expand Slade Brewing International in a new direction."

My spine stiffens and I feel my teeth clench together. I feel like I've been completely left in the dark about whatever the hell is going on right now and I don't like it.

"Blanc Wineries—"

"Oh, for fuck's sake!" I shout. "You gotta be kidding me!" I can't hide my anger.

"Something you want to share, Trent?" My dad looks at me, his words clipped.

"You already know the issue I have with Amelia Blanc and that I don't trust that woman."

"That sounds like a personal problem that you can address outside these walls of business, Trent. If you have an issue with their ethics, business practices, or financials, then let's talk about it. But if you've got your panties in a twist over some interpersonal conflict you had with her, deal with it on your own time."

Tyler chuckles, which gets Uncle Colton going. I sit back and roll my eyes, feeling like I'm 17 again, when I got caught sneaking into the brewery warehouse stealing beers.

"As I was saying, Blanc Wineries is a very established brand, and Amelia recently became the owner after using all her personal capital to buy it back. She came to me a few months ago with a proposition, and it's one I think can be profitable for both companies.

"Fine, I'll hear you out." I raise my hands in defeat and stand up to walk over to the coffee station in the corner of the room.

"That's great, son, but it's not me you're going to hear out. It's Amelia."

I spin around so fast that I slosh the freshly poured coffee out of the mug in my hand just as the conference room door opens and in she walks.

Amelia Fucking Blanc with a perfectly pearly-white smile plastered on her perfect face that says: *I win.*

Chapter 2

Amelia

"Good morning gentlemen. Thank you for having me."

"Morning." Drake tips his hat toward me. "My wife, Celeste, will be here any second," he says, staring down at his phone. "She had an appointment earlier this morning."

I nod and a second later, the door swings open and in walks Celeste Slade: blonde, with a touch of silver at her temples and a perfectly tailored Chanel tweed suit and nude pumps. From what I can gather, she's been the outside counsel for Slade Brewing for a long time—at least longer than she's been married to Drake, since that's apparently how they met.

"Apologies for my tardiness," she says politely with a sweet smile as she extends her hand to me from across the table.

The excessive jostling of a chair grabs my attention and I turn to watch as Trent pulls his chair out a little more forcefully than necessary. He glares at me as he grips the coffee cup in his hand and lets his body drop down into the chair.

"I won't be going over the full project today like I will in the board meeting," I say, "but I wanted to give each of you a full breakdown of the data and analytics that went into my research and presentation. In the folders I'm handing out, you'll find more than enough graphs and reports that will back up everything I mention today." I reach into my bag and pull out the reports I've had collated and bound for each member of today's meeting. I pass them out and then turn to Drake. "Well, looks like we're all here. Shall I begin?"

Drake nods and I turn to the screen in front of me where my presentation slides are displayed. This shorter presentation outlines how beneficial it could be to marry the Slade customers and the Blanc customers with a series of three different wines.

"I honestly don't see how this will benefit Slade. It only seems like it would benefit Blanc since we have a huge customer base." Trent crosses his arms over his chest, the veins on his exposed forearms bulging against the strain of his too-tight Oxford shirt sleeves.

"As I mentioned, in the folder in front of you, there are several graphs that break down the Blanc customer base." I smile and point to the untouched report that is still sitting in front of him. "Is there a specific fact or data point you're referring to, or just a general, unresearched observation?"

His jaw tics at my question and he lets out an audible puff of air. If he thinks he can get to me by trying to embarrass me or spout off nonfactual bullshit, he has another thing coming.

"As I was saying, this venture will not only be mutually beneficial in the immediate future, but long term, we can build an ongoing relationship that will introduce an entirely new customer base to each other's businesses."

I don't pride myself on being bitchy or petty—hell, I feel like as a woman in the business world, I have to play twice as nice just to be taken seriously, but Trent Slade has made it abundantly clear that he not only can't stand me and my family, but he also doesn't trust us and won't give me the benefit of the doubt, even when facts and data are on my side.

The funny thing is, I never once thought about Slade Brewing as *competition*. My parents never did either. We're both family-owned

That Feeling

businesses in the beverage industry, but we've never had any product crossover.

I finish my presentation and answer a few questions.

"Thanks again for this," Drake says, holding up the folder, "we'll be in touch about the board meeting."

"Thank you, sir." I shake everyone's hand except Trent's. He sulks silently in the corner of the room for a moment before brushing past me out of the room.

I think about how Trent stood against the back wall of the winery the other night, staring at me. At first, it was evident that he was glaring at me, given the way his eyes narrowed, but I swear, for a brief moment, it almost felt like he was checking me out. And when we went out to the back deck, the way his eyes couldn't stay focused on mine, I'd swear there was something—a spark or a moment between us.

I laugh to myself as I pack up the rest of my things and slide my bag over my shoulder. It wouldn't be the first time thoughts about Trent Slade swirled through my brain, leaving me confused and a little flustered. The way his eyes sparkle when he's smiling and that big, loud laugh he can't seem to control . . . a flutter runs through my belly as I make my way toward the elevator and out to the parking lot.

I reach for the handle of my car door, telling myself that it's just been too long since I've been with a man and that's my problem. After 11 long months of trying to get over my ex-fiancé, I'm just now back in the dating pool, and so far, I've been pretty lucky considering my first post-breakup date was with Jack Gregory, a real estate developer I met a few weeks ago.

"That was really fucking shady to go behind my back and talk to my father—even for you."

I spin around to see that Trent has followed me to my car. He holds his hand up over his brow against the morning sun.

"How was it shady? He's the majority shareholder of Slade Brewing."

"And I'm the CEO," he snaps back. "You could have come to me about this venture, but you didn't. Why?" He steps closer to me.

"Seriously? Because you screamed at me in front of dozens of people and accused my family of horrible things, then when you were informed that your accusations were inaccurate at that same event, you still stood by your defamatory remarks. Even this weekend, when you came to apologize, you downplayed it and said you were apologizing for raising your voice at me. As if I need an apology for that. I'm a grown, professional woman, Trent. I can handle myself and my emotions, but you clearly can't."

"This is why you were so quick to accept my apology, wasn't it?" He takes another step toward me and I step back, hitting my car. "Because you knew you were coming in here today to fuck up my world and you wanted to have the last laugh. Is this your version of revenge?"

I can't help but laugh at how ridiculous his accusations are. "You really think highly of yourself, don't you? You think I've been so consumed by your emotional outburst that I created an elaborate business scheme to . . . what? Get back at you?"

"No, not exactly, but I think you're deriving joy out of going behind my back and making me look like a fool in there."

"Why can't you believe that this actually has nothing to do with you, your accusations against me, or revenge, and realize it's completely about business, money, and the fact I now single-handedly own Blanc Wineries? I know this is probably hard for you to believe, but not everything is about you." I can feel tension building in my chest and I rub my temples to release it.

"Did you mean it when you said you accepted my apology the other night?"

"Yes."

"How can I believe you after what you pulled today?"

"Because believe it or not, Trent, I don't hold on to the past. I forgave you a long time ago, even when you didn't ask me to. Anger and hatred don't do anyone any good. You just let me live rent-free in

That Feeling

your head because you hold on to so much bitterness toward me. Meanwhile, I don't think about you at all."

I shrug nonchalantly but my throat constricts tightly as I swallow down the nervous lump.

"That right?" He drags his hand slowly over his scruffy jaw. It stands out against how clean-cut the rest of him looks in his tailored suit.

"Yes, that's right." I stiffen my spine, doubling down on my statement even though I'm so full of shit.

Do I ever think about you? Yes. When, you ask? Oh, when I'm lying in bed at night trying to fall asleep, but I'm so hot and bothered, I can't help but touch myself to the thought of you between my thighs.

"You never have a random thought creep in about me? Maybe wondering if I ever think about you?" His eyes stare into mine and a slow warmth begins to spread through my body. I pray it doesn't show on my cheeks as I feel them flush with embarrassment at the thought.

"I think you do. I think you think about me an awful lot, actually." He flashes me his signature flirty grin with a throat chuckle, but I narrow my gaze.

"What game are you playing here, Trent? Because I'm not interested."

"Game? What makes you think I'm playing any game, sweetheart?" He places his hand on the roof of my car and leans in.

I roll my eyes. "That right there . . . I'm not your sweetheart. I'm your business partner. It's like you're just trying to get a rise out of me for your sick pleasure."

"*Partner?*" He laughs again. "If anything, I'm your boss on this project. In fact, I'd highly suggest we go back to you calling me 'Mr. Slade.' Has a nice ring to it, doesn't it?" He winks at me.

I tilt my chin up to look at him as he towers over me, attempting to assert my confidence. He's closed the distance between us. In fact, he's so close that I can smell his spicy cologne and hear the sound of his whiskers against his hand as he laughs, dragging it slowly over his jaw.

I know exactly what you're doing, you sneaky bastard, and two can play that game.

"Whatever you want, *Mr. Slade*." I say the words slowly and deliberately, but I can't hide the mocking tone in my voice.

"So this is how it's gonna be then?"

"Doesn't have to be."

He crooks an eyebrow at me. "Meaning?"

"Meaning we can put this all behind us right now . . . and not like you apologized the other night then bit my head off today. I mean *really* put it in the past and move on."

"And then what? We're friends?"

"No, we don't have to be friends. We can simply be professionals who work together and treat each other with respect and trust." I emphasize the last word since I know he struggles with the idea of trusting me.

"Trust, huh?"

"What is that you think I plan to do? Take over your family's billion-dollar brewery?" I huff in exasperation. "That's complete insanity, Trent. All I want is to re-establish my family winery as a legitimate, reputable brand like it once was, so the next time I go to France to visit my parents, I can tell them they don't have to be ashamed of our last name anymore."

"You wanna know what I think?"

"No, but I have no doubt you're going to tell me anyway." I can't hide my frustration and it pisses me off even further that I've let him get under my skin.

"I think you need me. You need my family business and that pisses you the hell off because you want to hate me."

I roll my eyes, tired of this narrative already.

"Well, you know what I think, Mr. Slade? I think you're an arrogant, entitled rich boy who is intimated by powerful women. You can't stand the fact that I *don't* need your family money or business.

That Feeling

Blanc Wines was successful long before this business deal arose, and you know that. I think it eats at you that I don't need *you*." I say the last part slowly, making deliberate eye contact with him.

His eyes study mine, then they drop down to my lips as my tongue darts out to wet them. I swear it feels like he's inching closer. I can feel the heat radiating off his body, but just as quickly, he looks away.

"You have a deal," he says, holding his hand out toward mine. He's so close, the shake is a little awkward, but we manage. Not what I was expecting, but I'll take it. Maybe that's what we needed in this situation: to both just say our piece about each other—full transparency and move past it ... at least, that's what I'm hoping this is.

"See, that wasn't so hard, was it?" I give him a genuine smile as I release his hand, but he doesn't back away.

"I'm not saying I trust you yet, but I'll work on it and I'm open to it."

"That's a start," I reply as we stand chest-to-chest, almost touching. It feels weird and intimate at the same time. "I should get going."

He still doesn't move. "You going to move closer now that you'll be in my office regularly?"

"Hadn't planned on it, no. Fort Collins is only a 40-minute drive, and I don't foresee myself being in your office very often."

"What are you doing tonight? Want to grab dinner?"

His question takes me by surprise. "Uh, I have plans, actually, but I assume I'll be back in the office later this week for the board meeting. We can discuss things then?" I assume he meant a business dinner, because there's no way in hell Trent Slade is asking me on a date ... *right?*

He nods and takes a step to the side to reach around me and open my car door. I look at him, a little surprised as he places his other hand against my elbow and ushers me into my car.

"Thank you," he says, and I look at him questioningly.

"For?"

"Your patience and ... forgiveness."

I smile, even though it almost seems painful for him to say the words.

"You're welcome." We stare at each other again for a brief second. "Why are you being nice to me all of a sudden?"

"Nice? Who says I'm bein' nice?" He places his large hands on the open windowsill of my car and leans forward a little.

"So this is a game to you then? Just play nice enough so I let my guard down then you—"

"Then I what?" He laughs, waiting for me to finish the statement, but I don't. "I simply thanked you for accepting my apology is all. I can still be wrong in how I handled things with you in the past, but right about this deal not being a good idea. Either way, no reason for us to have bad blood between us." He winks at me and pats the edge of my car.

"Careful, Mr. Slade," I say teasingly, "I might get the wrong idea if you start playing nice."

He gives me a wicked grin. "I'd love to know what the wrong idea is in *your* head."

"That maybe underneath all that false bravado there's a soft spot." I blush. "Why, what did you think I meant?"

He laughs and shakes his head as he grips the edge of my car door and leans down till his face is near mine. "Now that's a conversation for another time, but trust me, it has nothing to do with being nice or soft."

I swallow down a huge lump and grip the steering wheel in my hands as I feel my thighs squeezing together.

"Okay, we're done here."

Just before he shuts my door and walks back toward the building, his voice deepens and he tosses me a sexy wink that has my stomach doing a little flip.

"Drive safe, darlin'."

PRE-ORDER THAT LOOK NOW!

Want to read where it all started with the Slade brothers?

Meet the Slade Brothers. Brooding. Protective AF. Rich and drop-dead delicious.

If you love small-town love stories full of alpha men who will stop at nothing to claim the women they love then grab this complete best-selling Slade Brothers Series.

Slade Brothers Series
Billionaire's Unexpected Bride
Off Limits Daddy
Baby Secret
Loves me NOT
Best Friend's Sister

Want a FREE book from me?

SIGN UP FOR MY NEWSLETTER AND GET *MY BEST FRIEND'S BROTHER* FREE!

It's no secret I've always had a crush on Damon Strickland.
My best friend's older brother and the center of every single one of my fantasies.

He's a walking, talking temptation.

That cocky grin and those broad, athletic shoulders.
You know what they say about a man with big hands right?

Growing up, we always tormented one another.
I was the nagging, annoying little girl he hated
And he was the man-whoring, douchebag I couldn't seem to get over.

Now as adults he actually came through and helped me land a job at my dream company.

That Feeling

How the hell am I supposed to focus when all I can think about is tearing that tight suit from his tempting body!

What's even worse?
He forgot to mention, he's my boss.

SIGN UP HERE

Also by Alexis Winter

Men of Rocky Mountain Series
Claiming Her Forever

A Second Chance at Forever

Always Be My Forever

Only for Forever

Waiting for Forever

Four Forces Security
The Protector

The Savior

Love You Forever Series
The Wrong Brother

Marrying My Best Friend's BFF

Rocking His Fake World

Breaking Up with My Boss

My Accidental Forever

The F It List

The Baby Fling

Grand Lake Colorado Series
A Complete Small-Town Contemporary Romance Collection

Castille Hotel Series
Hate That I Love You

Business & Pleasure

Baby Mistake

Fake It

South Side Boys Series

Bad Boy Protector-Book 1

Fake Boyfriend-Book 2

Brother-in-law's Baby-Book 3

Bad Boy's Baby-Book 4

Make Her Mine Series

My Best Friend's Brother

Billionaire With Benefits

My Boss's Sister

My Best Friend's Ex

Best Friend's Baby

Mountain Ridge Series

Just Friends: Mountain Ridge Book 1

Protect Me: Mountain Ridge Book 2

Baby Shock: Mountain Ridge Book 3

Castille Hotel Series

Hate That I Love You

Business & Pleasure

Baby Mistake

Fake It

**ALL BOOKS CAN BE READ AS STAND-ALONE READS

WITHIN THESE SERIES**

About the Author

Alexis Winter is a contemporary romance author who loves to share her steamy stories with the world. She specializes in billionaires, alpha males and the women they love.

If you love to curl up with a good romance book you will certainly enjoy her work. Whether it's a story about an innocent young woman learning about the world or a sassy and fierce heroine who knows what she wants you,'re sure to enjoy the happily ever afters she provides.

When Alexis isn't writing away furiously, you can find her exploring the Rocky Mountains, traveling, enjoying a glass of wine or petting a cat.

You can find her books on Amazon or here: https://www.alexiswinterauthor.com/

Printed in Great Britain
by Amazon